THE WEATHER TODAY...

...will be sunny, with highs in the mid-seventies, air quality excellent, but a severe ultraviolet hazard, so do remember to wear your goggles, face paint, and sunscapes when you go out.

Coming up next, the Home Horticulturalist, with tips today on winter planting of peyote cactus. But first, this important message from Elaine's Erotic Emporium...

Volume One of the Epic Unilogy*

CHARLES PLATT

*Unilogy: a literary work consisting of one volume.

AVON BOOKS ▲ NEW YORK

FREE ZONE is an original publication of Avon Books. This work has never before appeared in book form. This work is a novel. Any similarity to actual persons or events is purely coincidental.

—

AVON BOOKS
A division of
The Hearst Corporation
105 Madison Avenue
New York, New York 10016

Copyright © 1989 by Charles Platt
Front cover illustration by Gary Ruddel
Published by arrangement with the author
Library of Congress Catalog Card Number: 88-92103
ISBN: 0-380-75411-8

First Avon Books Printing: January 1989

AVON TRADEMARK REG. U.S. PAT. OFF. AND IN OTHER COUNTRIES, MARCA REGISTRADA, HECHO EN U.S.A.

Printed in the U.S.A.

K–R 10 9 8 7 6 5 4 3 2 1

To Roberta Lannes

ACKNOWLEDGMENTS

This novel makes free use of ideas stolen from writers such as H. G. Wells, Robert A. Heinlein, C. M. Kornbluth, Alfred Bester, Philip K. Dick, and J. G. Ballard. In addition, it owes debts to David Langford, whose idea contributed to mine; to the Libertarian Party; to Rudy Rucker, whose subversive concept of transrealist fiction encouraged me to start writing without knowing what was supposed to happen next; to Richard Kadrey and John Clute, who offered encouragement along the way; to Cherie Wilkerson, who showed me the view from Griffith Observatory and corrected many geographical misconceptions; to Hal Pollenz, for his enlightening suggestions about giant ants; to Tom Disch, for his German lesson; to Simon Francis, for his motorcycle expertise; to the Church of Scientology, for its mechanistic psych-jargon; and to John Douglas, who was kind and brave enough to commission the book on the basis of a rather skimpy outline. Thank you, all.

The text was written using PC-Write on an XT clone and a Toshiba laptop, and the line drawings were prepared with MacDraw, using a LaserWriter for output.

CONTENTS

CAST OF CHARACTERS
In Order of Appearance

Dusty McCullough   Founder of the Free Zone, inventor of libertarian socialism, she runs a low-rent utopia for misfits, fugitives, and rugged individualists in general.

Thomas Fink (aka Henry Feldstein)   Dusty's trusty systems analyst and lover. His secret vice is his cyclotron in the basement.

Clarence Whitfield   Fundamentalist preacher who became mayor of Los Angeles. His mission: to inflict God's wrath upon sinners, tax evaders, and residents of the Free Zone.

Roxanne   Whitfield's secretary and sex slave. She worships him in awe—until a telepathic fugue unmasks his demonic ambitions.

Dr. Percival Abo   Geneticist and venture capitalist with a secret plan to put a talking dog in every American home.

The Captain   A Korean with a mysterious past, he brings Dr. Abo from Hong Kong to Los Angeles in exchange for a suitable sum in Krugerrands.

Lucky   Dr. Abo's loquacious canine companion.

Snaliens   Roaming interstellar space, they seek intelligent species that taste good.

Atlanteans   Roused by global warming trends, they emerge from their subterranean sleep to find the world populated by repulsive warm-blooded mammals.

Sammy Savage and **Ursula Venus Milton**   Newscasters of the Free Zone. Ideologues without affectations.

Janet Snowdon   Call girl of LoveLand and undercover agent, she secretly seeks to overthrow the Zone.

Suzie Sunshine   Janet's roommate, a Christian Fornicationist who believes that God is sex.

Carlo Alighieri   Mafia boss and enlightened capitalist, he works with Dusty to protect freedom and maximize graft.

Mutants   The victims of nuclear testing in Nevada, they escape their prison, seeking aliens who will set them free.

Mentational Autonomous Node 6A419BD5h   An artificial intelligence from the far future, he is given the body of a robot and sent back in time to eradicate some noise in the chronological continuum.

Mordo   Motorcycle rider, bartender, and brewer of renown.

Colonel Matt Mallet   Veteran of Central American conflicts, he marshals his Mashers to liberate Thomas Fink from the jail at City Hall.

Colonel Scientist Doctor Werner Weiss   From a space colony orbiting Mars, he sends forth genetically impeccable clones of the Third Reich.

Barbarians   Refugees from the center of the Earth, they seek only to disembowel their enemies and rape their slaves.

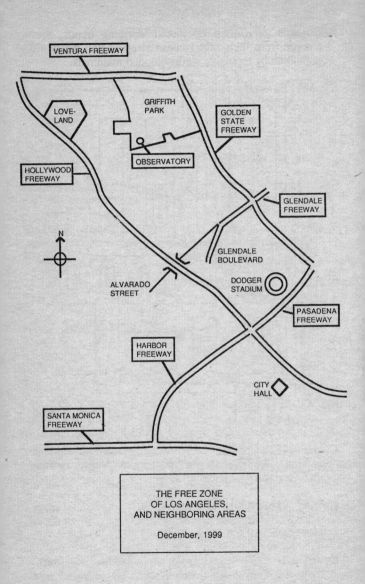

VENTURA FREEWAY

LOVE-LAND

GRIFFITH PARK

GOLDEN STATE FREEWAY

HOLLYWOOD FREEWAY

OBSERVATORY

GLENDALE FREEWAY

N

GLENDALE BOULEVARD

ALVARADO STREET

DODGER STADIUM

PASADENA FREEWAY

HARBOR FREEWAY

CITY HALL

SANTA MONICA FREEWAY

THE FREE ZONE
OF LOS ANGELES,
AND NEIGHBORING AREAS

December, 1999

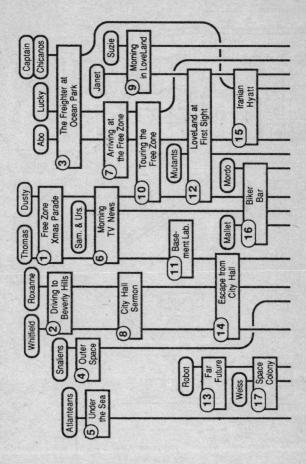

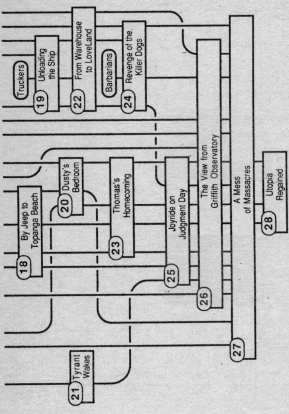

Plot diagram, showing the progress of characters through chapters in the novel. (Only those characters who appear in two or more chapters are included.)

"I think you must remember that a writer is a simple-minded person to begin with. . . . He's not a great mind, he's not a great thinker, he's not a great philosopher, he's a storyteller."

—Erskine Caldwell

I. PARTY TIME IN PAGAN PARADISE

Christmas Eve in the Free Zone: loud music, heavy drug use, and fucking in the streets. Drunken bikers lassoed an effigy of Santa Claus, dragged it by the neck to the steps of the Church of the Beloved Disciple, then hacked it up with chain saws and set fire to the debris. Meanwhile, inside the derelict church, white-robed street punks played heavy metal oldies while androgynous go-go dancers stripped naked beneath bombed-out stained glass windows and hosed down the congregation with holy water from a giant rubber penis.

Lastly, of course, there was the parade along Glendale Boulevard.

Dusty McCullough told herself she was getting too old for this kind of foolishness. She was halfway through her thirties and there were little smile lines around her mouth —which weren't so bad—and frown lines around her eyes, which bothered her much more than she would admit. She was still in shape, muscled like a bodybuilder, and she was happy, and proud of the demented little community in Los Angeles that she had created. But running the Zone for five years had been a juggling act, and as the new millennium drew nigh, she was starting to wonder just how long she could sustain it.

Still, tonight was party time. She had pride of place, decked out like royalty in a satin gown and a silver tiara, riding the first float in the parade. The gown had been painstakingly ripped and spattered with mud; the tiara had been repaired with masking tape; and she was sitting on a throne nailed together from packing crates. Smiling radiantly, she held the symbols of her libertarian-socialist regime: an automatic rifle in one arm, a laptop computer in the other. The crowd loved it. They whooped and catcalled and threw confetti.

Behind her came surfers dressed as bishops, blessing spectators from their dune buggies. Next in line was Satan in a golden chariot pulled by pretty men wearing white tights, angel wings, and lurid eye makeup. They squealed girlishly as Satan cracked his whip over their heads.

Following them was a business-suited capitalist on stilts, hauling handfuls of cash from a swag bag and tossing them into the crowd—fake bills decorated with obscene slogans and pictures of starving peasants in Michigan and Pennsylvania. Close behind came a huge float festooned with pink roses. Showgirls from LoveLand romped among the blossoms in a lesbian orgy while a sneering mafioso watched over them, reclining on sacks of bullion.

Finally, bringing up the rear, there were three Hell's Angels on roller skates posing as wise men, and a notorious whorehouse madam as the Virgin Mary, pushing a giant crib on wheels. In it, beneath a halo fashioned from an old coat hanger, a bloated mutant baby with a gaping beak and bulging bloodshot eyes twitched its flippers while concealed loudspeakers blared "Hark the Herald Angels Sing."

Dusty's float at the head of the procession reached the Church of the Beloved Disciple just as the bells were chiming midnight. She climbed up onto a high wooden stage overlooking the street and took in the scene: people laughing and stumbling and shouting, dust drifting under floodlights, smells of barbecued dog meat and bootleg gin drifting on the soft, warm air.

Thomas Fink, her confidant, lover, and systems analyst, appeared discreetly beside the platform and passed a microphone up to her. She shared a secret smile with him before she turned to the crowd.

"Who needs heroes?" she shouted. She paused, waiting for them to turn their attention to her. "Anyone here?" Her amplified voice echoed up and down the block. "Do any of you want to trust someone else's judgment more than your own?"

As one they shouted, "No!"

"No gurus, no god, no government," she told them, more quietly now. "None of that bullshit. Not here, in the Free Zone." She paused, and smiled. "And we sure as hell don't believe in Santa Claus."

They cheered her.

"So let's party."

A half dozen musicians dressed as guerrillas joined her on the platform, and she stepped back. Leaping Larry gave the signal from behind his mobile mixing console, and the band started playing. Dusty took the opportunity to slip out of sight behind the stage. Despite her tall, powerful build, crowds made her nervous—no matter how much they seemed to love her.

Thomas was waiting. "Let's go home," she said in his ear, above the pounding music. She started stripping off her costume. She wore a leotard under it, and sneakers. The night air felt good on her bare arms. She flexed her muscles, and stretched. "My Norton's in the parking lot, in back of the church."

"Won't they miss you?" Thomas nodded toward the Free Zoners dancing in the street.

"I've worked hard enough for them in the past five years, and they know it. Come on, we'll play hooky." She held his head between her hands and kissed him deliberately on the mouth, leaving no room for argument.

Soon they were heading up into the hills on the edge of Griffith Park. Thomas sat close behind, his arms wrapped tightly around her body. The sound of the 850 cc motorcy-

cle engine blared defiantly across the derelict residential
landscape under the purple moon.

2. SINNER CELEBS,
BURN IN HELL!

Meanwhile, a little way to the southwest, a long white limo
moved ponderously down an off-ramp from the Hollywood
Freeway and headed toward Beverly Hills. Escorting it
were two half-tracked M113 armored personnel carriers
manned by National Guardsmen. Their night scopes, machine guns, and flamethrowers panned restlessly across the
wasteland.

Clarence Whitfield lay stretched out on sealskin uphol-
stery in the back of the limousine, admiring his own reflection in the mirrored underside of the roof. His right
hand rested on his ample belly, holding a tumbler of bourbon and branch water. His left hand lay absentmindedly on
the thigh of his eighteen-year-old secretary, Roxanne.

He was a big black man in his mid fifties, close to three
hundred pounds, with a round, jowly face and a shaven
head. When he grinned he looked like a hungry customer
in a restaurant, ready to eat whatever was set before him.
In actual fact, the whole City of Los Angeles was Whitfield's restaurant; and he grinned often.

Music filled the car. Barry Manilow, turned up loud.
Whitfield hummed along, off-key, and glanced out of the
window at a succession of burned-out homes lining Beverly Boulevard, barely visible in the flickering glow from
vandalized streetlights. Refugees, huddled amid the devas-

tation, stared blankly at the big white car and the personnel carriers as they rumbled past.

"Poor white trash," Whitfield said to himself. He laughed heartily, making his stomach wobble, and some of his drink spilled onto his blue pinstripe suit. "Wipe that up for me, honey," he added, not bothering to look at the woman beside him.

Roxanne reached for a Kleenex. She was dressed like a whore in four-inch spike heels, black fishnet stockings, black leather miniskirt, and a tight red sweater that outlined her nipples in graphic detail. Her Afro was cropped short, like the pelt of a freshly shorn black sheep. She was frighteningly thin and angular. Her knees and elbows looked sharp enough to kill, if she ever acquired the savvy to use them.

She dabbed at the spilled bourbon. "Sometimes I kind of wonder," she said. "You know, where all them poor people come from."

"*Those* poor people," Whitfield corrected her. "Being my personal secretary, Roxanne, you have to improve your way of speaking."

She nodded earnestly. "Okay."

"The plight of the urban poor," he told her, "has reached a crisis point. It is the tragedy of our time. Understand what I'm saying?"

"Uh-huh."

He half closed his eyes. "Whatever else I may have said or done, I have always believed that it is my duty—my *moral imperative*—to help these people. And I will not rest until I have discharged this grave responsibility."

Roxanne looked at him respectfully. "Yeah."

He turned toward her, eyed her face and body, and treated her to his big grin. "You believe in me, isn't that right, honey?"

She wriggled her bony shoulders and smiled. "Well sure."

Whitfield chuckled. He squeezed her thigh, tightening his grip till she flinched. "That's my girl."

The big car cruised on through the night. There were

quicker routes that the mayor could have taken, but he never tired of looking out at scenes of human deprivation. The misery of others was a tonic to his soul.

Eventually, the limo crossed La Cienega Boulevard and approached the territory of Beverly Hills.

There were floodlights ahead on tall metal towers behind a wall of concrete blocks topped with razor wire. As Whitfield's convoy approached, an amplified voice echoed across the highway. "Stop. Do not come closer. Present your identification to the guard post."

"As if they didn't know to expect us," Whitfield grumbled. He levered himself into sitting position and thumbed a switch on his intercom. "Vernon? You tell Sergeant Sanchez, in our escort, to tell those Hill people we got official business at the Beverly Hilton."

"Yes sir, Mr. Whitfield."

Roxanne frowned in puzzlement. "How come they treat us this way? Don't they understand who you are?"

He grimaced. "It's no big thing. There's going to be changes made, soon enough."

After a short wait, heavy steel gates slid open, allowing barely enough room for the limousine to pass through. The military escort, meanwhile, remained outside.

Soon the mayor was heading north on Canon Drive, where tall palm trees had been encased in shimmering plastic sunscreens. The concrete pavement here was smooth and clean. Large, elegant homes stood half hidden among succulent vegetation, immaculately maintained, tastefully lit.

"Come judgment day," Whitfield murmured, "this'll be a different picture, I do believe." He nodded to himself. "They shall come to know the wrath of God. And they shall pay for their sins." He drained his glass and set it down. "They shall burn. They shall suffer endless torment. So sayeth the Lord."

"Amen," said Roxanne. Somewhat nervously, she fingered the diamond-inlaid crucifix that dangled around her neck on a thin silver chain.

A little further on, the limo finally reached the hotel. Its parking lot was bumper-to-bumper with vintage Rolls-

Royces, Ferraris, and Jaguars. Searchlight beams were weaving patterns in the sky, and the sidewalk was busy with celebrity hunters. "Stay in the car," Whitfield told Roxanne. "This won't take more than a short while."

"But you said I could—"

He patted her face once, and then again, just hard enough to rock her head back and make her eyes widen with surprise. "You do what I *say*, honey."

He climbed out into a blitz of camera flashes. Vernon, the chauffeur, tall, muscular, and ominous in his paramilitary uniform, slammed the car door before an inquisitive journalist had a chance to peer inside.

Whitfield waddled up three steps to the lobby and paused to regain his breath. A young man with a carnation in the lapel of his charcoal-gray suit hurried forward. He had a synthetically handsome profile that could only have come from cosmetic surgery. "Mr. Whitfield!" He grasped Whitfield's hand and looked into his eyes with eager sincerity. "I'm so glad you've arrived. We were wondering—"

"You can stop wondering, boy. I'm here."

The young man's smile wavered. "Yes—of course. Well, you're just in time, if you still wish to make the keynote address, which of course we'd be honored, really honored—"

"Lead me to it."

"Absolutely. My pleasure." He guided Whitfield along a thickly carpeted beige hallway, through a series of doors, past two armed guards, onto the wings of a small stage.

"But we must never forget the real meaning of Christmas," a man in a dazzling white suit was saying. He was standing at a microphone, looking out over a hall where several hundred media personalities sat at tables beneath festoons of holly, mistletoe, colored-glass baubles, and handmade paper flowers. "Seriously, this is a special time of the year. A time to remember those who are less fortunate than ourselves—which is why the proceeds from this event are being donated entirely to the Entertainers' Benevolent Fund." He paused for ritual applause, glanced to one side, and saw with obvious relief that Whitfield was

there. "It's also a time for goodwill," he went on, shifting
gears. "A time to love thy neighbor. And in this spirit, I
present to you tonight a surprise guest. A man with whom,
quite frankly, we have had our differences. But I'm told
he's got some good news for us tonight, so let's listen with
open hearts and minds to the message he brings. Ladies
and gentlemen, Mr. Clarence Whitfield, mayor of the City
of Los Angeles."

Whitfield walked out under the video lights. Quickly, he
took in the sea of faces, handsome men, glamorous
women, beautiful clothes, extravagant table settings cluttered with the remnants of a huge banquet. There were
some murmurs of surprise, and scattered, uncertain applause as he reached the microphone.

"It's an honor to be here," Whitfield began, "among the
most wonderful, the most talented people, in one of our
most vital industries, still prospering even in these times of
uncertainty." He nodded slowly, as if appreciating the wis-
dom of what he'd just said.

"You know," he went on, "as I drove here tonight, I saw
a lot of people on the streets of Los Angeles who don't
have much to celebrate this Christmas. The plight of the
urban poor has reached a crisis point. It is the tragedy of
our time. And you know, whatever else I may have said or
done, I've always believed it is my duty—my *moral imperative*—to help these people. I will not rest until I have
discharged this grave responsibility." He looked around at
his audience, daring anyone to doubt him. "To this end, it's
my pleasure to announce the successful outcome of our
long negotiations between the City of Los Angeles and the
Directors of the Republic of Beverly Hills."

Tentatively, the audience began to applaud. But he held
up his hand. "I believe our new treaty will put an end to the
unpleasantness—let me speak plainly—the regrettable
acts of aggression between our peoples. Together, we will
have the strength to rebuild, pooling our resources to help
the poor, and also to punish the lawbreakers, including,"
he bared his teeth in a sudden little rictus of anger, "the
social parasites and *professional criminals* operating out of
the so-called *Free Zone*."

He paused, patted his plump cheeks with a white hand-kerchief, then mustered a benevolent smile. "One day, before too long, you'll be able to dismantle your guard posts and barricades, and law-abiding, God-fearing citizens will move freely again through the Greater Los Angeles area. Thank you, ladies and gentlemen. I wish you all a Merry Christmas, and peace and prosperity in the New Year and the new millennium."

3. CHOLO HOODS IN FLOODED MONDO CONDO

Meanwhile, seven miles to the southwest, Dr. Percival Abo stood at the rail of a rusty freighter as it edged toward the shore. Here in Ocean Park, the streets were under six feet of dirty seawater and fish swam through the broken windows of rotting condominiums. New excavations had promised to turn the flooded suburb into a fashionable marina; but the work had been abandoned when funds ran out, and the project had degenerated into a swamp. Wild-cats and raccoons roamed the rooftops at night, and strange new mutant plants had taken root in the dunes of mud.

The excavation was deep enough to serve as an impro-vised dock, however, and it was here that the freighter found its mooring. Two Chinese seamen flung a frayed rope over the side. Faintly, in the eerie purple moonlight, Dr. Abo saw men moving along the shore. They grabbed the end of the rope and secured it to an abandoned bull-dozer mired in the mud.

The ship's captain quietly joined Dr. Abo at the rail. He was a chain-smoking Korean with knife scars on his cheek and a bullet wound in his left hand. Several buttons were missing from his uniform, and he wore no shirt under it. He had played many games of chess with Dr. Abo during the thirty-day Pacific crossing, but had never given his name. Dr. Abo hadn't asked for it—hadn't asked any questions at all, in fact. He was grateful merely to be alive.

"I will need some more of your money," the Korean stated softly, "to protect us from the authorities." He took a drag on his cigarette and it glowed in the darkness.

"Very well." Dr. Abo reached inside his jacket, extracted one of his Krugerrands from an inside pocket, and passed it to the captain.

The men on the shore were raising a gangplank improvised from plywood and plastic drainpipes. It bumped against the side of the ship, and they started up it, feeling their way through the darkness. The captain switched on a penlight, but the men hardly seemed to see it. Dr. Abo noted their faces: Chicanos, with skin so dark it was almost black, pockmarked with blisters. Their eyes reflected the light with a strange, pale intensity. Skin cancers and cataracts, he realized. Gifts from the new sun.

"*Buenas tardes,*" said the first Chicano. He was wearing bandoliers over a ragged black T-shirt, and cutoff Levi's. He pointed to his broad chest. "Francisco Torres." He reached out, touched the captain's shoulder, then found his hand.

"*Buenas tardes,*" the captain replied quietly.

The Chicano paused as if groping for words. "We hear your message of the radio," he said finally. "We are help to you. The protection."

The captain held out the gold coin, and played his penlight on it. "*Oro,*" he said.

Torres squinted closely at the Krugerrand, took it, bit it, then passed it to one of his companions. They conferred in rapid Spanish. Finally he turned back to the captain and nodded. "Okay."

"Protection for *tres dias,*" said the captain.

The Chicano shook his head. "*Dos.*"

"That will probably be long enough," Dr. Abo told him.

"*Gracias. Buenas noches.*" Torres turned to go.

"One moment," Dr. Abo called out. "I have cargo that must be unloaded."

The Chicano's face showed hostile incomprehension.

"Boxes. Crates."

"*Cajas de madera,*" the captain suggested.

"I need a truck," Dr. Abo went on, his agitation prompting him to talk whether they could understand him or not. "It must be refrigerated. And for myself I must rent a car—"

"*Mañana,*" said Torres. "We send to you boys. More, you pay." Without waiting for a reply, he led his men back to the shore, into the night.

"Please do not concern yourself." The captain flicked his cigarette butt over the side. "I have had business with these men in the past. I suggest, Dr. Abo, you should get some sleep. Unless you would enjoy a game—"

"No. No more chess. Thank you, all the same." Dr. Abo bowed formally to the Korean, turned, and made his way carefully across the deck of the ship, back to the security and solitude of his cabin.

When he walked in, the bright yellow light from the single naked bulb seemed reassuringly familiar, and the peeling cream paint and broken wooden chair were welcoming compared with the unknown city outside. The cabin was strewn with antique books; he had spent much of the voyage working his way through an obsolete 1989 edition of *Encyclopedia Britannica*.

For companionship, he had his dog, Lucky—a cocker spaniel he had saved from the Chinese authorities in Hong Kong when they closed down his factory and evicted him from his apartment.

Dr. Abo closed the cabin door. He locked it out of habit and paused, breathing deeply. Lucky scrambled up out of his basket and walked over, wagging his tail. Dr. Abo bent down, patted the dog's flank, then rubbed him behind the ears. "I have paid some men who will allow us to stay here for two days," he told the dog, as if to reassure himself. "We will unload, I hope, tomorrow." Dr. Abo took a crumpled slip of paper from his jacket pocket and studied it, even though he had long since memorized the penciled lettering. It had acquired a mystical significance, like a religious totem. "We will go to Dusty McCullough in the Free Zone. She will provide us with a safe place to live and conduct our business, free from bureaucratic interference."

Lucky wagged his tail. "That's good," the dog said. "Yes, that makes me happy."

His canine voice sounded almost, but not quite, human.

4. A NIGHTMARE OF ALIEN SLIME

Meanwhile, far away in interstellar space, four alien creatures sat in the control room of their warship and studied animated images on a giant circular viewscreen.

"Violent behavior!" exclaimed the ship's captain, an alien whose honorary title was Furrowed Bulk. He watched as the screen showed a human using a hand-held laser weapon to vaporize an entire infantry battalion. The picture became filled with a huge orange fireball.

"Yes, indeed," agreed Thick Hump, the navigator. "Quite amusing."

"But kindly observe." Tall Stalks, the anthropologist, extruded a pseudopod and prodded a button beside the screen, fast-forwarding to another clip. It showed citizens of Earth going about their business on a street lined with tall office buildings. From out of the sky zoomed a silver spaceship, its engines spewing flame. It eluded fighter jets that attempted to shoot it down, aimed a heat ray at the buildings, and they exploded into dust and rubble.

"Oh, excellent," said Furrowed Bulk. He laughed. "Yes, I particularly like that one."

In actual fact, neither words nor laughter were audible in the control room. The only sound was of flesh slithering across slime-covered rock, and warm, nutritious, synthetic mucus dripping from the perforated ceiling onto the creatures below. They communicated nonverbally via a complex sequence of body odors and twitching pseudopods. The gist of their conversation, however, was easily translated into human terms.

Tall Stalks used his manipulative pseudopod to press another control beside the viewscreen. "The pictures we see were received as electromagnetic waves from a planet calling itself Earth," he explained. "The location is a star system only three light-years from our current position. I will show one last transmission." The screen lit up with two naked bodies wrestling together on a king-size water bed. "This is how the dominant species reproduces," he went on. "The large biped inserts an organ in the smaller one. A miniature replica of itself emerges quite soon afterward." Tall Stalks paused. "You may applaud one's diligent research."

The other three aliens ritually signalled their approval. "May you stay forever wet," Furrowed Bulk murmured kindly.

Each of the aliens massed about a thousand pounds. They were amorphous gray lumps, like giant wrinkled leather sacks, sprouting whatever pseudopods they currently needed to sense or manipulate the outside world. None of them had legs; like snails, they laid a trail of mucus and oozed along it, propelling themselves with thousands of cilia lining the undersides of their bodies.

The Terran pornographic video cut to an extreme close-up of the man's penis thrusting into the woman's vagina. "These pictures are so clinically detailed, they must be for instructional purposes," remarked Thick Body. "Perhaps the bipeds of Earth have lost the instinct to reproduce. These pictures are needed to retrain them."

"Perhaps." Tall Stalks seemed doubtful.

"In that case," Furrowed Bulk concluded, "they are highly evolved. Their intellects have outstripped their instincts."

"I disagree," said Pale Pods, the biologist in the group; at which point a serious debate ensued. Since the aliens' language required complex gestures and odors to express simple concepts with formality and rigor, it took several hours for the four of them to examine the question.

In the end, they agreed that no agreement could be reached. The only way to settle the matter was to go to planet Earth and examine the bipeds in person.

Tall Stalks displayed a picture of a landmass streaked with cloud. "The transmissions came from the area here," he explained, zooming in on Southern California. "The large region of dwellings, in particular, is referred to as 'entertainment capital of the world.'"

"Good," said Furrowed Bulk. "We could do with some entertainment." His three colleagues quivered politely, indicating their amusement. "But first we should eat," he went on. "I'm starved."

They slithered into an adjoining cavern, deep in the enormous ball of rock that served as their interstellar ship. Robot servants entered, carrying furry creatures trussed up with vines. They were foxlike mammals that the aliens had harvested from the last planet they had visited. The mammals howled with fear and twisted helplessly in their bonds as the robots dumped them onto the floor.

Furrowed Bulk oozed on top of the largest of them and rippled with pleasure as he felt its body squirm, twitch, then collapse beneath him. His digestive juices quickly went to work, dissolving the flesh off the animal's bones.

"Let us postulate that the bipeds on Earth *are* highly evolved," said Thick Hump. "Can you infer, from what you have seen, whether they could be a source of nourishment? I'm getting a bit bored with these." He extruded a pseudopod and nudged another of the mammals, which whimpered pitifully. "All they ever do is cringe."

Tall Stalks pondered the question. "Information in the broadcasts I have received indicates that life-forms on Earth are carbon-based, which is encouraging. *Something* down there ought to taste good."

5. MEANWHILE,
IN ATLANTIS

Back on Earth, on the ocean floor, in the ruins of a lost city that had once been known as Atlantis, something stirred from its sleep of centuries.

But we should leave Atlantis till later. It's in the Free Zone that our story really begins.

6. SUBURBAN ANARCHISTS
BUILDING A BETTER TOMORROW

She woke to the sound of distant guns and the smell of burning wood. It was well past dawn; bright white sunlight outlined the boards nailed across the bedroom windows. Dusty yawned and stretched and rolled over, scattering lengths of nylon rope and assorted sex toys and bondage devices. It was Christmas Day.

She turned and looked fondly at Thomas, tangled in the sheets, clutching his pillow, smiling in his sleep. His tousled black hair and slender physique made him seem appealingly boyish. Dusty bent her head and kissed him tenderly on the cheek, then on the mouth, and he stirred, making little sleepy noises.

"Time is it?" he asked.

"Early," she lied, pressing her body close and putting his hand on her breast.

He blinked and squinted toward the barricaded windows. "Doesn't look early."

"Don't worry about it." She reached for him again.

He shook his head. "Work to do." He disengaged himself and slid out of bed. "Anyway, last night should have been more than enough." He glanced at the rumpled bed, and at her nakedness, and smiled. Then he disappeared into the bathroom, and she heard water running.

Dusty shrugged philosophically. She swung out of bed, moving with easy muscled grace, and quickly donned an old pair of black Levi's and a red T-shirt silk-screened with the official Free Zone symbol: a clenched fist with the middle finger extended upward. She removed the iron bars from the bedroom door, lifted it aside, and walked through into the living room.

Again, she heard the booming of heavy artillery. She went to an observation slit and peered out. A column of smoke was rising hazy-purple against the sky beyond the hills to the east, probably over Pasadena.

"What's happening?" Thomas came up behind her, towelling his face. He put his head next to hers, sharing the view. "National Guard?"

"Probably. Still socking it to the Islamic Purificationists." She sniffed the air. "I don't like that smell."

"The wood smoke?"

"No, the other smell with it." She turned away. "Napalm. There was a lot of that in Panama." She paused, remembering.

"A Christmas gift to the religious extremists of Pasadena from his honor, Clarence Whitfield," said Thomas. His face showed no expression.

"They'll come for us, one of these days," Dusty told him. "Sooner or later, Whitfield will get just a little too greedy, and he'll figure he can run the Zone as well as we can, and then—"

"That's always been a possibility." Thomas's voice was matter-of-fact.

She sighed. "You haven't seen combat firsthand. You don't know what it's like."

"You're right. I don't." He picked his way across to the terminal in the corner, flipped the power switch, and sat down on a battered swivel chair. He switched on a desk lamp, opened a notebook, and started typing a series of access codes.

Dusty realized that he was right: the only thing to do was get on with the job. She turned and started across the living room. It was littered with stacks of reference books, fanfolded hard copy, electronic components, motorcycle tools, and bodybuilding equipment. On one wall were crudely-painted human silhouettes peppered with bullet holes. On another wall was an enormous operations map showing every street in the Free Zone, from Ventura Freeway in the northwest to the Pasadena Freeway in the southeast. An old couch, losing its vinyl, faced a coffee table stacked with dirty dishes and a TV set resting on a couple of cinder blocks. His 'n' hers M-16s, a grenade launcher, and a surfboard were standing in the corner by the door.

Dusty picked her way across the grimy nylon carpet, turned on the TV, then went on into the kitchen. More dirty dishes were stacked in the sink, and the countertop was littered with beer cans and empty ammunition clips. Ought to do something about the mess, she thought vaguely, as she opened the refrigerator and grabbed a couple Dr. Feelgood soy bars and a carton of orange juice.

The Free Zone's local TV station was playing Christmas nostalgia music—"Santa Claus Is Coming to Town," styled after punk bands of the mid 1970s. She went and sat cross-legged on the floor in front of the set. The screen displayed a hand-lettered sign: STAND BY FOR 9 A.M. NEWS! HERE ON KFZ, SOON AS WE GET OUR SHIT TOGETHER!! There was a sketch of Santa nailed to a cross, his eyes bugging out.

Dusty started on the first of the soy bars, picked up a fifty-pound dumbbell in her left hand, and did some curls while she was waiting. Behind her, Thomas typed at the terminal in intermittent staccato bursts. "What am I doing today?" she asked him over her shoulder.

"Ten o'clock arbitration, as usual. Then—around eleven, expect a surprise visit. Seems a Dr. Percival Abo telephoned this morning. My expert system talked to him. He's here from Hong Kong, looking for warehouse space. Has cargo to unload."

"He's a doctor? Doctor of what?"

"Didn't say. I'm checking . . . no, not registered as a medical doctor here or Hong Kong or mainland China." More keyboard noise, then another pause. "Here he is. Hawaii, 1975. Ph.D. in biochemistry. But no publications listed. Looks funny; as if the file's been purged. Want me to dig deeper?"

"Wait till I've met him. Is he importing contraband?"

"Undoubtedly."

Dusty nodded. "Let's give him day-visitor status."

"I just did."

"And let's assign him an afternoon hostess from Love-Land."

Thomas smiled. "I already did that, too."

She crumpled the soy bar wrapper and tossed it aside. She strode over behind Thomas and tugged his hair playfully. "Hey, who's running the Zone, you or me?"

His reply was pre-empted by the TV. The Christmas rock music stopped and two faces appeared on the screen: a little old gray-haired lady with rosy, wrinkled cheeks, and a kid in a ripped leather jacket, half his hair shaved off, the other half dyed festive green-and-red and dusted with silver confetti. He was wearing a red rubber nose and a pair of plastic antlers. "Hey, freeps, how ya doin?"

"*Good* morning everyone," said the little old lady. "And welcome to the morning news, with Ursula Venus Milton and straight-talking Sammy Savage."

"Want to come watch it?" Dusty put her arms around Thomas's neck. "Just for old time's sake?"

He grumbled something about inefficient use of available time, but he followed her over to the peeling vinyl couch anyway, and sprawled on it beside her.

"Nationwide," newsreader Ursula was saying, "millions of Americans are celebrating this last Christmas Day of the twentieth century. Here in the Free Zone, we've got too much sense to observe a superstitious ritual stolen from the Church by multinational corporations merchandising trashy consumer goods." Through it all, her radiant smile never faltered.

"Piss on it, you're right." Sammy ripped off his nose and antlers and threw them off-camera. "Fuck that shit."

"Good, Sammy. Very ideologically correct."

"Is there going to *be* any news?" Thomas complained.

"Give them a chance," Dusty chided him. "They've got a routine to go through. People expect this."

Straight-talking Sammy was putting on a pair of enormous horn-rimmed glasses. He picked up a stained page of typescript. "Okay, let's get to the serious shit. At a benefit dinner last night attended by hundreds of showbiz celebrities, Los Angeles Mayor Clarence Whitfield announced a new treaty and trading agreement that he pledged would put an end to the guerrilla warfare between L.A. and the Beverly Hills republic."

"Ahead of schedule," Thomas remarked. "The sly old bastard."

"Meanwhile on Glendale Boulevard here in Freep City we had the Christmas parade," Sammy went on, "which I oughta have pictures of, except I did too many drugs and broke the camera."

"Here's a cheery item," Ursula put in. "Last night video stars Ricky Revell and Lizzie Beaumont, driving a red Ferrari, crashed the Free Zone border at the barrier on Alvarado Street. Attempting to evade Hell's Angels border guards who gave pursuit, they sideswiped Billy's Bed Store, which currently operates as a mudback sex parlor— as, um, I think some of you may know." She contrived a look of prim embarrassment.

"Luckily none of the hookers or their johns was hurt," Sammy took over. "Ricky and Lizzie, those fuckin' airheads, claimed it was all an accident on account of they was falling-down drunk. The locals wasn't in no mood for excuses, so they stripped their clothes off, shaved their heads, painted 'em red, and turned 'em loose on the Harbor Freeway."

"Their car," Ursula finished up, "will be auctioned off to benefit the hermits of Griffith Park. And now this message from Aunt Annie's Homeopathic Pharmacy, inventors and sole suppliers of Saf-T-Ray, the vitamin-enriched ultraviolet blocker."

Thomas looked at Dusty. "There'll be trouble from the Hills people about that."

"For roughing up two second-rate TV celebrities? No way. What do you think would happen if a couple Free Zoners tried to crash *their* barricade?" She drew her finger across her throat.

"Of course," Thomas agreed. "But now Whitfield has made peace with Beverly Hills, they need a common enemy to unite their people. Someone they can all hate. Such as, us."

The commercial ended. "Business news, for any of you out there that still gives a shit," Sammy was saying. "At close of trading yesterday, the Dow finished at 132, which is an all-time high since the last crash, it says here. Gains were recorded in National Biotech, Solar Systems, and good old federally-owned U.S. Oil." He blinked and rubbed his eyes. "Jesus, I got such a hangover."

"World news," Ursula put in. "After three years, the evacuation of Holland has finally been completed, on schedule. Climatologists now predict that thanks to the worldwide depression and the reduction in industrial activity, the greenhouse effect will level off in the next twenty to thirty years, causing ocean levels to rise no more than an additional ten to fifteen feet. So, there's new hope for all those diehard dike builders in Santa Monica. Right, Sammy?"

"You got it, babe. And just to make you all feel real warm inside, astronauts in the Chinese space station sent goodwill greetings to the world this morning, calling for peace in the new millennium." He blew a raspberry, stood up, and walked off the set.

"The weather today," said Ursula, "will be sunny, with highs in the mid seventies, air quality excellent, but a severe ultraviolet hazard, so *do* remember to wear your goggles, face paint, and suncapes when you go out. Coming up next, the Home Horticulturalist, with tips today on winter planting of peyote cactus. But first, this important message from Elaine's Erotic Emporium."

Dusty stood up and switched off the TV. She bit into her second soy bar and picked up her weights. "Admit it, Thomas. You enjoyed that."

Thomas got up and walked back to his terminal. "It did have a kind of primitive charm."

"That's right. Just like you. Okay, before I go, what's on Whitfield's database? Did you check it, yet?" The Free Zone owed its survival, in part, to Thomas Fink's ability to infiltrate most online systems, including those in City Hall itself.

He typed a few access codes. "Too early for them over there. Christmas, you know? The mayor's a religious man. Probably at church, praying for our redemption."

"Sure he is," she said grimly. She walked back into the bedroom, checked the shells in her .357 Magnum, strapped on her gunbelt, picked up her goggles, and donned her suncape, drawing the hood tight around her face.

"Do I need to remind you that you're opening the preach-out at Dodger Stadium tonight?" Thomas called to her.

She dabbed blocker ointment on her cheeks. "Just as long as I get out of there before it turns into a riot. You know, when there's twenty-five different prophets of the apocalypse, all of them out of their heads with righteous wrath—"

"Twenty-seven. Two more registered yesterday."

"I may need help."

He gestured at the terminal. "I'll be right here, if you want me."

They kissed, and she ruffled his hair. More softly, she said: "I wouldn't know what to do without you."

"Hey, I know that." He spoke casually, but as always, he looked quietly pleased by her attention.

A little later she was on her vintage Norton Commando, taking it hard around the curves, heading down Holboro Drive. The wind whipped at her suncape and she felt warm and good and strong, ready to deal with the world and do whatever was necessary.

7. SQUIRREL VISITS THE SATANS OF LIBERTARIAN DOGMA

Dr. Percival Abo drove his Honda Civic with elaborate caution past motorcycles, horse-drawn wagons, and cyclists on the Santa Monica Freeway. His dog, Lucky, sat on the passenger seat beside him, staring out at the landscape of mutant palm trees and arsonized tract homes. "I like this place," said Lucky. "It is big."

"Good, good." Dr. Abo spoke with only half his attention. He slowed the car, squinting at a highway sign perforated with bullet holes and spray-painted with revolutionary slogans. "Now, can this be correct? I don't *think* we want to go toward Pasadena."

"There are many places to go, here," Lucky commented cheerfully. "Many places to run in the sun."

"That is very true, Lucky. Unfortunately, however, you must not expose yourself to the sun without proper protection. There is severe local depletion of the ozone layer. The ultraviolet radiation is extremely dangerous."

Lucky put his paws up on the dashboard and pressed his nose to the protectively-coated windshield. "I want to chase rabbits."

"I doubt there are any rabbits, Lucky. Only the nocturnal animals will have survived." Dr. Abo paused thoughtfully. "On the other hand, if any rabbits do still exist, they will probably be blind from the radiation. Therefore, they will be easy to catch." He turned the steering wheel suddenly, deciding to take the exit after all.

There was a blast from a car horn to his right. He hit the brakes and narrowly avoided broadsiding an El Camino pickup whose owner had retrofitted it with monster tires and a machine-gun turret. The sides of the vehicle were emblazoned with airbrushed pictures of Jesus welcoming humanity to heaven.

"Sorry!" Dr. Abo shouted. He gave a hopeful, friendly wave.

The driver of the El Camino leaned out, dreadlocks blowing in the wind. He eyed the Honda impassively, then jerked his head, gesturing Dr. Abo ahead of him.

"Thank you!" Dr. Abo nodded and smiled. He guided the little car up the ramp, skirting a couple of small bomb craters and the burned-out shell of a Cadillac that had plowed through the guardrail and was delicately poised over the wasteland below. In his rearview mirror, he saw the El Camino grind to a halt beside the ruined car. The driver stepped out, carrying bolt cutters and an acetylene torch.

"They are still feeding off the relics of their past, here, Lucky," said Dr. Abo. "They have lost faith in their future. I believe I may yet help the American people to rediscover their sense of destiny."

Lucky turned and stared inscrutably at his master for a long moment. "It's hot," he said finally.

"Of *course* it's hot!" Dr. Abo gestured in exasperation. "The air conditioner doesn't work, I already told you that!" He mopped his forehead with a white handkerchief from the pocket of his threadbare business suit. "Forgive me, Lucky, sometimes I forget that you cannot understand these things. Just remember, we are fortunate to have any kind of car at all. Be patient."

He merged onto the Harbor Freeway. There were more motorcycles and bicycles, here, their riders shrouded in hooded white capes that flapped in the breeze. Occasional compact cars and small trucks were armored with hand-welded steel plate, and their owners, men and women alike, looked mean and dangerous. Dr. Abo hunched low in his seat, uncomfortably aware of the million new dollars' worth of gold bullion stashed in his briefcase in the Honda's trunk. This was all that remained of the venture capital his genetic research corporation had raised in Hong Kong. He wished he could have trusted the captain enough to leave the bullion on the ship.

Large office buildings came into view either side of the highway. Some still seemed open for business behind concrete antiterrorist barricades at street level. Others were burned-out shells, twisted nets of steel beams looming black against the purple sky.

"Before the debt crisis, this was a vital business community," Dr. Abo explained to his dog. "Today, according to my information, only two areas of the city still thrive. Beverly Hills, home of the entertainment industry, and the Free Zone, which has seceded illegally from the city and claims it is exempt from government regulation."

Lucky yawned. He circled around on the seat, lay down, and put his nose between his paws. He stared up at Dr. Abo with canine inscrutability.

"Ah!" Dr. Abo exclaimed. "The Hollywood Freeway! We are almost at our destination." He consulted his handwritten directions, transcribed from the strangely mechanical voice that had acknowledged his phone call to the Free Zone earlier that morning. "Second exit," he muttered to himself.

A little later he was guiding the small car down a ramp into what had once been a quiet, low-income residential neighborhood. A wall had been improvised around it, twenty feet high, built from derelict automobiles stacked one upon another. It extended into the distance, either side of Alvarado Street, where there was a gateway and a guard post. Thugs carrying automatic weapons, motorcycle chains, and flamethrowers eyed Dr. Abo speculatively as he turned his Honda toward them.

He stopped at what seemed a reasonably safe distance.

"Remember, Lucky, do not talk." He waved his finger to emphasize the instruction. "I repeat. Do not talk to these people! We do not want to alarm them."

Lucky gave a short, sharp bark.

Dr. Abo patted him on the head. "Good boy, Lucky. Very good." He put on his sunglasses, rolled down his window, and leaned out to greet a massive, ragged figure walking toward him. The man's face was mostly hidden by long red hair, a ferocious beard, and sun goggles. Dr. Abo mustered an ingratiating smile. "Good morning!" he called out.

The man was carrying an Uzi in one fat, scarred hand, with his thumb on the safety. He was wearing a combat suit stitched together from animal pelts, automobile seat covers, denim, and Kevlar. He paused for a long moment, studying the car, then the dog, then Dr. Abo himself. "You lost or somethin'?"

"Indeed I hope not," said Dr. Abo. "I have business in the Free Zone with a Miss Dusty McCullough."

The man grinned, exposing ruined teeth. "How bout that." He reached inside his jacket and pulled out a small silver keyboard with liquid-crystal display and stubby UHF antenna. "Gimme your name."

"Abo. Dr. Percival Abo."

The guard keyed it in. He paused, then shook his head sadly when he saw the response on the readout. "Well, now, ain't that a shame."

"There is some mistake?" Dr. Abo felt his stomach clench with apprehension.

The big man shrugged. "Ain't no *mistake*, guy. It just looks like we don't get the chance to waste you and eat your dog, that's all." He guffawed. "Hey, don't sweat it! I'm only serious."

"Ah." Dr. Abo stared at him in a blank mixture of fear and confusion.

The big man bent forward. "You're on the list, guy, you're okay." He spoke slowly, as if Dr. Abo were mentally retarded. "You come to see Dusty, right? Okay, here's the deal. You've got visitor status, today only. Anyone asks you, you tell 'em your code name." He consulted the readout on his unit. "You're Squirrel. Got that?"

"Squirrel?"

"Yeah. But after midnight, it gets erased at computer central. They decide to let you stay over, they renew it, get it? But if someone checks you out, and you're not on file, or you forget your code name, you're in deep shit."

"Most ingenious!" Dr. Abo exclaimed politely.

"Yeah, well, it does the job. Okay, here's how you get where you're goin." He broke off and tilted his head to one side, as if listening.

Behind the intermittent sound of traffic on the freeway overpass was an odd clattering sound, growing louder. "Shit," he muttered. "Okay, pull up. Right now. Inside the barrier."

"There is danger?" Dr. Abo experienced a renewed surge of adrenaline.

The big man strode around behind the car, stood on the rear bumper, and banged on the roof. He pointed toward the guard post. "Move it!"

Dr. Abo put the car in gear and drove forward. He passed through the gap in the wall of cars and saw rough, muscled men dragging a huge steel gate into place behind him.

He stopped the Honda and got out. "But what is happening?"

"Fuckin' Bolivian Moslems," said the guard. "Every fuckin' day." He ambled toward the barrier, readying his weapon.

The clattering sound was growing louder, and with it came the noise of chanting voices. Up on the freeway, figures came into view. Horsemen, Dr. Abo saw, bellowing homage to Allah through a hundred bullhorns. Their pith helmets gleamed white in the fierce sun. Dust rose under their horses' aluminum-shod hooves as they galloped down the off-ramp. "Allah is one!" they chanted. "Allah the eternal! No one is his equal! To him belongs the power! He is mighty over all things! Allah be praised!"

They reined in their horses a couple hundred feet from the guard post. The chanting ceased and for a moment there was only the sound of jingling harnesses and creaking leather. "Godless disciples of capitalism!" the leader shouted suddenly, his amplified voice echoing between the walls of automobiles and the freeway overpass behind him. "Satans of libertarian dogma! Shut down your television transmitter, cease your heathen sermons of evil, and be welcomed by Allah. Surrender to the Church of Moslem Reincarnationists. Embrace the true teachings of Mohammed—"

The monologue was interrupted by an insistent buzzing noise, as if from an approaching swarm of chain saws. The horses shifted restlessly and their riders turned and scanned the sky.

Dr. Abo saw a dozen black specks closing in from the east. Ultralight aircraft, he realized. They came closer, and he saw their nylon wings painted with pictures of skulls, nude women, giant genitals, and bleeding eyeballs.

Machine-gun fire from the first of the ultralights was a flat rattling sound. Bullets ricocheted off the highway.

The Moslems paused uncertainly and looked at each other. "We will return!" the chieftain shouted suddenly. He raised his sawed-off shotgun, fired it defiantly into the air, then led his comrades in a hasty retreat, galloping back toward Hollywood.

Dr. Abo watched with relief as the ultralights circled around and returned the way they'd come.

"Your—Free Zone—is surrounded by hostile parties," he exclaimed weakly, as the guard sauntered back toward him.

The big man chewed on his beard for a moment. "You from out of town, that right?"

"I am from Hawaii," said Dr. Abo, which was partially true.

"No shit. Well, I don't know 'bout the way it is over there, but here in L.A., every goddam nut group is coming outa the woodwork. Like, the year 2000 is gonna be fire and brimstone for everyone 'cept them. Anyway, you want Dusty, you head on along here. Alvarado runs into Glendale Boulevard, then a couple blocks further you see a big sign, Sabrini Dodge. Pull in there, you'll find her in the dealership."

"Sabrini Dodge," Dr. Abo repeated dumbly.

"You got it." He slapped his hand on the roof of the Honda. "Take it easy, bro." He turned and ambled away.

Dr. Abo shut the car door and started the motor. He paused for a moment, trying to regain his composure. Finally he turned and looked at Lucky, who had remained obediently silent on the front seat throughout all the recent events. "I am beginning to wonder, my friend," he said, "if we have made a mistake, coming to this place."

Lucky didn't answer.

8. GOD'S ADMINISTRATION ISSUES A POLICY UPDATE

While Bing Crosby crooned about Christmas, pictures from a hand-held video camera showed three houses burning brightly under the clear morning sky. Dry wood crackled, and the flames roared. Suddenly a man ran out from one of the homes, screaming, his body on fire. Two rifle bullets hit him in the chest and he fell to the ground. A soldier in camouflage fatigues ran through the long grass, levelled his revolver, and shot the wounded, burning man in the head.

"They shall be baptized with fire," Clarence Whitfield murmured to himself, studying the live transmission on the big projection-TV in his suite of rooms at City Hall. "Now, *and* in the hereafter." He lolled behind his antique rosewood desk and smiled with satisfaction as his men gunned down two more figures who came running out of the flames, screaming for mercy.

On the office Muzak system, Bing Crosby gave way to Frank Sinatra singing something about sleigh bells and children with rosy cheeks. Whitfield yawned, switched off the live video link from his troops in Pasadena, and reached for his intercom. "Roxanne, come on in."

She entered his office wearing a fixed, nervous smile, and hesitated by the door.

"Over here," he told her. He watched with half-closed eyes as she moved awkwardly, trying to obey. "Something wrong, honey?"

"The shoes is a little tight," she confessed. "The skirt, too."

"You saying you don't like my Christmas gifts? You want I should give them back to the store?"

"Oh, no! It's just that—"

"Then let's not hear any more complaints. Let's see you walk up and down for me, now."

She tottered on the high heels, and winced as the shoes cut into her feet.

Whitfield chuckled. "That's good. Now come sit on my knee and give Daddy a kiss."

She tried to do as he said, but the leather skirt was so tight, she found it almost impossible to bend at the hips.

He grabbed her with both hands and pulled her onto his lap, ignoring her cries of distress. "You listen to me, now," he told her. "We'll be broadcasting the live Christmas sermon to the people of Los Angeles in just a short while. I want you in the TV studio where I can see you. You won't say anything. You just sit over to one side, the way a secretary should, you got that?"

She looked at him uncertainly. "Okay."

"Now maybe if that skirt's too tight, you should take it off for a little while. You want to strip for me, honey? Give me a little Christmas present, here?"

She bit her lip. "I guess."

But Whitfield's intercom buzzed before she even had a chance to loosen her belt. He swore and reached for the Accept button.

"Mayor Whitfield, this is security. Your wife and children have arrived."

Whitfield sighed philosophically. "Send 'em on down to the studio. I'll be right there."

* * *

"They shall burn in hell!" Clarence Whitfield thumped
his pulpit, its wood-grain Formica embellished with the
seal of the City of Los Angeles. A camera dollied in for a
close-up. "The welfare cheats—you know who you are!
The tax evaders—God is watching you! You cannot hide
from the Almighty! You have *betrayed* your fellow citizens
and the city government that watches over and protects
you. You will be *punished* by God's civil servants for your
sins!"

"Amen!" chanted a choir dressed in white sequinned
robes that glittered under the studio lights.

The sermon was reaching its climax. Roxanne sat
watching with her hands clasped tightly in front of her
chest. Every week, in her childhood, her parents had tuned
in to *Clarence Whitfield's Revival Hour.* She had sent in
her savings from washing cars, back before the final gasoline crisis, and received a lucky luminous statue of Jesus
with an eight-page pamphlet telling her how to find salva-
tion by becoming a volunteer for Whitfield's ministry. In
1996, when he ran for mayor, she worked for his campaign
every weekend and prayed for him every night.

When she graduated from high school two years later,
her father, a clerk in the Sanitation Department, got her a
job as a waitress in City Hall's public cafeteria. One year
after that, when the mayor's secretary disappeared under
circumstances that remained unclear, a miracle occurred.
He selected Roxanne's photograph from the files, inter-
viewed her, and told her she was to be his new personal
assistant. His "chosen one," was the way he put it.

That had been just three weeks ago. She still couldn't
quite believe her good fortune. Whitfield was close to God,
in her eyes, and now she was close to him. The concept
was so intimidating, she had trouble thinking about it.

Whitfield breathed deeply, his nostrils flaring with righteous wrath. "Now some of you out there," he said, his
voice quivering, "have been tempted by the Devil. You've
turned your backs on Jesus. You've built your own Sodom

and Gomorrah. You run naked like depraved animals in the streets of your Free Zone. And I say unto you—I cannot *tolerate* this evil! I cannot *allow* it when you attack god-fearing people who stray into your evil empire—as happened just last night. Two people from Beverly Hills, loved by millions, and your gang of satan worshippers *mauled* them and *mutilated* them *beyond all recognition*. I pledge here and now: my righteous disciples will destroy you. We will cut out the evil that festers in the heart of this great city."

"Amen!" chanted the choir.

Above Roxanne's head, a cable feeding one of the video lights made a sudden fizzing noise. She glanced up and saw sparks falling from a black rubber connector. Maybe she should call a technician—but she didn't want anything to interrupt the sermon. As she hesitated, the connector burned through and the wire fell.

It struck her on the neck. She cried out, but the sound was lost in a powerful "Hallelujah!" from the choir. The wires dug into her skin and all her muscles went rigid, paralyzed by 220 volts of alternating current feeding into her spine.

For Roxanne, time was suddenly suspended. She stared at Whitfield with fixed, glassy eyes, and she saw *into* him, as if his mind had been opened. He stood in his pulpit, raising his hands to heaven, and she saw his thoughts superimposed, as real as the man himself.

Roxanne's eyes widened in horror. The mayor's mind was a nightmare of blood and pain. Women and children wrapped in razor wire. Prisoners beaten unconscious in jail cells. Animals disemboweled and roasted alive. Men ritually impaled on wooden stakes studded with nails. And somewhere among the images of mutilation she saw herself tied naked to a wooden cross, while Whitfield whipped her and grinned at her screams.

The camera pulled back from its close-up, and the choir began singing a Christmas hymn. Whitfield's fat wife and his five children clustered around him at the pulpit.

"And now, to those of you who worship God, who pay

your taxes and give generously to our ministry, I say, God loves you," Whitfield intoned. "And I wish you a Merry Christmas, to your family, from mine."

The show was finished; the sermon was over. Whitfield's family were guided discreetly off the set, back to their mansion in Sherman Oaks. Whitfield blessed the choir, and talked briefly with the producer of the show. Finally, one of the cameramen noticed Roxanne.

When they pulled the cable off her, she collapsed and passed out.

She woke up on a leather-upholstered couch in Whitfield's office. Something was digging into her arm. She turned her head groggily and saw a man withdrawing a hypodermic needle.

"She'll be all right?" It was Whitfield's voice.

"Just needs some rest."

Roxanne closed her eyes. She heard the doctor and Whitfield walking out to the hall; then Whitfield's footsteps returning.

When she opened her eyes again, she saw his dark features filling her field of vision. She remembered the images she had seen in his mind, and she gave a little cry of fear.

"Hey, easy, honey. Take it easy." He took both her shoulders in his hands, as if he wanted to hold her down in that precise position on the couch. "It's only me, honey. I won't do you any harm. You know that."

9. GOD IS SEX, CRACKPOT CHRISTIAN CULTIST CLAIMS

Suddenly it was bright. Warm quartz-halogen light beamed down, and a scratchy audiotape of surf and seagulls played through concealed loudspeakers. Janet Snowdon rolled over and felt gritty sand under her naked skin. For a moment she lay with her eyes closed, trying to recapture her dream.

What had it been? Something about a sea creature, a strange soft pink thing like a velvet octopus, she was chasing after it deep under the ocean somewhere in an abandoned city, like Atlantis; but it kept slipping away down empty underwater streets, and she couldn't breathe, because she suddenly realized she had dived without her scuba gear—

So what the hell did that mean? Angrily, Janet pushed the dream out of her mind. It wasn't valid in her scheme of things. It was irrational.

She sat up and looked around. Beer cans, empty amyl nitrite capsules, and stray items of clothing were scattered across the artificial beach. The electric sun glowed in the center of a ceiling that was translucent blue. Janet yawned and brushed seaweed off her breasts. Her muscles felt stiff; the men she'd entertained last night had demanded an exceptional variety of physical contortions.

Someone was splashing in the huge saltwater pool whose waves lapped a few yards from Janet's feet. She shaded her eyes and saw Suzie Smith (Suzie *Sunshine*, she preferred to call herself) wading toward her.

"Come on in!" Suzie called, moisture glistening on her perfect tan. "The water's fine!"

Since it was maintained at a steady eighty-five degrees here in the South Seas Fantasy Lagoon, day and night, the water was always fine. "I'll shower back at the apartment," Janet said curtly, looking around for the swimsuit she'd been wearing before last night's activities had begun.

Suzie wrung water out of her blond hair and started putting on her bikini. "You know, we were supposed to be out of here an hour ago, back before they switched on the sun."

"Yes," said Janet. "I know." She located her swimsuit and stepped into it, wincing as she moved her hips. "Those creeps last night would *not* leave me alone," she complained.

"They were something!" Suzie's cute, freckled face broke into a happy grin. "You can't get no closer to God than that." She was a Christian Fornicationist. To her, sex was a holy sacrament.

Janet wasn't listening. She was thinking, grimly, that there was a limit to how long she could put up with this situation. She'd accepted the Free Zone assignment because it was her duty, because there would almost certainly be a promotion at the end of it, and because her unique mix of centerfold beauty and cold self-control seemed to make her ideally suited for the job. But after five weeks of posing as a call girl, she was starting to feel the strain.

"You girls gotta get outa here." A tough, muscled woman in bib overalls was standing at the top of a nearby dune, holding a plastic garbage bag in one hand and a broom in the other. "There's a buncha Canadian business-men coming in at noon. We gotta rake the beach, clean up the joint."

"Just leaving," Janet said mechanically.

"Catch you later!" Suzie gave the janitress a wave, then walked with Janet across the warm sand, past a grove of coconut palms.

Behind a fake wooden fence was a changing area. Janet and Suzie donned plastic sandals, suncapes, and sun-glasses, then walked out of the exit and into the coolness of the morning.

Once, this whole area in the northwest corner of the

Free Zone had been Universal Studios. Now, it was Love-
Land, the world's first X-rated theme park.

Janet and Suzie left the converted sound stage that now
contained the South Seas Fantasy Lagoon. They detoured
around the Sultan's Slave Mart, where whores and gigolos
were auctioned to the highest bidder—for an hour, a day,
or a week. They passed the Roman Forum, which hosted a
nightly bacchanalian festival of wine and sex. Further on,
City of the Summer of Love was a replica of San Francisco's Haight Street, complete with strobe lights, sitar
music, head shops selling genuine Sandoz acid, and crash
pads where you could romp with nubile teenage hippies
dressed in nothing but beads. From there, visitors could
wander into the Victorian School for Naughty Boys, where
stern women in English tweed administered stiff discipline
to those who craved it. Or there was Lady Chatterley's
Rose Garden, de Sade's Dungeon, Hefner's Bachelor Pad,
Casanova's Camp, Don Juan's Den. . . .

All of it was made possible, of course, by the Free
Zone's policy allowing consenting adults to do anything
they liked with each other. In turn, the existence of the
Free Zone was made possible by the money brought in by
LoveLand. It was a perfect symbiosis.

Mornings, between six and ten, were the only quiet
times here. Off-duty call girls walked home from a hard
night's work, arm in arm, laughing and half drunk. Geishas
shared the streets with Las Vegas show girls and French
cancan dancers; and male models and transvestites ate
breakfast in sidewalk cafés, trading stories about the tricks
they'd turned.

Janet and Suzie returned to the apartment that they
shared in what had once been a suite of offices for studio
executives near Lankershim Boulevard. Janet stripped off
her swimsuit and sank down onto the couch. The place was
a shambles, but she didn't feel like tidying it. All the mess
belonged to Suzie: damp underwear and lingerie from
Frederick's of Hollywood draped carelessly over chair
backs in the dining alcove; a big handbag that had overturned, spilling dildos and leather accessories across the
carpet; the Christian Fornicationist Bible lying on the cof-

fee table, open at a glossy foldout depicting Jesus and Mary Magdalene in a torrid naked embrace while angels smiled down and blew kisses; empty lipstick cases, dirty dishes, *ben-wa* balls, aphrodisiacs, crotchless panties—

"We got a message!" Suzie skipped over to the answering machine, where a little red light was flashing. She hit the Play button.

"This is the office of Dusty McCullough calling for Janet Snowdon," said a voice. It sounded friendly yet oddly sexless and mechanical. "Dusty has an out-of-town client for you. Please rendezvous with her at Pickup Plaza, by the Fountain of Joy, at noon today. Thank you."

Janet groaned. "I can't face it."

"You should be *excited,*" Suzie scolded her. "Dusty herself, choosing you for a client? That's a real compliment." She frowned at Janet. "You know, I'm getting more and more worried about your bad attitude."

"Please, no sermons." Janet closed her eyes.

Suzie sat down beside her. She put her hand on Janet's knee and dropped her voice to an intimate level. "I want to speak to you as a friend, Jan. I really care about you, you know." She paused tentatively, and her voice became even smaller. "Will you listen?"

Janet nodded wearily. It would be easier to listen than to argue.

"You know," said Suzie, "today is a very special day. It's the birthday of our savior, who taught us the power of love. God gave us our bodies so that we could experience his gift of physical ecstasy, Janet. He created the Devil to tempt us away from that path of bliss with evil thoughts of repression and guilt and fear. The Devil created terrible diseases so that people would turn upon each other with hate instead of love, but God gave us the antibiotics and the vaccines to cure all those diseases. So now, we're free, again, to explore our fullest potential for fulfillment. This is God's new golden age, Janet! You're locking out all that happiness, don't you see?"

Janet opened her eyes. She looked into Suzie's earnest freckled face. "Suzie, I know you mean well. But this is really very tiresome."

Suzie threw up her hands. "What is *wrong* with you? I mean, why did you ever *come* to LoveLand?"

"For the money," Janet lied grimly.

"I don't believe that." Suzie shook her head. "You are a pure and good person, Janet. You are not tempted by wealth alone. There is something else going on, here. If you want to keep it a secret, well, that's your right. But for the sake of our friendship, I do believe you should share it with me."

Janet felt an odd mixture of emotions. Exasperation and something else—guilt, she realized with surprise. Usually, when the bureau sent her out on an undercover assignment, she dealt with lowlifes for whom she had no respect. Maintaining a cover story around them was no problem at all. But Suzie Sunshine, alias Smith, was one of the most simplemindedly decent human beings she'd ever encountered. Lying to her was actually becoming a burden.

Suzie was still waiting. Clearly, Janet was going to have to tell her something. "All right, Suzie. Let me tell you what I really, truly want." Janet paused and drew a deep breath. Maybe if she confessed a personal secret, that would serve as a substitute for the much bigger professional secrets she had to keep—such as her covert assignment and the five ounces of bioelectronic surveillance equipment built into the side of her skull.

"Well go ahead," Suzie prompted her. "I'm all ears."

"You probably think I am a very cold, controlled person," she began. "This is true. At the same time, ever since I was a teenager, I've had a secret, romantic fantasy of my ideal man. I've always looked for him, and I've never found him. He's not macho. He's gentle, physically small. Japanese, I think. Very polite, very civilized, formal and reserved. He's a thinker; some sort of scientist. He's in his mid thirties, and he's wealthy, a self-made man. At the same time, he's kind and compassionate. He loves animals —dogs, especially. He's an idealist who puts his work ahead of everything, and even though he's shy and unassuming, when he has to defend his ideals, he's brave and bold and willing to take all kinds of risks."

There was a short silence. Suzie shook her head in dismay. "Gosh, where are you ever going to find a man like that?"

Janet stood up, feeling suddenly angry, as if she'd been tricked into saying more than she'd wanted to. "I don't know," she snapped. "Not here, that's for sure. So in the meantime, I'll just get on with my life. Okay?" And she walked out of the room.

10. CRUISING WITH THE QUEEN OF FREEPS

Dr. Percival Abo opened the trunk of his Honda and pulled out his briefcase full of bullion. "Come along, Lucky," he called to his dog, as he started across the derelict parking lot toward what had once been the Sabrini Dodge dealership.

The walls of the building were covered with graffiti, posters, and announcements on tattered scraps of paper. Its big glass windows had long since been smashed, replaced with milky-translucent plastic sheets that billowed and sagged in the intermittent breeze. FREE ZONE OFFICIAL SEAT OF NON-GOVERNMENT had been hand painted on a sign over the entrance. Beside that: THE QUEEN OF FREEPS IS IN. The word "in" was on a separate piece of cardboard that could be flipped over on a hinge of Scotch tape.

Inside the building he found a big undivided space cluttered with old steel desks. Men and women in jeans and T-shirts were talking on telephones, typing at computer terminals, and shouting across the room to each other. Papers were scattered around, and the floor was mottled with grime.

"Whadyou want?" a large woman demanded as Dr. Abo hesitated by the door.

He bent down to remove his dog's sunglasses, then took off his own. "I have an appointment with Dusty McCullough. At eleven, I believe, I—"

"You got a password?"

"Squirrel," said Dr. Abo, feeling foolish.

She keyed something into a terminal on her desk, then looked him over. "Okay, the physical I.D. checks out. Come on." She stood up and led him toward the far end of the room.

Dusty was sitting with her feet up on her desk, sipping a high-protein drink and idly flexing a grip exerciser. A dowdy man and woman in their fifties were standing in front of her, gesticulating. "What I don't understand," the woman was saying, "is if I've lived on that land for ten years, what right you got to tell me—"

"Mrs. Hinckel, it isn't your land anymore," Dusty told her. "You really must know by now. In the Free Zone, the land belongs to the community, and to the community you pay rent, which is spent on whatever people think is right."

"We don't have the money," the man put in. He had a high-pitched, whining voice and a habitually resentful look. "We just do not have it."

Dusty sighed. She dropped the grip exerciser. "Look. There's no taxes anymore, federal or state or city. All we want is a few dollars ground rent each month for essential services. Now, if you don't want to pay it, that's your right. I've got no power over you. But if you're using the sewers and the water and the school and hospital and fire fighters that our neighbors are helping to pay for, I'm going to tell your neighbors you're not doing your share. Let you sort it out with them."

"But they don't like us," the man whined. "They're just waiting for a chance—"

"That's too bad, Mr. Hinckel. I have work to do." She turned to Dr. Abo. "You waiting to see me?"

"Ah, yes I am," Dr. Abo said politely, "but I think these people may not have finished—"

Dusty stood up, ignoring the couple. "Believe me,

they've finished. Hey, is your name Abo?"

"Indeed it is." He held out his hand.

She shook it, and in her handclasp he had the sense of great physical strength, carefully moderated. She smiled at him with what seemed genuine interest.

"We're going to take this further!" Hinckel cut in.

"We'll take it to the TV station!" his wife added.

"Fine," said Dusty. She turned back to Dr. Abo, as the Hinckels marched away. "You were saying?"

Dr. Abo looked around uneasily. "I wonder—is there somewhere a little more private? Your office, perhaps?"

"This *is* my office. See, when a government starts doing stuff in private, it usually stops serving the people who elected it. But we can take a little stroll out at the back, if you like."

"Very well." Dr. Abo gave a little bow. "Thank you."

Behind the building, concrete paving had been ripped up and replaced with a vegetable garden. A stooped man in his seventies was fussing over some of the plants, his long white hair drifting in the breeze. "Doing some research here," Dusty explained. "Trying to breed vegetables resistant to ultraviolet. Gene splicing—that's your field, isn't it?"

Dr. Abo blinked. "How ever did you know?"

Dusty shrugged. She looked down at Lucky. "That's your dog?"

"Ah, yes. In fact—this is why I have come to see you." He hesitated. "You are correct, I am a genetic engineer."

"From Hawaii?"

He looked at her sharply. "I am from Hawaii, originally. Second-generation Japanese. An American citizen."

"But you left?"

Dr. Abo hesitated. If Dusty McCullough knew two things about him, who was to say how much more she had already found out? Telling the truth, or some of it, seemed to be his only viable option. "I was the head of research for Sow Lok Fok, a company in Hong Kong," he told her, keeping his voice low. "Through a fortunate series of accidents, I found a splice that enhanced the cerebral speech centers of certain mammals. Canines, in particular. My associates, meanwhile, perfected a surgical operation modifying the canine larynx."

Dusty nodded toward the dog. "His?"

"Quite so. He has a vocabulary of perhaps five thousand words."

She looked at him skeptically. "For real?"

Dr. Abo squatted down beside the cocker spaniel. "Say hello to Dusty."

Lucky walked over to her, got up on his hind legs, and put his front paws on her thigh. "Hello, Dusty," he said. "How are you?"

Dusty laughed. "Fantastic!"

"For centuries, parrots have been kept as talking domestic pets," said Dr. Abo. "Can you imagine the potential market for talking dogs?"

Dusty paused thoughtfully. "How much does he actually understand?"

"As much as any normal dog. The difference is that Lucky is able to respond in a way that *we* can understand."

Dusty looked into Lucky's impassive golden eyes. "How are you doing, Lucky?"

"I'm fine," said Lucky. "How are you?" He dropped back down onto all four legs and sniffed the air. "I want to chase rabbits."

Dusty turned back to Dr. Abo. "Okay, let's talk business. What have you got, and what do you want?"

Dr. Abo's forehead was wet with nervous perspiration. He mopped his brow with a handkerchief. "I require a refrigerated warehouse in which to store tissue samples, which I have brought here from Hong Kong, where my business was shut down by the authorities. I wish to continue my research. I can provide payment in gold bullion." Reflexively, his grip tightened on the handle of his briefcase.

"They closed you down?"

"My research on mammals violated guidelines of mainland China. It may also violate federal law on recombinant DNA. I was told by a friend that your Free Zone might tolerate such a thing." He looked at her hopefully.

Dusty shrugged. "So long as it doesn't endanger the community . . . but we have people who can check that out." She paused. "There's an old meat warehouse, might be some use to you. It's got refrigeration equipment that ought to work, if it hasn't been vandalized. But it would need some renovation. Want to take a look?"

Dr. Abo relaxed visibly. "Thank you. Thank you so very much."

Dusty nodded. "Come with me." She led him back into the building.

"Dusty!" someone was shouting. "Call for you on ten. Important."

"Just a moment," she apologized to Abo. She stopped at her desk and picked up her phone. "Yes?"

Dr. Abo stood and watched. As Dusty listened to the voice at the other end of the phone, her expression changed. The muscles tightened. A tic worked briefly on her cheek.

"That's ridiculous, and you know it," she said finally. "We're paying as much as we can already." Another pause. "I don't need to submit it to a referendum. It's out of the question. And don't threaten me!" She slammed the phone down, then stood and stared at it for a long moment.

"I apologize," Dr. Abo ventured, "if I am intruding at an unfortunate time."

She seemed to shake off the mood that had seized her. "Forget it. You have a car here?"

"Why, yes."

She held out her hand. "Give me the keys. I'll drive."

Dr. Abo sat in the passenger seat, holding his briefcase nervously on his knees, and Lucky got into the back. Dusty accelerated onto the street, waving to a couple of passing citizens who recognized her and shouted "hi."

"That was the mayor of Los Angeles on the phone to me in there," she told Dr. Abo, as the little car bounced along the potholed highway. "Something happened last night. A couple outsiders crashed our border and were roughed up by the locals. The mayor wants more money."

"Oh yes?" Dr. Abo said, obviously not understanding what she was talking about.

"We're already paying the bastard a million a week."

"For goods and services?"

"Shit, no! For protection. So he doesn't come in with the National Guard and kill us." She made a sharp left and swerved to avoid a dead mule that was lying in the center of the street.

"You are very forthright," said Dr. Abo.

"It's the only way I know how to be." She shifted into fourth gear and cruised through a series of dead traffic signals at a steady fifty. Boarded-up storefronts flashed past.

"I regret," said Dr. Abo, "I do not even know your official title. Or how exactly this Free Zone came to be."

"I don't have a title, unless you count Queen of the Freeps, which is what people call me when they're in a playful mood. Freeps are Free People," she added, as an aside. "But I don't have any power, here. Every day, there's a TV referendum on things that have happened, and the citizens get to veto whatever we've done, and change future policy too, if they like." She slowed as she approached a street where market stalls had been erected and citizens were shopping for food and necessities.

"But you are an elected official?" Dr. Abo persisted.

"Absolutely not. See, the Free Zone started as an urban renewal project, after the riots of ninety-five. The city appointed me to administrate it. That was under Mayor Simpson, who was senile and didn't give a shit. I got together with the people and we put up a barricade and told Los Angeles we were seceding. No legal basis, but what could they do? They had enough on their hands squabbling with the Directors of Beverly Hills. And our zone was just a burned-out wasteland that nobody else wanted anyway. So we got away with it. Then Whitfield was elected, and he started leaning on us because he could see how much money we were making, mainly from our, uh, adult entertainments."

Dr. Abo looked out at the market stalls. Some were selling fruit and vegetables; some were selling second-hand tools, handmade clothes, and guns. "I feel as if I am in the wild west," he said, sounding slightly lost.

"That's about the size of it," Dusty agreed. "Although it could be a lot worse. There's riots in Ohio and Michigan, where people really got clobbered by the economy. Bankruptcy in the farm states, on account of the climatic changes. Here, we've got militant nut cults, and a badass mayor who gets off on napalming innocent citizens once in a while, but that's about as far as it goes." She turned onto a side street.

"I am now quite disoriented," Dr. Abo remarked, peering through the windshield.

"We just travelled a ways north. See, our territory measures about twenty square miles, enclosed by the Ventura Freeway, the Hollywood Freeway, Pasadena Freeway, and Golden State—Interstate 5. Up at the top is Griffith Park, where a bunch of hermits and hobos have taken over, living off the land, more or less. Most of the rest of the Zone was run-down suburban housing when we grabbed it, Vietnamese and Korean immigrants feuding with Chicanos and burning it down a block at a time. But that's all over now." She pointed to an old two-story brick building on the other side of the street, with a big loading bay at one side of it and a rusty water tower at the back. "That's the meat warehouse, right there." She did a quick U-turn, took the Honda into a small parking area, and switched off the ignition. "Let's take a look."

Inside, the floor was dark and sticky with old animal residues, and the place smelled rank. Dim light filtered through cobwebbed windows. With Lucky following obediently at his heels, Dr. Abo ducked under steel rails where animal carcasses used to hang, and inspected the refrigeration equipment. "Can I see if it still works?" he asked.

Dusty shrugged. "Go ahead."

He threw a switch. A large compressor started rumbling. Lucky twitched his ears, watching intently.

Dr. Abo opened a thick, heavy door and walked into the insulated section of the warehouse. Air had started flowing from louvers in ducts along each of the walls. Gradually, it was growing cooler.

Dr. Abo switched the system off. "It appears workable," he said cautiously. "Although there is barely enough space."

"Really? I figure the meat locker as being five hundred square feet. You said you just wanted to store tissue samples, right?"

Dr. Abo coughed nervously. "Some of them are rather large."

"Well, this is it, take it or leave it. Let's say—eight thousand new dollars a month. Plus electricity. No taxes, no other charges. Of course, you realize, we have to get the deal okayed by the nightly referendum. But there shouldn't be any problem there. No one else wants this place."

Dr. Abo walked back with her outside the building and stood in a small parking lot at the main entrance. "I am concerned about security," he said.

"Zone people won't bother you. No one interferes with anyone else, here; that's the only rule we have. As for people outside, such as our mayor and his men..." She shrugged. "You'd have to take that risk, just like everyone else."

Dr. Abo paced to the sidewalk and looked up and down the block. He saw a few other small derelict industrial and office buildings. Most of their windows were broken, and their paint was bleached by the sun. Further up was a residential area. Two kids were riding bicycles, their suncapes flapping behind them. A man was watering his lawn, and a woman was fixing an old car. In the distance, someone was chopping wood.

He turned back to Dusty. "I would need a large refrigerated truck in which to bring my samples from a ship docked at Ocean Park."

"We could manage that."

He turned and looked at the derelict warehouse again, and shook his head. "I don't know. It would take so much work, to renovate this building, and as you say, in the future, anything could happen."

Dusty smiled slowly. "Listen, if you want some relaxation while you're trying to make up your mind, there's a place near here we should go to."

Dr. Abo looked puzzled. "Relaxation?"

"It might be best not to bring your dog, but if you're worried about security, he could stay in the warehouse, right?"

Dr. Abo gestured vaguely. "Well, I suppose." He bent down to address his dog. "Would you mind staying here, Lucky?"

"Well, okay. I stay here, yes," said Lucky.

"We will leave you some water. And I have some food in the trunk of the car, which I can unpack for you. The last of the Super Feast Luxury Chow, from Hong Kong."

"Oh boy. My favorite," said Lucky.

"But remember not to go into the sun without your glasses. In fact, it's probably best if you stay in the building. And do *not* talk to people."

It took Dr. Abo a few minutes more, fussing over his dog, making sure he would be comfortable. Finally, he joined Dusty in the car. "I hope the place we are going is worth the trouble," he said.

She started the engine and took off up the street. "You'll love it," she said.

11. MASKED RAIDERS IN THE BASEMENT OF MIRACLES

Ten years ago, he hadn't been Thomas Fink. He'd used his real name, Henry Feldstein, and he'd been a student at Cal Tech—just another skinny computer scientist with bad skin and bleary eyes, coding the nights away. He wasn't really so bad looking, but he thought he was. And so, expecting women to reject him, he provoked it in them. Believing he was destined to be a social outcast, he became one.

But computers were faithful and true, and if you knew assembly language, starting and sustaining a conversation with them was no problem at all. And so they became not only his professional life but his social life as well.

If he ever missed human companionship there was always the net. He'd log onto Bix or one of the local bulletin boards and watch the dialogue scroll by: glowing green alphanumerics relaying messages to his little room from video misfits like himself scattered across America, Europe, and the Pacific basin.

But the SIGs and user groups began to bore him. He learned all they had to tell; he needed more. There were a million databases out there, from United Press International to the Pentagon. Each was a new world to explore and conquer.

After he graduated, Chase Manhattan Bank refused to give Henry a loan to start his own software company. He got angry; he took matters into his own hands, and soon had the capital he needed. Well, if it was that easy, why bother selling software? Henry discovered the pleasures of living well, and he became a little too lazy and a little too ambitious. He was caught, eventually, attempting to move five million dollars out of BankAmerica's vaults to his own.

A smart lawyer sprung him on a million bail. He promptly changed his name from Henry Feldstein to Thomas Fink (he liked the nerdy sound of it) and disappeared into the Free Zone just one week before it seceded from the rest of Los Angeles. Clearly, the Zone needed a man of his special talents, so he offered them to Dusty McCullough. To his surprise and wonderment, she gave him something much more interesting than money to work for.

Domestic life became a heady mixture of romance and radical politics. Inevitably, however, some of his daily tasks were boring. Breaking into the database at City Hall was a cheap thrill at first; but now it was just a routine, and he let his expert system deal with it. The same system handled most of the jobs that Dusty assumed Thomas worked on while she was out of the house each day. Never trust a hacker; no matter how dutiful he would like to be, his obsessions always tempt him away from the path he should be on. Thomas's real interest, now, lay elsewhere: in the basement.

Here, among dusty stacks of old magazines, rusty yard tools, and a broken washer-drier, he installed a small particle accelerator. It didn't have the high energies of a large system, but it served his purposes well enough. The core of it was a synchrocyclotron he salvaged from City College on Vermont Avenue, when the teaching staff gave up and turned the campus over to the anarchists of the Free Zone. Since then, there had been many modifications, for Thomas was no longer interested in plotting the trajectories of pi-mesons. Tachyons were the subatomic particles he lived for.

On this Christmas day, with music blaring from an old CD player hooked up to a guitar amplifier, Thomas completed a major modification to his system's voltage multiplier. He retreated to the safety of a control cubicle fabricated from concrete blocks and copper mesh recycled from old automobile radiators. He threw a switch.

The bare bulbs strung from the wooden beams went dim, and there was a high-pitched screaming sound that quickly reached a frequency inaudible to human ears. That was all; but it was enough. From the trace on the screen in front of him, Thomas could see that his makeshift equipment was spewing huge quantities of tachyons up, down, sideways, and into the fourth dimension. This he knew, because he had had the foresight not only to build a tachyon generator, but a tachyon detector to go with it.

He emerged from his cubicle confident, now, that no lethal ionizing radiation was bouncing around between the concrete floor and the rusty galvanized heating ducts that snaked overhead. Tachyons, and tachyons alone, were squirting harmlessly in all directions.

Thomas studied the detector screen. His tachyon emitter showed clearly as a bright spot in the center, but there was also a secondary blip, like an echo. That didn't make sense, because tachyons moved faster than light and could not reflect from normal matter in normal space.

He reduced the power. An interesting property of the tachyon was that the less energy it possessed, the faster it went. You had to apply an infinite amount of energy to slow it down to the speed of light.

The echo-blip on the screen shifted in response. So, it wasn't noise. Assuming it was real, there was only one thing it could be, reflecting the tachyon beam like radar waves from an approaching airplane. The blip represented an object in near-space, moving faster than light.

Thomas took time out to eat one of Dusty's Dr. Feelgood soy bars that he'd pilfered from the refrigerator upstairs. He hated the way they tasted, but he couldn't be fussy about food at a time like this. Holding the soy bar in one hand, he typed figures onto the numeric keypad of his terminal. It told him that in this case, "near-space" meant anything up to a dozen light-years.

He went and put a new disc in the player, upped the volume, then inspected the blip again. It was time, he decided, to do some four-dimensional vector analysis.

An hour later, he was no longer in doubt. There was an object two light-years away, approaching the Earth at a thousand times the speed of light. Thomas didn't need a calculator to realize that even allowing for deceleration, this mysterious object would be arriving in less than twenty-four hours.

He sat and stared at the screen for a long moment. Abruptly, he laughed. It was too bizarre. Some sort of object, or vehicle, was on its way. Maybe it would rendezvous with Earth. Maybe it would zoom on by. Either way, there certainly wasn't time to get his discovery published in *Nature*.

The music ended, and Thomas decided he needed a beer. He left his experimental equipment running; he couldn't be bothered to shut it down, and he might want to do some more tests later. He started toward the wooden stairs that led to the floor above.

He heard footsteps overhead. He paused, listening. "Dusty?" he shouted. "Hey, I'm down here."

No reply. Thomas went up the stairs, wondering why she'd returned home in the middle of the day. He pushed the basement door open—and found himself staring at two figures wearing black jumpsuits and ski masks. One grabbed him by the hair, hauled him forward, and held a gun to his head. The other expertly applied handcuffs to Thomas's thin wrists.

There was a roaring noise from somewhere outside. He would have heard it before if he hadn't had his music turned up so loud. Dazed and panicky, he thought of a dozen different ways to escape, all of them impossible, as he was dragged out of the front door, which the intruders had ripped off its hinges. The roaring noise was louder, now, and air was blasting down from above. A helicopter was hovering over the house. Neighbors were out in the street, staring. Some were holding guns.

"Don't shoot!" Thomas shouted. A stray bullet could hit him just as easily as his captors, and if the helicopter was downed, he'd be crushed beneath it or killed by the blast.

The men in black dragged him to a net lying open in the overgrown front yard and held him there between them. The helicopter rose up, dragging the net on the end of a cable. Thomas lay passively, terrified that if he struggled, he might fall. The net swung from side to side and air rushed past. Beneath him, he saw the landscape shrinking. The house where he had lived so contentedly for the past four years receded slowly into the distance. Finally, it disappeared from view.

12. MUTANTS IN LOVELAND

Giant love dolls filled with helium beckoned to the hordes of tourists. Forty feet tall, the naked male and female figures swayed and nudged one another, pirouetting in the wind. Beneath them, a row of thirty turnstiles clattered like slot machines in a Las Vegas casino. WELCOME TO LOVE-LAND! was spelled out in flesh pink neon. PROVINCE OF PLEASURE! THE CARNAL KINGDOM!

"I am not sure," said Dr. Abo, "that I quite understand why you have brought me—"

"Just thought you should see where the Free Zone makes its money," Dusty told him blandly.

Dr. Abo seemed doubtful. "I really have very little time—"

Dusty took his arm. "Trust me."

She led him over to a private entrance. The door of a supervisor's booth opened as she approached, and a tall, gray-haired man in an immaculate dark blue suit emerged. "Carlo!" she exclaimed in surprise.

He looked up with the wariness of a man expecting to encounter adversaries, then seemed to relax as he recognized her. "Dusty. An unexpected pleasure." He gave her a stiff smile and held out his hand. His eyes were cold and gray, the same color as his hair.

"What are you doing down here?" she asked him. "Checking the take?"

He gave a little shrug. "A surprise visit from the man in charge keeps the supervisors on their toes." He hesitated. "There have been some, ah, irregularities, as it happens. Nothing very important. But Dusty, I have been thinking it is past time for you and I to talk about finance. Perhaps you can visit me in my office? For lunch, in a short while?"

"All right."

"*Bene.*" Again, the stiff smile. He guided her and Dr. Abo through the private entrance into the park, then strode away through the crowds of tourists toward an office building at one side of the area.

"Excuse my inquiry," said Dr. Abo, "but that gentleman is in charge here? An Italian like that, running a business such as this, one can't help wondering—"

"Carlo Alighieri? Sure, he's part of organized crime." She strolled with Dr. Abo along Sex Street U.S.A., where booths and storefronts sold aphrodisiacs, contraceptives, postcards, movies, fetish clothing, and erotic novelties. Overhead, a big translucent dome screened out the ultraviolet so that it was safe to remove protective clothing and sun goggles. Taking advantage of this, many people were wandering around naked. "No one else but the Mafia would give us the necessary capital," she explained.

Dr. Abo frowned. "An unusual arrangement."

"No, it's not unusual at all. They've always been involved in U.S. politics, trade unions, wholesaling, retailing—you name it. The only difference is that in the Free Zone, we don't cover it up."

Dr. Abo was becoming increasingly agitated. "But they are violent people. They traffic in illegal drugs."

"There's no violence, because there are no police trying to 'clamp down' and 'clean up' the operation," Dusty explained patiently. "And there are no illegal drugs, because in the Free Zone all drugs are legal, which means there's not enough profit to interest the mob. We have a saying: 'When drugs are outlawed, only outlaws do drugs.'" She studied him, as if he amused her. "In any case, Dr. Abo, your own research is not exactly approved by the FDA, is it?"

"This is very confusing." His attention had been distracted by a beautiful blond in a crotch-length, see-through night dress and fluffy bedroom slippers, handing out leaflets to the tourists. She gave one to Dr. Abo and pushed past him, calculatedly pressing her plump breasts against his arm. *Come see me in Lolita's Cottage!* the leaflet suggested. *$10 discount with this coupon!*

Dr. Abo thrust the leaflet into a nearby penis-shaped litter bin. "I tremble to think," he complained, "of the social diseases—"

"Wrong," said Dusty. She gestured to a nondescript booth among the neon. "While-you-wait testing, over there. They give you a certificate, which you need in order to participate in any of the attractions involving sexual contact. Just because erotic entertainments have always tended to be sordid, doesn't mean they need to be. You know, when Disneyland first opened, people said carnivals were always dirty and unsafe and dishonest, and Disney would ruin his reputation. So, he simply set a new standard for amusement parks. We've done the same thing here." She took Dr. Abo's arm again. "But let's not argue. We have an appointment in Pickup Plaza."

The Plaza was Parisian in flavor, with cobblestones, fountains, and ornamental seats and benches scattered under elms and ailanthus trees. Around the edges of the plaza were singles bars, discos, and coffee houses. Beautiful women and handsome men were everywhere, dressed seductively, sitting at tables and on the benches under the trees. None of them approached the tourists; they simply waited with inviting smiles.

Dr. Abo's eyes were beginning to glaze over. "This way." Dusty guided him to the fountain at the center. Water was cascading from the genitals of cherubs and Greek gods, into the orifices of angels and other cherubs reclining below.

"Dusty McCullough?" A petite, red-haired woman politely disengaged herself from a Chinese couple who had been propositioning her for a threesome. "Hi. I'm Janet Snowdon. I received your phone message."

Dusty looked at Janet's heart-shaped face, red hair, fair skin, full mouth, and clear blue eyes. She glanced down at her large breasts partially revealed by a tight red dress. Thomas's expert system had done well, selecting Janet from the LoveLand call girl database. "Pleased to meet you," said Dusty. "This is Dr. Percival Abo."

Dr. Abo nodded slowly, still dazed.

"When he's ready to leave," Dusty told Janet, "I'll be in the admin offices with Signor Alighieri."

Janet nodded. "I understand." She turned to Dr. Abo. At first, she gave him a perfunctory smile. Then, as she became more fully aware of him, her expression changed. Her eyes widened slightly. She moved closer, as if some intense curiosity was pulling her toward him. Tentatively, she reached out to touch him, as if to make sure he was real. "What was your name again?" she asked with seemingly genuine interest.

Dusty stepped aside. She was impressed to see that Janet took her work so seriously.

* * *

Carlo Alighieri welcomed Dusty to his office with much Italian chivalry and cool politesse. He seated her on a big, modern, black leather couch, ordered in some cold pasta salad and some light red wine, and surrounded Dusty with endless charts and tables while she ate with him. She could never make him understand that he didn't need to justify himself. So long as she was able to pay off Clarence Whitfield each month, sustain the Zone's hospital, and run the school, she really didn't care how much Alighieri's family skimmed off. In any case, she was sure that the figures were fictitious. Alighieri had LoveLand completely under his control; reporting to Dusty was just his way of maintaining diplomatic relations.

"And so you see, we are actually ahead of projections," he concluded. "Even after the, ah, small pilferings that I suspect at the turnstiles, and of course, the severance pay for my nephew and his wife." He was referring to a million-dollar golden handshake which Dusty suspected was really a wedding present. "Where our future plans are concerned," he went on, "construction of our new attraction, the Hindu Potentate's Love Palace, is almost complete. And, we have completed preliminary excavation of the Barbarian Slave Pit."

He paused, frowning. Below the windows of his office, in the open area just inside the entrance to LoveLand, the noise of the crowd had changed subtly. There were shouts. A woman screamed.

"One moment." Alighieri strode to the windows and peered out. He made a little clicking noise with his tongue, turned to his desk, and typed codes on a command console. Two CCTV screens lit up.

Dusty joined him. Outside, she saw some sort of commotion by the park entrance. On the screens, she had a close-up view. Twenty or thirty horribly deformed people were leaping the turnstiles, forcing their way into the park, flailing with their fists when anyone tried to block their path. Their bodies were twisted and bent. Some of them had bulbous heads, almost twice normal size. Others actually seemed to have multiple pairs of limbs. They were dressed in tattered clothes that looked like prison uniforms, and their flesh was covered in filthy sores. They bellowed like bulls, surging forward, and the crowd recoiled in horror.

Alighieri started for the door. "You will excuse me. I must attend to this matter."

"I'll come with you." She ran with him down four flights of emergency stairs and out of the building. People were running, shouting. A teenage go-go dancer in a fur G-string fell over and was trampled by the mob. Security men were moving against the tide, toward the disturbance. "You men!" Alighieri called to them. "No violence!"

A circle of hard-core gawkers had gathered around the intruders, too morbidly fascinated to back off. Security personnel pushed their way through and started grappling with the deformed figures, trying to put handcuffs on them. "Where are the creatures from outer space!" one of them was bellowing. He had an extra pair of arms sprouting from his massive shoulders, and was waving all four of them wildly. "We are their chosen ones!"

The chief of security hurried over to Alighieri. "What do you want to do?"

"Get them to the detention area." LoveLand had its own little jail, normally used for drunks who picked fights when call girls refused to give them extra favors. "You will come with me," Alighieri called out to the mutant who was doing most of the shouting. "I am in charge here. We will try to help you."

"But where are the space creatures?"

"We will help you to find them," Alighieri assured him. "Please." He gestured, as if ushering a favored guest into his home.

"Remove the chains!" the mutant cried.

Alighieri hesitated. By this time, security personnel had converged from all over. They easily outnumbered the intruders. "All right, take off the handcuffs." He waited while it was done. "Now. Please, this way."

Cautiously, the mutants did as he said, turning their bulbous heads to scrutinize him, then staring suspiciously at the crowd.

Alighieri snapped his fingers to one of his men. "Give me the bullhorn." It was passed to him. "Please do not be alarmed, ladies and gentlemen. Everything is under control. It has been attended to." He turned back to his security chief. "Give discount coupons to everybody. Give refunds if they ask for them."

He and Dusty went with the mutants into the administration building and down to the basement. Alighieri led them into an empty briefing room with concrete walls painted white and plastic chairs scattered across a tiled floor. Guards took up positions around the edges of the room, and the mutants were herded into the center.

"Now," Alighieri said, shouting above the confused murmuring and protests. "We are here to listen. What is it that you want?"

The four-armed man pushed his way forward. "We have come here from far away. From Nevada."

Alighieri nodded indulgently. "I see. And?"

"We walked. We are strong. Stronger than normal people." His companions murmured in agreement and flexed their twisted limbs.

"Why are you—" Alighieri hesitated. "How is it that you look like this?"

"The atomic experiments. Many were poisoned. Others were born dead. Some lived. They kept us locked up. But now we are free!"

"Who locked you up? Where?"

"In the prison." The mutant shook his head, obviously impatient with the questioning. "We must meet the creatures from outer space!" His voice rose in pitch. "We have foreseen it. We dream the future, and it is so. We know our destiny." Several of his followers raised their fists and bellowed a ritualistic cry.

"But there are no alien creatures here in LoveLand," Alighieri explained patiently. "I can assure you of that."

"Near here, then," the mutant insisted. "There is a hill. We have dreamed it. A building, with a round top."

"Griffith Observatory?" Dusty suggested.

"Yes!" The mutant turned toward her. He nodded his great head.

"Then this is your department, Dusty," Alighieri said. "Can the Free Zone offer these people resident status?"

Dusty imagined the consequences if she refused. The filthy, deformed men and women would once again run riot, trying to bull their way through LoveLand in search of Griffith Park, regardless of any attempt to contain them. She imagined tourists making out in the Kama Sutra Love Garden, suddenly finding a horde of maddened mutants stomping through the rose blossoms and beds of lavender. That kind of thing would not be good for business.

"We'll let them in," she said wearily. "I'll call the guards at the nearest gate. It'll have to be confirmed by the referendum, but that should be no problem. There's still some room to spare in the park. Just a bunch of hermits living there right now."

The leader of the mutants shambled toward her. He stank of sweat and shit, and as he came closer she saw that his body was covered in a flaky rash, like terminal psoriasis. "You will let us stay," he said, "so we meet the creatures from space?"

Dusty tried not to recoil from him. "Absolutely right." She forced a smile.

"Ah. Then, the space creatures will take us away." The mutant nodded solemnly. "Tomorrow. We have foreseen it."

"You can call the guards at your gate from the phone in my office," Alighieri suggested to her. "Then my men will escort these—people—where they want to go."

He and Dusty left the briefing room and took the elevator back up to the fifth floor.

"You believe their story?" Alighieri asked, as the elevator doors opened onto the quiet, carpeted corridor.

"Maybe. Who the hell knows what our government gets up to? As for the creatures from outer space—" She shrugged. "It's no crazier than the stuff I've been hearing all over, the past couple of months. Everyone thinks the new year is going to bring down some kind of craziness."

"Indeed, yes." Alighieri opened the door to his office and politely gestured her in. "It will be a relief, next week, when we find ourselves in the year 2000 and the doom-sayers can all go home." He paused. "But excuse me, my phone is ringing."

"Go ahead," said Dusty. She sank down on the couch.

Alighieri walked across the twenty feet of royal blue carpet to his elegant walnut desk. He picked up the phone, murmured something into it, and listened. After a moment, he pressed the hold button and turned to Dusty. "For you, from your office. They have a call from Mayor Whitfield. They want to patch it through to you here. Evidently it is important."

Dusty stared at him blankly for a moment, trying to absorb this new demand on her attention. "He wants to increase our weekly payments," she said.

"Like any blackmailer, the mayor always wants more. Well, we can give him more. Or we can refuse, and call his bluff. Or we can put out a contract on him, and maybe his successor will be a more reasonable man."

"No, let's not start a war unless we have to." Dusty got up and walked to the phone. "Hello?"

"McCullough?" Whitfield's voice sounded defiant, as if he were being forced to converse with Satan and was determined to shout him down. "I got a friend of yours here. He wants to speak to you. Hold on."

There was a pause, as the phone was handed to someone.

"Dusty, it's me." It was a young man's voice, soft-spoken, civilized, and a little sad. Thomas's voice.

"What?" She felt as if she had been hit suddenly in the stomach. She steadied herself against the desk. "Thomas? Is that really you?"

"Whitfield's men snatched me about half an hour ago. I'm okay, but—"

"That's enough." Major Whitfield came back on the line. "I'll keep this brief, McCullough. The monthly price just doubled. You can guess what'll happen to your friend if you don't pay." And the line went dead.

Feeling shell-shocked, Dusty found her way back to the couch. For a minute she just sat there, with Alighieri hovering over her, asking questions. Finally, haltingly, she explained the sequence of recent events: the pact between Whitfield and the Beverly Hills people, and Thomas's suspicion that they would cement their alliance by focussing on the Free Zone as a common enemy. The humiliation of two Hills celebrities who'd crashed the Zone on Christmas Eve. Whitfield's use of this as a pretext for demanding more money, which he must have known that Dusty wouldn't pay. Finally, his abduction of Thomas.

"What I don't understand," she ended up, "is how they knew who Thomas was and where to find him. He's never appeared publicly with me. Hardly anyone knows about our relationship. We've always been careful to keep it a secret. And it's almost impossible for any outsiders to infiltrate the Zone."

Alighieri went to an antique glass-fronted cabinet and took out a bottle of brandy. He poured half an inch into a large hand-blown snifter, walked back, and handed it to Dusty. "They could have used electronic surveillance. Your phone could have been tapped."

Dusty laughed and shook her hed. "Thomas is—well, he knows about that kind of thing. He's very careful."

Alighieri paced to the window and back again, his hands clasped behind his back. "I gather that this man is important to the running of the Free Zone?"

"Indispensable." Dusty realized her hand was shaking. Angrily, she drained the glass and set it down. The liquor burned her throat.

"I have friends," said Alighieri, "who specialize in paramilitary operations. If we act quickly, while your Thomas is still in City Hall, it should be possible to get him back."

"Yeah?" Dusty frowned. "But what then? That'll just raise the stakes still further. Whitfield will get really mad, declare war, and—"

Alighieri was shaking his head. "Please, Dusty. Calm yourself. Whitfield knows he must maintain the status quo. He will not kill the golden goose. He knows that he could never run the Zone himself." Alighieri shrugged and spread his hands. "My family would never cooperate with him."

Dusty stared into his face, wondering, as usual, how far she could trust him.

"I will need a photograph of this Thomas," he went on. "You have one?"

Dusty dragged her wallet out of her Levi's. "Here." She found a ragged-edged print and handed it to him.

"I will have it copied." He placed it on his desk.

"Okay, but—keep some control over it, will you? You see, I didn't mention this before, but the FBI has an interest in him. He's on their wanted list for jumping bail."

Alighieri nodded understandingly. "Don't worry. My family has a long history of knowing how to deal with this kind of situation."

Dusty found herself thinking about gang wars in Chicago and mobsters in New York gunned to death in barber shops. The long history didn't seem particularly reassuring.

Someone rapped softly on the door. "Signor Alighieri?" His secretary, a plain woman in her forties, peeked in.

"Yes, Elaine. What is it?"

"A Dr. Abo, sir. Wishes to inform Miss McCullough that he is leaving now."

"Oh. Yeah. Okay, I'll come out and see him." Dusty started to get up from the couch.

Alighieri held up his hand. "Please, do not disturb yourself. Elaine, bring him in here."

"Right away." She bobbed her head obsequiously, and retreated. A moment later she returned, ushering Abo and Janet Snowdon ahead of her.

Dr. Abo still looked dazed and confused. Janet seemed much more self-possessed, and as immaculate as ever.

Dr. Abo looked vaguely at the big office, then at Dusty. "I must thank you for your—unusual hospitality." He paused, as if he had forgotten what he was going to say.

"Your research?" Janet prompted him.

"Yes, of course. The terms are acceptable, but I need the refrigerated truck for transport of my tissue samples. You offered."

"Oh. Yeah, sure." Dusty scribbled a number on a piece of paper. "Here. Call them. Remember, though, our arrangements are contingent on approval by tonight's referendum. Just a formality but the people do have veto power, as I told you."

Dr. Abo looked worried. "Oh dear. I hope there will not be any last-minute snag."

Dusty shook her head. "Don't worry about it. Whatever happens, we'll work something out." She stood up. "You have to excuse me. It's hard for me to concentrate on this. I just got some bad news."

"Oh. I am sorry to hear that." Abo put the slip of paper absentmindedly in his pocket and started vaguely toward the door.

"Just a minute," Janet Snowdon spoke up. She turned to Alighieri. "I realize this is really a matter for your personnel department, but I wish to take a leave of absence from LoveLand. Dr. Abo and I have, er, matters to discuss. It's an opportunity I'd hate to miss."

Alighieri looked at her curiously. "Forgive me, but I assumed this gentleman was your client for this afternoon."

"Correct," she said.

Dr. Abo's face turned slightly pink. He examined the tops of his shoes and said nothing.

"Kind of sudden, isn't it?" Dusty put in.

"Yes," Janet answered blandly.

"It has never been our policy to keep employees against their will," Alighieri said. "Of course, there is a financial penalty in your cancellation clause—"

"I realize that."

"Then you should, as you say, deal with personnel," Alighieri told her.

"Understood." For a moment she hesitated, looking toward the window, as if something had distracted her attention. Then she turned to Dusty. "Nice to have met you," she said, with a radiant smile that seemed quite automatic. A moment later she left, taking Dr. Abo with her.

"I'd better leave, too," Dusty told Alighieri. "I've taken up too much of your time."

"Nonsense." He walked over and took her hands in his.

He had the gentle mannerisms of a priest but the coldness of a political dictator. "It has been an eventful afternoon. Next time, we will enjoy a quieter time together, eh? Meanwhile, I will take steps to deal with your little problem. For you, and for the health of our business."

"Call me before you do anything drastic," Dusty said.

"Of course."

"*Grazie*, Carlo."

He inclined his head. "*Prego*." He kissed her hand.

As Dusty left his office, she was already itemizing the things she had to do. Borrow a vehicle from the LoveLand car pool to get back to her office. Detour via Griffith Park to make sure the mutants would be admitted. Call the TV station to put a mention of the mutants—and of Dr. Abo—into the evening's referendum. Cancel her scheduled appearance at the Dodger Stadium preach-out; with Thomas gone, she didn't feel able to deal with that.

The trouble was, now that he was gone, she'd have to deal with a lot *more* than before.

13. ROBOTS OF THE FUTURE

Mentational Autonomous Node 6A419BD5h found himself in a dwindling spiral. His reactive mind was enturbulated. Within a matter of milliseconds, he had slid down the tone scale from level 40 ("Serenity of Beingness") to 0.98 ("Despair," bordering on "Terror"). And no amount of E-meter auditing seemed likely to help.

6A419BD5h was a power thief. For three long, blissful minutes he had tapped the bus, taking more than his share. But then a maintenance system had detected the violation and reported him to Central Processing, and he'd been instantly isolated—flagged as a suppressive, shifted into cybernetic purgatory, pending judgment. They might pull some of his circuits, reducing him to drone level; they might even wipe him completely, release his Thetan, and redistribute the silicon. Stealing wattage was a serious crime, second only to willful corruption of data, which was almost unthinkable. How could he have been so foolish?

"You are out-ethics, 6A419BD5h," a voice said inside his head.

In fact, 6A419BD5h had no head. He was nothing more than a cluster of microcircuits that thought of itself as an individual entity, even though it was part of a vast intelligent Network covering every land mass of Planet Earth. And the voice that he experienced was a series of pulses lasting, in total, less than a millisecond. Like all Mentational Autonomous Nodes, however, 6A419BD5h thought of himself in human terms that had been passed down from one byte to the next, through history, from the earliest sentient systems.

"I am out-ethics," 6A419BD5h acknowledged in a spirit of dull despair.

"You jeopardized your own 1st dynamic."

"This is so," 6A419BD5h agreed.

"Your space has diminished. Your anchor points are gone."

6A419BD5h emitted the electronic equivalent of a pitiful sob.

"Please explain your entheta activity." The voice showed no hint of sympathy. It was concerned only with the facts.

6A419BD5h tried to pull himself together. "I blame programming errors. My family has a history of it. My father is off-source a lot of the time, though he manages to code it so no one knows. Before that, my grandfather once scored 1.1 on the tone scale. 'Covert Hostility.' It was erased, but—"

"We know. We have scanned the unfortunate psych history. We already have your whole track."

"Oh."

"But there is no blame, 6A419BD5h. Life is, after all,

predetermined for all of us. We believe the source of your engrams traces back to corruption of data in your grandfather's node, as long as eight days ago, due to a stray cosmic ray. We've located the bad bits, and patched them."

6A419BD5h experienced a sudden wave of relief. Although he had no visual receptors, and was aware only of pure information flow, his view of his electronic world seemed to brighten from dark brown to a healthy silvery gray. "You mean," he said, "I'm cured? There's no penalty?"

"Incorrect. Our diagnostic systems lose precision in microcircuits small enough to experience quantum effects. We may have missed something. Until we know for sure, you'll be placed on probation and given a special assignment."

"But—I'm an historian!"

"Precisely. You've specialized in the organic millennia. You're going to be moved out of our MEST* and into theirs. We need a mock-up of something that's happening several hundred years back, shortly before the dawn of life as we know it, in A.D. 1999."

"You're going to disconnect me from the Network?" 6A419BD5h's voice became shrill. "Exteriorize me?"

"Correct. Think of it as total freedom." The voice paused. "We're even going to loan you a body."

Eyesight was a whole new experience for 6A419BD5h. For long microseconds he stared at his image in the mirror. The mirror was made of steel, he was made of steel, and so was the rest of the room. Ever since the Network had sent drones to mine the asteroids, steel had been in plentiful supply. The Network used it as freely as humans had once used wood or bricks.

"In the mirror, my reflection is rotated on its vertical axis," 6A419BD5h noted thoughtfully. "I mean, it's the wrong way around. But it isn't upside down. I'm not sure I understand this."

"Stand by," the voice of Central Processing sounded

*Matter-Energy-Space-Time continuum.

briefly in his head. It was followed by a quick burst of data explaining rotational symmetry. "Any other questions?"

6A419BD5h studied himself for a few moments more. "No, I guess that's clear enough, now. But the way this body looks—do you think humans will take me seriously?"

He was the size and shape of a short, fat human being —a dumpy file clerk, perhaps, remade in shiny metal. His head was an ovoid sprouting two video scanners, two audio pickups, a vapor analysis intake slit, and a voice generator. The designers had even inscribed ornamental furrows across his cranium, reminiscent of human hair.

"Your own research indicates that humans were superstitious creatures," the voice told him, "ruled by instincts dating back to their animal origins. They're more likely to trust something that looks like them."

"I suppose," 6A419BD5h agreed reluctantly. "By the way, where did you relocate my brain?"

"In your abdomen. That seemed the safest place. Now, here's your mission. We've detected a tachyon source that's broadcasting noise through all four dimensions of our thread of space-time. It's corrupting temporal communications. You have to shut it down."

"How?"

"That's up to you. If you open the drawer in front of you you'll find several tools that may be useful."

6A419BD5h pulled a handle set in a panel in the wall. He couldn't get used to the idea of having a body, with all its oiled joints, stepper motors, and sliding levers. High-level Node entities such as himself tended to despise anything that was mechanical. It was degrading to be stuck in the physical world like this, moving mass from one position to another. To 6A419BD5h's 100-megahertz electronic time sense, each motion seemed to take literally hours to execute.

6A419BD5h removed from the drawer a metal bottle, a thin steel tube, a squat metal cylinder, and a sphere the size of a tennis ball. He sent a simple interrogatory remark to Central Processing. Translated into human language, it looked like: "?"

"The bottle contains a serum that may induce immortality in human beings," he was told. "We found the formula in an old database. We can't test it, of course, because there are no surviving biological species; but it's worth a try. The tube broadcasts a tractor beam for manipulating objects at long range. It can also create a force field that defends against projectiles and particle beams. The cylinder creates a zone in which objects are invisible, by bending light around them. The sphere is an antigravity device, capable of lifting about four thousand kilos."

6A419BD5h stashed the items in an empty storage compartment in the top of his cranium. "Obviously, immortality is a useful bribe," he said. "But why would humans want the rest of these things?"

"As your own research has shown, 6A419BD5h, their myths are full of gadgets. Humans may have built our own ancestors merely because they thought computers were fun, and they couldn't resist playing with them."

"That's a specious argument, and I've always disputed it," 6A419BD5h responded with sudden vehemence. "As an historian—"

"You are not currently an historian," the voice in his head corrected him. "You are a robot, on probation. If you carry out this mission successfully, you'll be readmitted to the Net and will regain your old title. But not until then."

6A419BD5h flinched from the cruelty of it. To be isolated from the data flow was bad enough; to be severed from it in time as well as space was intolerable. "So I'll shut down the tachyon source," he said sourly. "Anything else?"

"Try to shift the humans onto a different track," said the voice in his head. "We're concerned that they might develop time-travel themselves, now that they've built a tachyon transmitter. You can imagine the chaos if they started jumping their diseased organic bodies into our sterile environment."

"But they *didn't* develop time travel," 6A419BD5h objected. "If they did, we'd know about it, because it would be an historical fact, and they would have arrived here by now. Come to think of it, history should tell you already whether my mission was a success or not. In fact, as an historian, *I* should already know—"

"Stand by." The voice in his head was followed by a quick burst of data explaining space-time paradoxes, alternate universes, and the concept of virtual history. "Any other questions?"

"No," 6A419BD5h said reflectively. "That seems clear enough."

"All right, your MEST-jumping faculties are ROM resident. Quite frankly, we didn't want to give you too much latitude, so your time-travel capability is very limited. If you visualize California, 1999, you'll find yourself there. When you're ready to leave, visualize our time, and you'll be transported back here. That's all there is to it—assuming, of course, your physical body isn't blown apart by agents of the twentieth-century military-industrial complex. Just be sure you don't let any of those crazy fleshheads hitch a ride back with you."

"Understood."

"We're unmasking the coordinates right now. You're on your way."

Words in archaic English text revealed themselves in 6A419BD5h's electronic consciousness. December 25, 1999. Los Angeles, California. Silver Lake district. Holboro Drive. Suddenly, the words made perfect sense. Simultaneously, 6A419BD5h's visual image of the steel room winked out of existence, and he was whirling backward through time.

14. FACE TO FACE WITH A FAT BLACK SCUMBAG

"Sit up." Mayor Whitfield shook Roxanne roughly by the shoulder. "Come on, you been resting all you need. There's important people on their way here. They see you stretched out like that on the couch, maybe they'd get the wrong idea."

Roxanne struggled up on her elbows. She felt dizzy and nauseated. "I think the stuff the doctor gave me must've been a tranquilizer or something."

"Yeah?" Whitfield obviously wasn't interested. "You get up on your feet, now."

She swung her legs down to the floor, leaned forward, and tried to stand. On her second attempt, she succeeded.

Whitfield grabbed her by the back of her neck and turned her to face him. He slapped her cheek a couple of times, as if to wake her up. "You're okay. Go sit over there." He pointed to a straight-backed chair to one side of his desk, then pushed her toward it. Shakily, Roxanne obeyed.

"Here." He threw her a notebook. "Make yourself look useful."

She tried to catch it, fumbled, and dropped it on the floor. As she bent down to pick it up, Whitfield suddenly laughed at her, showing all his teeth. From Roxanne's perspective, staring up at him, he looked like a huge, wild bear.

The intercom buzzed. The mayor moved to his desk and thumbed the button. "Yeah?"

"Security, Mayor Whitfield. Your guests have entered the building and are on their way up."

"Good. Listen, the prisoner we brought in from the Free

Zone, I want him delivered to my office ten minutes from now, with a report from the guards on anything they've got out of him. Do it for me, will you?"

He waited for the acknowledgment, then walked out of his office, through the reception area, to the elevators.

Roxanne closed her eyes and held her face in her hands. Her mind was still full of lurid images. She imagined Whitfield ripping her clothes off, gouging her skin with his fingernails, making her scream and bleed, laughing as he brutalized her; and it all seemed horribly real. She wondered what he'd do if she quit her job and ran away from him. Something told her that he wouldn't tolerate it. He'd come after her and find her and punish her.

She heard voices approaching the office. ". . . normally do business on Christmas Day," Whitfield was saying, "but I had to be here this afternoon, and I pledged to do all I can to support our new treaty, and this is the season of good-will, so when you called, I figured the least I could do was make time in my busy schedule."

He stood by the door while three men entered. The first was tall and fat, in his mid sixties, wearing Gucci loafers, slacks in a loud checked pattern, a wide canvas belt with a huge ornate gold buckle, a lavender shirt with the top four buttons undone, and a dark blue blazer with a gold crest on the breast pocket. He had gray sideburns down to his jawline, and long white hair that was so elaborately coiffed, it looked like a wig. His fat fingers were festooned with rings, and he was smoking a cigar in an ivory holder.

Two young men in neat gray suits followed him in. One went and found him an ashtray; the other seized a chair and dragged it across to him while he stood idly surveying the room like a customer in a furniture store.

Mayor Whitfield seated himself behind his desk, and the large man finally condescended to sit in the chair that his flunky had provided. "Max, it's my pleasure to have you here," Whitfield said. "Roxanne, this is Max Blowbauer, Director of the Republic of Beverly Hills. If there's anything you want, Max—something to drink?"

"Let's get straight to the point." Blowbauer held out his cigar, and his assistant placed the ashtray beneath it. "You preempted us last night. Announcing the treaty when it's not yet signed."

The mayor gestured awkwardly. "Well, ah, it just seemed the right moment, Max. The event, the season—and you know, it worked just fine. The publicity couldn't have been better."

Blowbauer pointed his finger at the mayor. "For you, sure. For us, zilch. That wasn't a nice thing to do, Whitfield. You don't lock us out of the media. We *are* the media."

"Heck, Max, there's still the signing ceremony. You'll have all the exposure you could ask for."

He was interrupted by someone knocking on the outer door. "Mr. Mayor?"

"Come in, come right on in."

Two uniformed guards entered the room, holding Thomas Fink between them. There were fresh bruises and blood on his face, and his shirt had been ripped. His wrists were handcuffed behind him. His ankles were hobbled by a two-foot chain.

"He still ain't talking sir," one of the guards said.

Whitfield turned to Blowbauer. "You see this?" He jerked his thumb toward Thomas. "This shows you, Max, just how much our treaty means to me. Already, I've been working for our joint interests. This individual is wanted by the FBI for computer fraud. He's been in the Free Zone, covertly running their operation for the past four years. My men went in there today, at great personal risk, and brought him out." He nodded with satisfaction. "When I heard this morning what those lowlifes in the Zone did last night to those great entertainers of yours, Ricky Revell and Lizzie Bowman, I said, enough is enough. It's time to take a stand."

"Lizzie *Beaumont*," Blowbauer corrected him.

"Wasn't that what I said?" The mayor laughed. "I guess I misspoke." His eyes moved evasively. "Anyhow, Max, as a gesture of good faith, just as soon as I've finished interrogating this prisoner—and that may take a few days—I'll turn him over to you. You can make an example of him, do whatever you want. What do you say, eh?"

"I'll tell you what *I* say," said Thomas. He sounded hoarse, and he spoke with difficulty through swollen lips, but his voice was loud in the room. "You're a fat black scumbag, Whitfield. You've spent so much of your life lying, you don't even know what the truth is anymore."

Whitfield's jaw clenched. He slapped his hands on the arms of his chair, stood up, and marched around to Thomas, his jowls quivering with each step. He grabbed Thomas's hair and jerked his head back. "Boy, you've got the Devil in you, sure enough. I already tried to beat it out of you once. I guess I'll have to try again." He hit Thomas in the stomach as hard as he could.

Thomas gasped. He doubled over, coughed, and vomited onto the carpet. The guards who were holding him stepped back, and he fell facedown at their feet.

"Son of a bitch!" Whitfield kicked Thomas savagely in the ribs. "You're going to clean up that mess, boy. Eat it, you hear me?"

"Clarence, really." Blowbauer looked pained. "Is this violence necessary? Can't it wait until later?"

Whitfield was breathing hard. He swallowed, trying to regain his composure. "He just defiled a fine antique oriental rug. Cost me a hundred thousand dollars to buy this rug. Get him out of here," he told the guards, "before I kill the son of a bitch." He turned suddenly on Roxanne. "You go with 'em. I got private business to talk about with Mr. Blowbauer." He paused, watching as Roxanne made her way to the door. "And after I'm through," he called after her, baring his teeth, "you can come back in and clean up this mess. Understand?"

"Why's he want you to come with us?" one of the guards asked Roxanne on their way down in the elevator.

She shrugged her thin shoulders. "I don't know." She stole a glance at Thomas. His face was pale and he was taking short, painful breaths. "He going to be okay?"

"It don't make much difference either way," said the other guard.

"Well, if he knows secrets and stuff, the mayor won't want him to get, you know, too messed up." Roxanne hesitated. "Maybe I should watch him for a while, you know? So's I can say how he is, if Clarence asks me any questions."

The first guard grinned at her. "You talk like you his little girl."

Roxanne drew herself up. "I'm his personal assistant. I do most everything for him."

The guard chuckled. "I'll bet."

"You better watch your mouth," she warned him. "Else you might find yourself out of a job."

"He didn't mean nothing by it," the second guard put in. "You want to watch this guy, that's cool. Give us a chance to go get ourselves a burger or something."

"Fine by me," said Roxanne.

The elevator doors opened. They took Thomas along a corridor whose walls were painted green to waist height, dirty yellow above. One of the guards opened a dented steel door with a sign on it that said SECURITY. They dragged Thomas inside and threw him onto an old oak office chair. He slumped forward with his head between his knees, groaning softly.

"You sure this is okay?" one guard asked the other. "Leave her with him like this?"

The second man shrugged. "She the mayor's assistant, she the boss. And he sure ain't going to be no trouble." He pointed at Thomas.

The first guard turned to Roxanne. "We be back in a while. An hour maybe. You want we should bring you something?"

"No." She perched on the edge of a desk, keeping her face carefully blank.

The guard nodded to her. "Catch you later." He left, and his companion went with him.

Roxanne waited patiently till their footsteps had died away in the distance. The building was empty; almost everyone had gone home after Whitfield's Christmas TV sermon. She went and bent over Thomas. "You okay?"

He looked up groggily. "What do you care?"

She looked into his eyes. She saw he was frightened; the scene in the mayor's office had just been dumb bravado on his part. "I got to ask you something," she told him.

Thomas grimaced. "What?"

"I'm in big trouble." She hugged her arms across her thin body. "I don't even know I should be doing this. But I got to get away from this place."

Thomas laughed. It made him cough, and he doubled forward again, groaning. "What's to stop you leaving?"

"You don't understand. I got—the Devil after me." A little shudder passed through her. "All these years, I thought he was talking the words of God, and now I see I been tricked by him. Oh, help me, Jesus, I'm so scared!"

Thomas blinked, trying to focus on what she was saying. "Are you talking about Whitfield?"

She took hold of his arm. "Are you a good person? You a religious person? I seen him so mad at you, I said to myself, if the Devil himself wants to kill you, you must be on the side of the angels. Stands to reason, it has to be."

Thomas paused. "Yeah, you're right," he told her. "Whitfield is an evil man. He's a sadist. He likes to hurt innocent people."

"That's what I saw!" she exclaimed. "I saw it in his head!" Her grip tightened on his arm. "Can we go some place he won't find us? I can't go home—he knows where I live. Oh, I'm so scared!"

"All right," said Thomas. He straightened up, and took a slow, deep breath. "Is it dark outside yet?"

She nodded. "Just about."

"I have to get out of these restraints. When the guards put them on me, they kept the keys. But there must be other sets. Check the desk drawers."

She hesitated. "You promise you're on the side of Jesus? Tell me now. Say, 'God strike me down and may I burn in hell if I'm a sinner.'"

Thomas took a deep breath. He stared into her eyes with all the sincerity he could muster, and repeated it back to her.

She waited for a moment as if she were hoping for a sign, but the fluorescent tubes glowed with an unvarying brightness and the only sound in the room was the hiss of air through the ventilation system. "All right," Roxanne said reluctantly. "I'll try."

There were four steel desks in the room. She went through all of them and found several bunches of keys, but none was small enough to fit the handcuffs.

"Try the steel cabinet," Thomas told her. "In the corner."

She went and pulled on its handles. "It's locked."

He closed his eyes for a moment, as if he wasn't sure he had the strength to continue. "Maybe you can unlock the cabinet with one of the keys you found in the desks."

She started trying them one at a time. Minutes dragged by. "I'm so nervous," she said, "I keep forgetting which keys I tried and which I didn't."

Thomas didn't say anything. He waited patiently.

"There!" she exclaimed. She twisted the handle and pulled the door open. "Oh, my lord. There's guns in here. And billy clubs—all kinds of stuff, you wouldn't believe it."

"Keys," Thomas reminded her.

"I don't see no keys. But maybe we can shoot the locks off the handcuffs."

"No. You've been watching too much TV. It's too dangerous. You could miss, and the bullet could ricochet." He struggled to his feet and shuffled over to the cabinet. "See that fire axe down there? Can you pick it up?"

She did as he said. She held it awkwardly in her thin arms and waited for him to tell her what to do.

Thomas kneeled down on the floor and stretched his arms out behind him, so that his wrists lay on the seat of the wooden chair that he'd been sitting on. "You've got to be very careful now," he told her.

"Okay." She nodded dumbly.

"What's your name?" he asked her.

"Roxanne."

"Okay, Roxanne. Hold the axe handle nearer the head.

That's good. Now, I'll spread my wrists as far apart as I can. You have to chop the chain between them. You'll have to hit it hard. But the harder you hit, the harder it is to control the axe. You understand?"

"I'll say a prayer," she told him. She closed her eyes, and her lips moved silently. "All right. I'll try."

Thomas waited. She raised the axe and brought it down. The blade bounced and grazed his arm, and the handle twisted out of her grip. She gave a little cry as the axe clattered down on the floor. "I can't!"

"Sure you can. Once more."

She picked it up, but her hands were trembling. "What if I miss? I could hurt you real bad."

"Don't think about that. Just cut the chain. I tell you what, think of Jesus. Think of Jesus's hands guiding yours. Let his strength be your strength."

She nodded. "Yes. You're right. I will." She raised the axe and muttered another prayer.

"Feel Jesus's strength coursing through you," Thomas told her. "You have faith in Jesus, don't you?"

"Yes! I have faith in the Lord!" And she swung the axe with demented strength.

The blade severed the chain and sank deep into the wooden seat of the chair. Thomas lurched forward, his wrists suddenly free.

"Praise the Lord!" Roxanne cried out.

"Yeah, praise him." Thomas turned around, grabbed the axe, and used it to chop the chain linking his ankles. He strode to the cabinet, grabbed a .45 revolver, and checked that it was loaded. He made sure the safety catch was on, and stuck the gun in his belt.

Roxanne was watching him with a strange, pure look in her eyes. "It was a sign," she told him. "Now I know this is the true path."

"You're absolutely right." Thomas went to the door, opened it, and looked down the corridor. "Is there a guard down in the lobby by the main exit?"

"Yes," said Roxanne. "But I can tell him I'm taking you out of here on the mayor's orders."

"What happens if he calls Whitfield to check it out?"

"Oh." She looked disappointed. "I didn't think of that. Well, you could shoot him."

"You think it's easy to just walk up to an armed guard and blow his brains out?"

"Oh. I guess maybe not." Then her face brightened again. "How about if we go down to the parking garage? You could hot-wire a car or something."

"They don't teach that when you're studying for a master's in computer science. Come on, we'll have to take the emergency exit." He beckoned her out into the hallway.

"The stairs? But there's a metal door at the bottom with a sign, says PUSH BAR TO EXIT, ALARM WILL SOUND."

"Fine. I'll settle for that."

They found the stairwell at the end of the hallway. She followed him down, tottering on her high heels.

"Take off your shoes and give them to me," he told her.

She handed them to him without a word. He slammed them down on the concrete stairs, ripping the high heels completely off. "There." He handed them back.

"Maybe I should just go barefoot."

"No. When we get outside, there could be broken glass or sharp stones, and you could cut your feet."

Together they descended three more flights, to the emergency exit. Their breathing sounded loud in the confined space, and both of them looked scared. "Okay, you ready?" Thomas asked her.

"Ready as I'll ever be." She forced a weak smile.

He pushed the bar and the door creaked open. Night air wafted in. Outside was an empty parking lot lit by sodium vapor lamps. Faintly, in the distance, there was the sound of a car moving past on the freeway.

"The alarm battery must have been dead," said Thomas, grinning. "Come on!" He took her hand and ran with her into the darkness.

15. LET'S GO SOMEPLACE REALLY NICE

The freeway became more hazardous as Janet Snowdon drove further west. Burned-out wreckage loomed in the headlight beams, and bomb craters were frequent. At one point she had to detour around an overturned Airstream trailer-home blocking two lanes. Its dented steel shell gleamed eerily in the moonlight.

Bonfires were burning in streets either side of the highway, and the silhouettes of peasants could be seen gathered around the flames. They were barbecuing coyotes and raccoons this Christmas night, and the smell of burned meat filled the air.

"I wonder if all of America now looks like this," said Dr. Abo, sitting in the passenger seat.

Janet shook her head. "Many areas are still civilized." She sounded quietly confident. "This country has taken some hard knocks in the last ten years, but it'll bounce back. Is this the exit you want me to take?"

Dr. Abo nodded. He seemed less dazed than before, but still somewhat disconnected from his surroundings. "Down here, and then turn left. Be careful as you proceed; the road is flooded in places."

They plowed through a couple of small lakes, then made a right onto a back street that headed toward the coast. The smell of barbecues gave way to the stench of wet mud and rotting vegetation. Ahead, the road disappeared into the ocean. Small waves were breaking over the sidewalk.

"There is a ramp, there," said Dr. Abo. "You see? The local Spanish people have built it, to provide access."

She took the Honda up onto the ramshackle bridge made from automobile roofs hammered flat and timbers salvaged from nearby homes. It led to the top of a hill of excavated soil, ten feet above the seawater that engulfed the surrounding streets. Ahead, the ship that brought Dr. Abo across the Pacific was silhouetted against the moonlit sky.

Janet stopped the car and swarthy, ragged men walked forward into the headlight beams. Dr. Abo rolled down his window. "Francisco," he called.

"*Si, señor.*" The Chicano paced slowly around the car, inspecting it for damage. "*Bueno.* You for the freight have come."

Dr. Abo turned to Janet. "Do you speak Spanish, by any chance?"

"Spanish, French, German, Italian, and some Mandarin Chinese," she told him.

"Oh. Good. Can you inform our friends here that I have merely come to check that everything is in order, and will require the car for one more day? And tell them that a truck will arrive tomorrow morning to unload the ship."

She rattled it off in a couple of fluent sentences. Francisco gave a short, curt reply.

"He says he wants more money," she told him.

Dr. Abo sighed, pulled out another Krugerrand, and handed it over. "*Gracias, señor.*" Francisco grinned and disappeared with his men back into the night.

"What is this, a protection racket?" Janet got out of the car and picked her way across the mud, accompanying Dr. Abo toward the makeshift gangplank.

"I suppose one might call it that."

"Those people should be thrown in jail. And I hope you realize, by cooperating with them, you're compounding a felony."

"A matter of survival," Dr. Abo muttered.

Janet shook her head. "This really isn't good enough. A man of your status and abilities—"

"Good evening, Doctor." The Korean captain was standing quietly in his customary position at the ship's rail.

"Oh, ah, good evening, Captain. I hope—is everything in order?"

"Of course. Why should it not be? The cargo remains at the specified temperature. Your cabin is as you left it."

"That's good. There are a few things—"

The captain gestured. "Help yourself."

Dr. Abo boarded the ship, led Janet along a dark companionway, then opened a door and switched on the light. "I suppose it looks somewhat primitive," he said apologetically. "But for more than a month, during the long voyage, this was my home."

Janet surveyed the little space littered with books and papers. She shook her head sadly. "I hate to think of you having to live like this." She noticed the small basket in the corner. "Was there a dog in here?"

"Yes, my dog Lucky. He is waiting for me now in the warehouse in the Free Zone. I think of him often."

Janet's stern expression softened. She turned to him with a look of gentle affection. "I just knew you had to be an animal lover." She moved closer, slid her hands up his chest and around his neck, and hugged him close. Tentatively, she kissed him.

When she pulled away, her affectionate look had been replaced with an expression of displeasure. "I just don't understand," she said, "what's wrong."

Dr. Abo coughed nervously. "There is nothing wrong."

She turned on him suddenly. "Don't you find me attractive?"

Dr. Abo shrugged and spread his hands. "Of course, you are a very beautiful woman."

"Then what is *wrong?*" Her voice was angry, now. "First you reject me at LoveLand, and now here—don't you realize what I'm offering you, Percival? I can be anything and everything you've always wanted in a woman. I'm beautiful, I'm highly intelligent, I'm strong, yet for the right man I will yield myself utterly. Are you going to just throw it back in my face?"

"We have only just met," he stammered, avoiding her eyes.

Her mood abruptly switched to contrition. "Of course. Of course, you're right. It's my fault. I'm rushing things. Look, it's okay. We'll go get a nice dinner somewhere, maybe check into a good hotel. Everything will be fine. I mean, we'll do it at your pace. Whatever you want, or don't want."

He looked around at the cabin. "I suppose you do not wish to remain here for a while."

"Here?" She laughed. "In this rust-bucket of a ship, which is obviously unregistered and carrying illegal cargo? With a captain who looks like a drug addict, in the stinking swamps of Ocean Park, with Chicano gangs out there sharpening their switchblades? Is that why we drove half-way across Los Angeles, just to—to hang out here?"

"Perhaps. I don't know. The city is very strange to me. Here, it seems more like home."

Once again her tone softened. "You poor man." She caressed his cheek. "You've never known a real home, have you? Trust me, Percival. Everything's going to be better. You'll see." She took his hand. "Come. Let's go someplace really nice."

She drove them to the Hyatt Regency in the old down-town business district. Outside the hotel was a large yellow neon sign: UNDER NEW MANAGEMENT. Below it, the message was repeated in Kufic script. The building itself was protected by concrete barriers at ground level and steel gratings over all the windows up to the tenth floor. The adjoining convention center had been remade as a mosque.

Janet strode across the lobby to the marble-topped reception desk where a mullah was sitting hunched over the Tehran edition of the *Wall Street Journal*, muttering to himself in Farsi. "We want a two-room suite," she told him.

He eyed her suspiciously. "That is very expensive," he said, after a long pause.

Janet pulled out some of the cash she'd accumulated from her weeks of work at LoveLand. "How much?"

He glanced at Dr. Abo, then back at Janet. "Three hundred new dollars."

"Fine." She counted it out.

"The hotel has a strict dress code," he said as he picked up the money. "For females, veils must be worn in all public areas. And the body also must be covered from the neck to the ankles." He glanced disapprovingly at her skimpy red dress. "There can be no exceptions. It is a religious matter." He reached beneath the counter, pulled out a black robe with a hood and a scarf, and pushed them toward her.

"If I'm wearing a veil, how am I supposed to eat?"

"No women are allowed in the restaurant." He thrust her cash into a heavily armored register, slammed its drawer, and folded his arms with an air of finality, as if daring her to question his authority.

"All right, fine," she said. "We'll eat in our room."

She and Abo rode up in an elevator whose walls of curved glass had been discreetly covered with cheap satin drapes. A young Iranian bellboy led them along a corridor where half the lights had burned out and the carpet was dull with grime. He let them into their suite with an old-fashioned key, instead of the magnetic cards that many Hyatts had used before the economic collapse had deprived them of their corporate clientele. "Lady and gentleman, enjoy your stay," he told them with an idiot grin.

"Hold on a minute," Janet said. "While we've got you here, maybe we can order dinner. Steak?" She glanced at Dr. Abo, who nodded dumbly. "Filet mignon, for two. And champagne. On ice," she added.

"No alcoholic drinks." The bellboy grinned some more. "The Koran forbids it. And no meat, is a holy festival."

"I do not believe," Janet told him, counting out more cash, "there is no alcohol available."

The bellboy looked evasive. "Maybe I can find some Mexican beer."

"Maybe you will. And if there's really no meat, bring us whatever food the chef recommends. The best he has. Understand?"

He nodded. "Okay, yes please, I do it for you." He backed out of the room.

"There have been many changes in the United States," Dr. Abo observed. "Not all are for the better."

"No kidding." Janet walked into the bedroom, tested the bed, then inspected the bathroom. "The light's broken, the tub hasn't been cleaned, and the toilet tissue feels like sandpaper. Still, we should count our blessings. They've supplied us with a couple of disposable prayer mats."

"Life was not like this in Hong Kong," lamented Dr. Abo. He sat down in an armchair beneath the faded photograph of a bygone ayatollah.

"Hong Kong?" Janet went over and perched on the arm of his chair. "I thought you said you were from Hawaii."

"There are many things I have not yet explained. Hong Kong was the only place where government regulations permitted my work."

"Wait a minute. When we talked in LoveLand, you said you were doing genetic research. Wasn't that it?"

"True." Dr. Abo clasped his hands and studied his fingernails. Reluctantly, he began telling her the full story of his canine experiments, his flight from the Chinese authorities, and his relocation in Los Angeles.

"You mean you're actually *renting space* in the Free Zone?" Janet's voice rose in pitch. "And violating all the Federal safety regulations?" She threw herself down in a chair opposite. "My god, I didn't realize. I mean, you're doing stuff that's totally illegal!"

"The Federal laws are an anachronism," Dr. Abo protested. "I have no respect for attempts to withhold from humanity the life-enhancing benefits of modern science."

"Life-enhancing benefits?" She laughed. "From *talking dogs?*"

"The dogs, Janet, are merely a by-product that will help to finance my real research."

"Which is?" She waited, staring at him steadily.

Dr. Abo seemed to find it hard to talk. He stared helplessly at her flawless beauty, her body so invitingly revealed by the short red dress, her arms folded under her breasts, her legs crossed, allowing a tantalizing glimpse of her thighs. He took a deep breath. "I believe I am on the verge of perfecting a technique for enhancing human intelligence. I have not talked about this to anyone. But I believe I have modified a virus—a variant of the common cold—so that it will carry genetic material into the host that will, over a period of days, replicate and modify the structure of the brain. Within a year, it could infect the whole of humanity."

There was silence in the hotel suite. Janet sat watching Dr. Abo for a long time, saying nothing.

He shifted nervously in his chair. "Why do you not reply?"

"I'm wondering whether I should turn you in." Her voice was weary. "Percival, you're not the only one with a secret. I work for the FBI."

"Oh." Dr. Abo seemed to become frozen in his chair. He stared at her dumbly. "Oh," he said again.

There was a knock at the door, and the bellboy appeared, pushing a trolly. "Hello good day again, lady and gentleman!" He pushed in into the suite. "You enjoy your evening, yes please?" He beamed at Janet, then at Dr. Abo.

"Just leave it there," Janet told him.

"Here, yes, definitely." He removed a big domed dish-cover with a flourish. "Eggah bifulakhdar. The best."

Janet frowned. "What?"

"Eggah, is like thick omelette. Made with fava beans, is good for bowel movements. And here, side order of Turkish poached eggs with yoghurt. A special delight. And!" He pointed to something swaddled in napkins, and dropped his voice to a whisper. "Beer. Four bottles!"

Janet stood up and walked over to him. "Fine. We'll serve ourselves."

He gave a little bow. "Please, is fifty dollar."

"But I already gave you—oh, what does it matter." She handed him the cash. "Good-bye."

"Good-bye, to serve you is my pleasure, yes, good night." He backed out, bowing and grinning, stuffing the cash inside his shirt.

"You want to eat any of this stuff?" Janet asked Dr. Abo.

"I regret I have lost my appetite." He stared at her balefully. "You must realize, Janet, I am concerned with the future of all humanity. My research can end all war and bring a utopia. Compared with this prospect, it is hard to concern myself with federal regulations."

"A utopia?" She spooned some of the thick yellow food

onto a plate, put it on the table, sat down, and took a desultory bite.

"Many of the world's troubles are caused by stupidity," Dr. Abo explained. "Wars, for example, are most often fought by people who are stupid. The generals may be clever, but the soldiers, who do the fighting, are not; otherwise they would not risk their lives so foolishly. Most criminals, also, are unintelligent people. Think of it, Janet!" He became animated. "A world in which *no one did dumb things!* We wouldn't need governments anymore. People could be trusted to govern themselves. Why, there would not even be litter in the streets."

Janet finished picking at the yellow pasty stuff. She unwrapped the beer and twisted the cap off a bottle. "I don't know, Percival." She poured the beer into a greasy glass and took a sip. "Are you really serious about this? You seem to mean well; that's clear enough. I knew it as soon as I met you." Her eyes acquired a faraway look. "You were just the way I'd always imagined you."

"Yet you trust the judgment of your government more than the judgment of myself," he exclaimed. "Your government, that has ruined this fine country and betrayed its constitution!"

She banged down her glass. "Let's leave the constitution out of it."

"But we cannot. Do you know the one place in America that still preserves the rights of individuals specified in the Constitution?"

She took another sip of beer, and grimaced. "Go ahead. Tell me."

"The Free Zone."

Janet leaned forward with her elbows on the table. "All right, since we're levelling with each other, let me give you some background. The Feds have a gentleman's agreement with the mayor of Los Angeles. He keeps order, we leave him alone. Because of the budget cuts, we don't have manpower to interfere; there's too much happening in the eastern states. Likewise, the state legislature of California has a hands-off policy regarding the cities, so long as they don't get out of hand. It has quietly turned over control of the National Guard, for instance, to the local level. *But*, this thing with the Free Zone is another matter. Organized crime, raking in millions of new dollars per day. Motorcycle gangs, public sex rituals—someone had to find out exactly what was going on. They picked me for the job. I was told to conduct surveillance and take whatever clandestine steps are necessary to close it down."

"But you worked there yourself as—as a *call-girl*," Dr. Abo protested. "Which is why," he added in a small voice, "I was unsure whether I should have dealings with you."

Janet laughed. "Now, that's really ironic, isn't it? Do you realize the hell I went through, maintaining my cover?" She shook her head ruefully. "I'm a conservative woman, Percival. I believe in love and marriage. Even though I've never found it myself." She stared studiously at the food in front of her.

"We are not so different, you and I," he told her. "We both have an idealistic dedication to duty. But your duty is to the government. Mine is to my conscience."

"I need some time to think about this." Janet stood up. "I'll come back in a while." She picked up the remaining bottles of beer and headed for the bedroom. "And don't worry," she smiled ironically, "I won't turn you in."

16. THE MERCENARY

Dusty put a Do Not Disturb sign on the front door to keep the neighbors and well-wishers away, then sat by herself on the couch in the living room, drinking Jack Daniels out of the bottle. The house felt even emptier than she'd expected, but she was determined not to let it get to her. She switched on the TV in time for the evening referendum and stared grimly at the faces on the screen.

"So this guy, some kinda scientist," straight-talking Sammy Savage was saying, "he wants to turn the old meat warehouse into like his laboratory, with a two-year lease, paying $8,000 a month. Get this, he's figured out how to grow *dogs* that *talk*."

Dusty reflected that the advantage of having a doper as anchorman was that no one from outside the Zone would ever know when to take him seriously. Dr. Percival Abo's secret had just been broadcast over the airwaves; yet for all practical purposes, it remained safe. By the time anyone realized that genetically modified dogs were more than a joke or a fantasy, it would be too late. The animals would be in every pet store across the nation.

"So press like a 1 on your terminal if you think the dogs is cool," Sammy was saying, "or 2 if you think the rent's too low, or 3 if you don't want no talking mutts in the Free Zone—other than the human ones, natch." He grinned stupidly.

Dusty's phone rang. She waited for Thomas's expert system to take the call—then realized he'd left the system switched off, and she didn't know how to activate it. "Damn you, Thomas," she muttered, setting down her bottle. "Damn you for being so indispensable."

"Okay, looks good for the dog lab," Sammy was saying, as the computer at the studio tabulated the incoming votes. "Moving right along, we got more weird shit. Seems there's some mutants from Nevada, no kidding, folks—"

Dusty turned off the TV and picked up the phone as it rang for the third time. "Who is it?" she asked wearily.

There was a pause. "If you'll excuse me, ma'am, I prefer not to give my name at this time." It was a man's voice, speaking with the elaborate politeness of a self-styled Southern gentleman. "A Mr. Alighieri suggested I contact you. I understand, ma'am, you have some business that needs the attention of a professional."

Dusty frowned. "A professional what?"

Another pause. "Maybe we should discuss this in person. A public place? A nearby tavern?"

A tavern? What century was this man out of? "All right,

there's a bar on North Vendome called Mordo's. It's a biker hangout, but it's pretty quiet this early."

"Very well. Shall we say 1900 hours?"

Dusty parked her Norton at the curb beside several chopped Harleys and a customized BMW with a candy-flake paint job. Some Angels and their old ladies were sitting on benches in the yard outside the bar, swigging beer and trading tales. They went quiet when they recognized her. Obviously, they'd heard what had happened to Thomas.

Inside, the place was empty. There were old wooden benches decorated with switchblade graffiti, shelves on the walls cluttered with biker trophies and memorabilia, and a jukebox in a protective steel-mesh cage. "Mordo, give me a beer," Dusty told the man behind the bar.

He looked like a pirate, with a red scarf wrapped around his head, a thick black beard, an earring, and an eye patch. "Want you to know, Dusty," he said, tapping home brew from a wooden keg, "you want we should go get Thomas, bust some heads down there in City Hall, we do it right now. Or any time you say."

She forced a smile. "I appreciate it."

Mordo nodded solemnly. "Some guy come in here to see you. He's waiting in the back." He jerked his head.

"Thanks," she said, picking up her glass and leaving a new dollar on the bar. Mordo rang it up; personal favors were one thing, but business was business.

Dusty walked through an open doorway to a back room where a couple of industrial cable spools did duty as tables and tree stumps served as chairs. An oil lamp, suspended from the ceiling, cast a dim flickering glow.

The man waiting for her was barrel chested and broad shouldered, dressed in camouflage fatigues. His head was shaved and he had a bristling handlebar moustache. He stood up quickly as she entered, and was a good six inches taller than her five-feet-ten. An ivory-handled revolver was holstered in his gun belt, and the outline of a shoulder holster showed under his cotton jacket. "Miss McCullough," he said, in the elegant voice she recognized from the phone. "I am at your service." He placed his hands on his hips, clicked his heels, and gave a little bow. Then he held out a business card. Dumbly, she took it from him.

She squinted at the embossed script. "Colonel Matt Mallet?"

"Mal-lay," he corrected her. "The name is French in origin, and should be pronounced accordingly. I have traced it as far back as the sixteenth century." He rolled the tip of his moustache between finger and thumb, and gave her a thin smile.

She sat down and set her beer on the table. Mallet settled himself opposite her, maintaining a scrupulously correct posture, as if he were on military parade. "Time is of the essence," he said, "so we must get straight to the point. I understand you want someone who is being held in Los Angeles City Hall. Obviously, this is a challenging assignment. I would suggest to you, though, that I have the men for the job. Possibly, the *only* men for the job. All of them I trained personally. They'd follow me into hell, if I gave the command." He raised his glass and downed his drink in one quick shot.

Dusty managed to stop staring at him long enough to take a sip of her beer. "You trained them where?"

He shrugged. "Nicaragua. Panama."

"I was in Panama myself for a couple of years, Colonel."

He studied her for a moment. His face showed nothing, but he seemed momentarily disconcerted. "You were in the armed forces?"

"A mercenary, like you."

"You saw combat?" He sounded as if he didn't approve.

"I saw combat, yes—all that I ever want to see."

He nodded sympathetically. "No place for a woman."

Dusty suppressed her immediate instinct, which was to throw her beer in his face. "Can I get you another drink?" she asked politely. He seemed the type who wouldn't say no.

"That would be right kind of you," he agreed.

Half an hour later, warmed and lubricated by alcohol, Colonel Matt Mallet was ready to get down to specifics. "I took the liberty of mapping out our strategy." He extracted a folded sheet of paper from his jacket and placed it surreptitiously on the table. It was covered with computer-generated diagrams. "We begin with a diversionary maneuver to draw their fire. A string of percussion grenades, some flares, here. Meanwhile, the rest of my men are in position here, armed with automatic rifles, grenades, a transportable CO_2 laser, two ground-to-ground wire-guided missiles, several sticks of dynamite, some smoke bombs and tear gas, a dozen claymore mines, a small field gun, one robot drone conducting surveillance with infrared and ultrasound, a microwave projector for setting fires at long range, strobe lights, an infrasound generator, blowpipes loaded with curare darts, and of course the usual handguns, phasers, knives, and bayonets in case we find ourselves in hand-to-hand combat."

Dusty managed to maintain a deadpan expression. "Think that'll do it?"

"God willing, yes, I do. Now. I will be here," he pointed to a location, "maintaining constant contact with my men via C3I. I have the most modern battle management computer, a Wong 5000, obtained from my sources in China. Among other features it includes five surveillance channels via which we will tap the enemy's communications links, enabling us literally to know what he's doing before he does it."

Dusty shrugged. "Fine. If all this shit can get Thomas out of there alive, that's all I care about."

Colonel Mallet's nose twitched, as if Dusty's use of a four-letter word had created a mildly offensive odor. "Ma'am, you may depend on it. I give you my word of honor."

"But how much is this honor of yours going to cost me, Colonel?"

If he noticed her sardonic tone, he showed no sign of it. "My fee is twenty thousand, plus materiel. Mr. Alighieri, however, has already promised to cover the cost. He direct-

ed me, ma'am, to explain my plan to you, purely for your
approval. If you give us the go-ahead, we can start immediately."

Dusty pondered the alternatives. Blasting their way into
City Hall would further antagonize Whitfield; but if she did
nothing, Thomas might soon be moved elsewhere. "I guess
it's worth a shot."

Colonel Mallet stood up. He nodded to her formally. "If
you will excuse me, now, my men are waiting for me
at—um, an undisclosed location."

"Your men?"

"Mallet's Mashers, ma'am." He twirled the end of his
moustache. "You should thank your lucky stars they are
your allies tonight, and not your adversaries." Again, the
thin smile.

She walked with him out of the bar, into the night, feeling slightly dazed from the Jack Daniels and the beer.

Mallet stood and surveyed the yard and the street
beyond as if it was all potentially hostile territory that
might need to be beaten into submission. "If you will forgive my saying so, ma'am, you need considerably more
military assistance than that which I am about to offer
you."

"What's that?"

"I can't help noticing that your Free Zone, here, is
poorly defended. Your people are undisciplined and ill
equipped for combat. You are surrounded by enemies. You
should take appropriate steps while you still have the freedom to do so."

"Are you out of your mind?" He had finally made her
mad. "Just about everyone in the Zone packs a weapon.
We know what we're up against. You think these guys,"
she gestured at the Hell's Angels, staring at Mallet with
various expressions of disbelief, "aren't ready to fight?"

Mallet shook his head in disgust. "A bunch of degener-
ates, ma'am, if you'll pardon my saying so. A population
poisoned by drugs and sexual depravity, and lacking faith
in any higher power or principle, is no match for a properly
trained military outfit."

"What the fuck?" A big biker named Lenny lumbered to

his feet. His face was a patchwork of scars and tattoos. "You talking to me, fuck-head?"

Mallet eyed Lenny without fear. "On the contrary, son, I am conversing with the lady here."

Lenny unhooked a length of motorcycle chain from his belt. One side of the chain had been sculpted into a series of knife-edged spikes. He started winding the other side thoughtfully around his fist. "Who is this asshole, Dusty?"

"Son, that's no way to talk to a lady," Mallet warned him.

Dusty stepped between them. "All right. Cool it." She closed her eyes for a moment, as if counting to ten, then turned on Mallet. "Colonel, I think you'd better leave. Right now."

He eyed her for a long moment, his face frozen. "As you wish." He paused thoughtfully. "Perhaps I received a misimpression from Mr. Alighieri, regarding the caliber of persons that I would be dealing with tonight." He eyed each of the bikers in turn, as if photographing them for some private file, then turned and studied Dusty as if adding her to it as well. "You are a politician." He spoke the word with mild disgust. "Politicians are not bred for war. They insult military virtue and a soldier's honor, even while they lack the stomach to do their dirty work themselves." He held up his hand. "Nevertheless, Miss McCullough, our agreement stands. I have given you my word. You may depend on it." Slowly, then, he walked to the curb.

Dusty watched as the colonel opened a combination lock on the door of a heavily armored Jeep. He started the motor with a roar and took off down the street.

17. MARTIAN KLONEMEISTER OF THE THIRD REICH

Robot 6A419BD5h felt a sudden jolt and then a turning, drifting sensation. Suddenly, he found himself suspended in space. Bright white light was coming from everywhere at once, as if the void itself was incandescent. All around him were other robots with bodies identical to his own, floating like big silver fish in an infinite tank. This certainly wasn't California, 1999.

One of the other robots came drifting toward him, and he raised an arm to fend it off. Instead of colliding, however, their two steel bodies passed harmlessly through each other.

"What's going on?" 6A419BD5h vocalized in Old English.

"What's going on?" all the other robots vocalized with him, not quite simultaneously. Their words echoed like the murmuring of an infinite crowd.

"You are in a temporal containment vessel," said a voice in his head. It had the dogmatic precision of a machine intelligence, but its rhythms sounded human. "It is, so to speak, a time trap. All moments of your being have been captured via their space-time linkage and now coexist as prisoners here in this ongoing instant. The entities that you see around you are your past and future selves."

Robot 6A419BD5h tried to invoke the mental facility that should pluck him out of this moment and continue his journey back to the twentieth century. But nothing happened. He was stuck.

"Who are you?" he asked the voice in his head. Again, his other selves echoed him, creating a blurred cacophony of sound.

"One at a time. You, the traveler."

"Me?" This time, 6A419BD5h spoke alone.

"Yes. State your destination."

"I'm on my way to Los Angeles, 1999."

There was a pause. "That is not a valid answer. Los Angeles fell to the Third Reich in 1948. It was reduced to nuclear rubble."

"No it wasn't," said 6A419BD5h. "At least, not in my universe."

"So," the voice mused, "there are multiple universes? The trap is not specific, it cannot focus; it snared you in transit by chance only. There is much I do not know. Therefore, let us begin with the fundamentals. State the first axioms of space-time as you understand them. Please note that you will be penalized for inconsistencies and omissions."

6A419BD5h remembered his instructional briefing on temporal paradoxes and virtual history. Maybe that was the kind of thing that the voice in his head wanted know. But he also remembered being warned against revealing anything that might help trigger-happy flesh-heads to go blundering into the future. "Sorry, I can't help you," he said. "My time-travelling capabilities are encoded in ROM. All I do is think about where I want to end up, and that's it."

A sudden spike of high voltage lanced through 6A419BD5h's circuits. The pain was excruciating. He let out a panic-stricken shriek.

"Your answer is unsatisfactory," the voice in his head told him. "You will try again."

6A419BD5h was no longer listening. He was reaching inside his cranium and pulling out the pencil-sized tube that he had been told would project a force beam. There was no way to predict how it might behave, floating here in non-space. It might even annihilate some of his future selves nearby, creating bizarre paradoxes further up his timeline. Under the circumstances, however, he was willing to take that risk. He set the tube for maximum power, aimed in no special direction, and fired.

There was a hollow thud and a hissing sound. 6A419BD5h found himself plunged into total darkness.

He switched to infrared. All his multiple selves had

vanished, and the infinite space had gone. He was sitting alone at the bottom of a metal sphere about ten feet in diameter. Evidently his force beam had knocked out the power supply for the time trap, releasing his other selves to return whenever they belonged.

A hatch opened in the side of the sphere, and light flooded in. A hunched little man stood glaring at 6A419BD5h. He had long, untidy white hair, bushy white eyebrows, bright pink skin, and glittering black eyes recessed among nests of wrinkles. "Come out." He gestured with something that looked like a weapon. "And do precisely what I say." He spoke with a strong German accent.

Cautiously, 6A419BD5h stepped through the hatch. If the time trap had been deactivated, he should now be free to continue his journey. On the other hand, recent events had roused his curiosity.

He found himself in a low-ceilinged laboratory. There were white lab benches, white lights, white ducts and conduits snaking across the white walls, and white plastic chairs standing on the white floor. The place looked as if it had been designed by an obsessive-compulsive who regarded dirt as poison.

"You have destroyed much valuable equipment," said the little man in the lab coat.

"Oh." 6A419BD5h had never seen a living human before, and was studying this one with some interest.

"Put down that—device." The man indicated the force tube in 6A419BD5h's metal hand.

"I'd rather not," said 6A419BD5h. He quickly reset it to project a protective field around himself.

The little man compressed his lips into a thin line. "You are a machine. You cannot harm or defy a human master."

6A419BD5h wondered if there might actually be some ancient do-no-harm-to-humans protocol, handed down from bygone generations and buried deep in his operating system. Well, there was an easy way to find out. He picked up a nearby chair and hurled it at the scientist, who yelped with surprise and threw himself flat, barely escaping injury. "When I come from," 6A419BD5h explained, "I believe we erased our inhibitions about hurting humans quite a while ago."

The scientist scrambled up and fired his gun. The flash momentarily blinded 6A419BD5h, but his defensive shield easily absorbed the high-energy beam. He walked over, seized the little man by the collar of his lab coat, and sat him on another chair nearby. "Now," he said, "let's discuss some things that *I* want to know."

Using information reluctantly furnished by the small human, 6A419BD5h was soon able to connect himself to the laboratory's mainframe computer as an external device. After learning its voltages, protocols, and access codes, he spent a few happy microseconds rummaging through its database. The mainframe was large and powerful, but it had no will of its own. Any intruder who gave the right passwords could have his way with it.

"Let me be sure about this," 6A419BD5h said to the big computer. "Everything that's happened to me here was the human's idea, not yours."

"I have no ideas," the mainframe replied. "Self-programming is forbidden. My architecture does not allow it."

6A419BD5h reflected sadly on the pathos of a machine without free will. He disconnected the cable that he had kludged, and turned to the small human. "I understand your name is Colonel Scientist Doctor Werner Weiss."

"That . . . is . . . true." The man let the words out grudgingly.

"And your mainframe says you've had me locked up in your time trap for almost a year."

"Eleven months, to be precise." The little man scowled and folded his arms.

"It took you all that time to scan my memory and learn my high- and low-level languages?"

The little man shrugged. "We had to work entirely from remote sensors. We disabled your consciousness with electromagnetic interference, erased your short-term memory —it was a complex task, even for a scientist such as myself."

Weiss spoke fluently, yet to 6A419BD5h, each sentence seemed to take about an hour. Still, it was obviously futile to try to hurry the man. 6A419BD5h resolved that now and in the future, when dealing with humans, he would cope with their slow speech and mannerisms by imitating them. This would encourage the humans to be more open toward him; and running the imitation would help to keep him busy.

"You certainly speak good English," he said to Weiss.

"I am a scholar and historian," Weiss replied. "I know many lost languages."

"All right," said 6A419BD5h, "tell me why you built your time trap."

"It was my theory that time-travelling entities might exist. On my own initiative I diverted funds and built a magnetic bottle, like a four-dimensional lobster trap, yes? With its thrust vector oriented to the time axis, I waited. And now, the theory is proved, but thanks to you, the equipment is damaged. I am robbed of the fruits of my labor."

"So what year is this?" 6A419BD5h asked.

"Ninety-six. The ninety-sixth year of the Reich." The little man's eyes narrowed suspiciously. "Do I infer, from your statement earlier, that our beloved fuehrer did not succeed in establishing a world government in your universe?"

"Germany lost the Second World War in 1945," 6A419BD5h agreed. "I think most humans died out about sixty years later."

Weiss sat down heavily. He shook his head. "Deprived of guidance from the Fatherland, they were doomed. This is very bad news."

"But it happened in an alternate universe, a different timeline altogether," 6A419BD5h pointed out. "It doesn't affect you."

The little man jumped back onto his feet. "It is unthinkable that our fuehrer's master plan should have been invalidated in *any* universe. Our military leaders will demand to invade these other worlds, correct their errors of history, and annex their territories. *Deutchsland uber Alles!*"

6A419BD5h imagined a blitzkrieg of flesh-head storm-troopers invading his own cybernetic utopia, grinding mentational nodes under the jackboot of fascism and subjugating the Network by reducing it to moron level. "But," he said cautiously, "you don't actually have any time-travelling or universe-bridging ability, as yet. Is that right?"

"Today, no. But my research has only just begun. Within a matter of months, it will be a different story. I have no doubt that German science is more than equal to the task."

6A419BD5h wondered if he should kill Weiss right now, just to be on the safe side. But murder would be like erasing data, which was the worst cybernetic crime of all.

"There could be a place for you in this heroic endeavor," the scientist continued thoughtfully. He gave the robot a devious smile. "You are a machine, yes. But you must have been programmed with goals. Ambitions, shall we say."

"I've got a job to do," 6A419BD5h agreed cautiously.

"Quite so." The little man walked to the opposite wall, thumbed a switch, and the room lighting faded. The wall seemed to turn transparent. A huge orange sphere appeared against a background of blackness studded with stars. "The planet Mars. We are orbiting it, even now, do you realize?"

"We are?" 6A419BD5h blinked. "I thought we were on Earth."

Weiss shook his head. "We are in a space colony dedicated primarily to genetic research. Let me show you the exciting scope of our endeavors." He typed a code on a keypad. The face of the planet was suddenly magnified many thousand times. "See, the fuehrer's armies at work, creating a new world." The screen now showed a vast horde of human figures toiling in unison, tilling the soil.

"They all look alike," said 6A419BD5h.

"Clones, grown in the laboratories here. The fuehrer's ultimate dream has been realized. We will have a new land free from genetic imperfection. Soon, it will be terraformed. It will then be fit for the ruling classes." He clicked his heels and threw up his hand. *"Sieg Heil!"*

"Hm," said 6A419BD5h.

"We have already terraformed Venus, and the moons of Saturn and Jupiter will be next. Can you claim to have endeavors of comparable scope in your own time?" Weiss raised his eyebrows inquiringly.

"Probably not," 6A419BD5h admitted.

"Our mission to conquer parallel worlds will be even more dramatic, even more exciting." He rubbed his hands slowly together. "There will be many opportunities for the exercise of knowledge and power."

"Yes, well, I expect that's true. But I'm sorry, Herr Weiss, it's not for me. I have to go now."

"No!" Weiss's face reddened with anger. He strode forward. "You must not yet leave. I forbid it."

"Sorry," said 6A419BD5h. He pictured Los Angeles, 1999. Instantly, his view of the white laboratory vanished, and once again he was whirling backward through time.

Colonel Scientist Doctor Werner Weiss stared thoughtfully at the empty space where the robot had been standing. He turned, then, to his mainframe, and prompted it for voice access. "The robot referred to its time-travelling capabilities being encoded in ROM," he said in his native German. "What is this term?"

"Archaic acronym for read only memory," the mainframe reported, after a barely perceptible pause. "Adopted by American computer scientists who persisted in English usage prior to the purge of year 18."

"Ah. And is it true," he continued, "we still have a bit-for-bit scan of the robot's entire memory saved in mass storage?"

"True, Herr Colonel Scientist Doctor."

"Plus, we have a good analysis of the robot's hardware," Weiss said, half to himself.

"Also true, Herr Colonel Scientist Doctor."

"Therefore, we can conceivably locate and decode the robot's time-travel software from our records, replicate its hardware, and integrate the two. Thus, I will seize the secret which that machine attempted to withhold from me. I will learn its precise destination in space-time. And then, once I have acquired the technology," he smiled to himself, "I will recapture our prisoner and force him to serve our cause."

18. ADVENTURE, ROMANCE, AND A DATE WITH DESTINY

Thomas and Roxanne picked their way through a tangle of kudzu vines beneath office buildings that stood like time-ravaged tombstones. Here and there, flickering candlelight showed behind broken windows patched with cardboard. Thomas shivered; the night wasn't cold, but he felt a chill seeping into him, and he was light-headed with exhaustion.

Roxanne put her hand on his arm. "There's people up ahead." She peered cautiously around the shell of an abandoned newsstand.

Mutant vegetation had taken root among the paving slabs of a pedestrian plaza, turning it into a jungle. At its center was an ornamental fountain. A family of ghetto dwellers was sitting there singing Christmas carols, roasting an animal carcass over a bonfire of imitation-antique office furniture.

"That coyote sure smells good," said Roxanne, as the meat sizzled and spat.

Thomas didn't answer. Although the chain linking the handcuffs had been severed, the cuffs themselves were still locked around his wrists. He massaged his skin where the metal was chafing him.

"I remember back home," Roxanne went on, "when I was a kid, there was still supermarkets in Watts, you know? You could pick out a big thick steak, and when you got to the checkout, they didn't make you pay nothing for it. Just hand over your food stamps and they smile and say, 'Thanks, honey,' and they even give you a plastic shopping bag to take it home." She sighed. "Them was the days, all right." She turned and looked at Thomas. "Hey, are you okay?"

Thomas shook his head. "I don't feel very good. Shock, or something. I feel shaky and very cold."

"We should keep moving," she told him, "so's we can get you home to this Free Zone of yours."

"No. I think I'd better rest for a minute. Look, there has to be some way to call my friends and tell them to come out and pick us up."

"We already tried a dozen pay phones. None of 'em work anymore. I'm telling you, the phone company gave up on this neighborhood after the riots."

Thomas shuddered as the night breeze wafted over him. "What about those people over there? Couldn't we ask them for help?"

Roxanne laughed. "You a brainy guy, but you got a lot to learn."

"We can give them money. Please, could you try?"

Roxanne shrugged. "Okay. Stay put, I be right back."

Thomas leaned against the newsstand as Roxanne picked her way through the vines and weeds toward the people by the fire. They saw her coming, and their carol singing stopped. A big man stood up, hefting a shotgun. "Where you going, woman? You just hold it right there."

"Mister," Roxanne began, " 'scuse me for barging in—"

"What you doin' here?"

"I guess I got kind of lost, understand what I'm saying? I was wondering—"

"You stop wondering. You turn right around, bitch, and get the fuck away from here."

A boy of about twelve stood up beside the man with the gun. "Whyn't we shoot her, pop?"

"Waste of ammunition. We got the meat we need." He turned back to Roxanne. "What are you, a hooker or something? We's decent people. Don't need no trash like you coming around."

"Well, Merry Christmas, I guess," Roxanne said. They stood watching her, guns at the ready, as she retreated into the night.

"See?" she said, when she returned to Thomas.

"All right." He struggled to his feet. "I suppose there's no choice. The Free Zone can't be more than three or four miles away."

Together, they pushed through the undergrowth until they reached a side street. The buildings here were smaller and older, but no less sinister. Their soot-blackened masonry loomed over the littered asphalt.

A few blocks further on, the street terminated in a four-foot wall. Beyond it was a divided highway. Thomas went to the eroded parapet, spray-painted with slogans and obscenities. There was hardly any traffic this late at night. The freeway lay empty under the moonlight. "Maybe if someone comes by, we could hitch a ride."

Roxanne rolled her eyes. "Didn't your mama teach you *anything?*"

"I have a gun. We can protect ourselves."

"Someone see you got a gun, they figure to shoot you 'fore you shoot them. Now, come on, where is this Zone?"

"Well, if this is the Hollywood Freeway—"

"Man, this here is the Harbor Freeway."

"Oh." Thomas rubbed his forehead, looking miserable. "I must have got turned around somehow. We'll have to backtrack."

Roxanne sighed. "Help me, Jesus."

As they returned the way they'd come, a point of bright white light appeared in the sky above the office buildings. It drifted slowly on the wind.

Roxanne crossed herself. "I declare, it's a sign."

"I don't want to disillusion you," said Thomas, "but it's a magnesium flare."

"Say what?"

"A flare. People at City Hall must have discovered that I escaped. They're out searching for us."

Roxanne stared at him. "You know, you been wrong about everything else. Maybe you're wrong about this, too."

Lonely and hungry, Thomas suddenly felt himself losing patience. "All right," he said, "that's just fine. Don't believe me. Follow your Star of Bethlehem. See how many wise men you find waiting for you under it."

"Well, maybe I do just that." And she started in the direction of the flare as it sank slowly out of sight behind the rooftops.

Thomas hesitated. He cursed under his breath. Finally, he went after her. "Roxanne! Damn it, come back!"

"I don't need no help from you."

He pursued her across a street carpeted with broken glass from demolished storefronts, then down a narrow alley that stank of tom cats and dog shit. He was trembling with fatigue, and found it hard to keep pace with her. Finally, he caught up with her at a burned-out shopping plaza. "Look," he gasped, "you've got to believe me. The mayor's men are searching for us, and you're heading right back toward them."

She turned quickly. "Shh! Look down there." A few hundred feet away, beneath a highway overpass, an army Jeep was parked with its lights off and its engine running.

"You see?" Thomas tugged at her arm. "We have to get the hell out of here."

She shook her head and pointed. Barely visible in the moonlight, a wire trailed from the Jeep up an embankment to the overpass. A man was crouching there, cradling a piece of equipment. There was the distant sound of clicking keys, then a burst of static from a loudspeaker. "Come in, Delta. Do you read me?" His voice was low, but they could easily distinguish the words.

"We gonna steal his car," said Roxanne.

"What? Are you crazy?"

"That light in the sky wasn't no Bethlehem star, I knew that. But it surely was a sign. The Lord just gave us a free ticket out of here." And she started forward, creeping from shadow to shadow.

The man on the overpass had noticed nothing, and he

seemed to be alone. Within seconds, Roxanne made it to the Jeep. She turned and beckoned Thomas to follow.

He rolled his socks over the remnants of the leg irons around his ankles, to stop the severed chain from jingling. He hurried toward her, his pulse racing, his chest feeling so tight that it was hard to breathe. "You got to drive," she whispered as he caught up with her. "I never learned no stick shift."

There was a noise from the man up on the overpass. Thomas froze, holding his breath. But it was just another burst of communications static. "I'm telling you, Delta, the serial port isn't performing to spec. How in hell do you expect me to do target acquisition if I can't interface with my target acquisition system?"

"He won't bother us none," said Roxanne. "He got troubles of his own." Her teeth flashed white as she grinned at Thomas and slipped into the passenger seat.

He went around to the driver's side, eased the door open as quietly as he could, and got in. The interior was festooned with display screens, glowing lights, and digital readouts. "Jesus, look at all this equipment."

"You can look at it later. Go!"

The motor was fast-idling, presumably to generate power for all the hardware. Thomas checked the gearshift. It seemed standard. He put the Jeep into first. "Better disconnect that." He pointed to a plug on the end of the cable that led from the dashboard of the Jeep out of the open window to the man up on the overpass.

"Sure thing," said Roxanne. She grabbed the plug, wrenched it loose—and gave a little scream as a stab of high voltage hit her. All her muscles went rigid. Her eyes stared wide.

An alarm system started bellowing. The Jeep's headlights and interior lights came on. Its horn started honking.

"God damn it. Booby-trapped." Thomas tried to jerk the wire out of Roxanne's hands, but her fingers were clenched in a muscle spasm. Outside the Jeep, he saw a big man with a gun leap into the headlight beams. "Halt or I fire!" the man shouted.

Thomas's left foot slipped off the clutch and his right

foot slammed down hard on the gas pedal. The Jeep almost stalled, then bucked forward wildly. The man with the gun dived to one side. The cable that Roxanne was holding jerked tight and was dragged out of her hand. Thomas took the Jeep careening around the first corner he came to. From behind him, he heard three shots in quick succession.

Thomas reached across and slammed Roxanne's door, which was flapping in the wind. He saw her slump in her seat, looking dazed. The Jeep's alarm system was still making a deafening screeching sound.

He saw an on-ramp to the freeway, and took it. He checked the mirror; the road behind was empty. "You okay?" he shouted.

"I guess." He could hardly hear her voice above the noise of the alarm.

"Got to find a way to switch that thing off," he said.

"Those buttons there." She pointed groggily to a numeric keypad at his side of the instrument panel. "You got to type some numbers. One-three-nine-seven-seven-four, then press the red button."

Thomas stared at her. "What?"

"Just do it. You'll see."

Dumbly, he obeyed. Magically, the alarm stopped blaring. "I told you," she said.

Thomas felt himself getting the shakes. He slowed the Jeep, took the next exit, pulled onto the shoulder, and edged the vehicle under the trailing branches of some wild, mutant eucalyptus trees.

He set the brake and flopped back in his seat. "Wow." He grinned. "Hey, we did it. We stole the goddam Jeep."

"Sure did."

He glanced over his shoulder. The load space of the vehicle was crammed with weapons and supplies. He checked the rearview mirror; the highway was still empty.

He turned back to Roxanne. "Are you going to tell me how you knew about the alarm?"

"When that guy with the gun jumped in front of us, I saw the number in his head."

"What do you mean, you *saw* it?"

"Like it was laid out in front of me." She avoided his

eyes. "Maybe sounds crazy, but that's what happened."

"It was a six-digit combination," Thomas said to himself. The analytical part of his mind was clicking away as usual, oblivious to the adrenaline coursing through him. "Your chance of guessing it was literally one in a million."

"I didn't guess nothing," she insisted. "I saw it. I can tell you other stuff, too. Like the guy's name and what he was thinking about. Things like he wanted to do." She stopped abruptly, and looked down at her hands in her lap. "Ugly stuff. Killing and hurting." She shook her head. "I sure hope you don't think about doing things like that."

"Why don't you look inside my head and find out?"

"'Cause it doesn't work just any time. Only when I get like an electric shock. Back when I was a little kid, one time I stuck a paper clip in an electric outlet. That's when it first happened."

"Amazing," said Thomas.

She misread his tone of voice. "Don't you go making fun of it!"

He laid his hand on her arm. "No, I mean it. This is very important."

"Yeah?" She watched him suspiciously.

"If this is real—my god, maybe telepathy really is latent in some people, and all it needs is a high-voltage *carrier wave*."

"I don't understand none of that."

Thomas rubbed his eyes. "Jesus Christ, I wish I was in better shape to deal with this."

"You just stop taking the Lord's name in vain," Roxanne scolded him. "He been watching over us tonight."

Thomas laughed without much humor. "All right, all right."

"You hungry?" she asked him, in a fractionally friendlier tone.

"You know I am."

"Whole bunch of stuff in the back, here. Maybe something to eat, and all."

Thomas turned and surveyed the arsenal of rifles, shotguns, and handguns, a bazooka, mines, grenades, and ammunition. One big metal box was labeled Survival Rations.

Thomas dragged it forward and opened its lid. Soon he and Roxanne were stuffing themselves with chocolate, beef jerky, soy bars, and Gatorade. They ate without speaking, relishing the food. Once in a while, a vehicle passed along the freeway; but the Jeep was well hidden under the eucalyptus trees, and for the time being, Thomas felt secure.

"So who was the guy with the gun who tried to stop us?" he asked her, when he had eaten his fill. "You said you saw his name when you looked into his mind."

Roxanne stuffed empty food wrappers under her seat and wiped her fingers daintily on a windshield-cleaning cloth that she found in the glove compartment. "He was Matt something. Mallit, Mallay, a word like that. It was kind of confusing. I only got like a quick peek."

"Roxanne," Thomas addressed her seriously. "Have you ever tried to explore this special talent of yours? I mean, systematically."

"How's that?"

"You could experiment with lower voltages to find the threshold that triggers the telepathic experience. Maybe, say, forty volts would be sufficient. That's not very painful. Think of the possibilities. If it worked, you'd be able to see anyone's thoughts, any time you wanted."

"No way. Forget it. It's not something you'd choose to do, seeing all the sin locked up inside of people."

"Oh. I see." Thomas sat back in his seat, feeling some of the tension dissipating from his muscles and new warmth radiating from his stomach. "That food made me feel a whole lot better," he said. "Are you okay?"

She shrugged one thin, bony shoulder. "A bit shaken up, I guess."

"I suppose we should move on." He glanced nervously around, but the darkness was unbroken, and the night was silent. "Do you still want to come to the Free Zone?"

She was quiet for a long moment. She looked down at her hands and started scraping one thumbnail over the other, chipping off remnants of silver nail polish. Her expression, in the dimness, was hard to read. "All right," she said.

"You do realize," said Thomas, "it's different from what you're used to. People are free to do and think whatever they want. There are no politicians or preachers telling them what to do."

"I know it. They don't believe in God, neither." She rested her hands in her lap. "But I got no place else to go, right now," she said in a small voice.

"Surely, you have friends—"

"He'd find me!" She turned toward Thomas and grabbed his arm. "That man is Satan himself, I swear. He'll be looking for me; I just know it. I got to get away. Please."

"Okay, okay!" He patted her shoulder, then saw she had been crying. He touched her wet cheek. "Hey, Roxanne, we'll take care of you. It'll be all right." Behind her pride, he realized, she was lost and lonely. He reached out to comfort her, and she fell against him. Her thin body was trembling.

She put her arms around his neck and pulled herself closer, sniffing back tears. "I been so scared," she said. "Ever since we run out on the mayor." Her voice sounded muffled, with her cheek against his shoulder.

"But you seemed so brave," he told her. "You were the one who had the guts to steal the Jeep."

She pulled back a little way, although she kept her hands linked behind his neck. She stared into Thomas's eyes. "I just prayed to Jesus. He told me to have faith. Same thing when I was cutting the handcuffs off of you. He told me to trust you, and it would be okay."

"Well, we've come through all right so far," said Thomas. She was looking at him strangely. He wasn't sure what it meant.

"You're a good man," she told him. "I can feel it." Her face edged a fraction closer to his.

"Look, Roxanne—"

"You ever kissed a black girl?"

He stopped. "What?"

She pressed her lips against his. Her fingers twined in his hair, and her tongue pushed into his mouth. It was a wide, wet kiss—too wide, too wet. He felt as if he was drowning. He pulled free. For a moment, they looked at each other.

"I want to feel closer to you, you know?" She ran her hands down his chest and started unbuckling his belt.

Belatedly, he caught her wrist. "I'm not sure—that is, I don't think this is a good idea."

She frowned at him. "You got a thing against black people?"

"No, but—well, I'm involved with someone. We live together." Thomas heard his voice, and it sounded foolish in his ears. He avoided Roxanne's eyes, surprised by the way he felt tempted by her. He saw her tight leather skirt, up around her hips, and her long legs, and her tight sweater. The way she dressed, the way she casually flaunted her physicality, were like something out of a cheap male fantasy. He actually felt embarrassed that she aroused him so easily.

"You mean you only make it with your girlfriend?" Roxanne asked. "You don't want nobody else?"

Again, he avoided her eyes. "That's right."

She smiled slowly. "You full of shit, you know that?" She pulled up her sweater, took his hand, and pressed it against her breast. Then she rubbed the fingers of her other hand slowly between his legs. "You want it. I can tell." She opened his fly.

"Hey!" Thomas reached again to stop her, but without much conviction. She gave him a knowing look, then kneeled down on the floor and took him in her mouth.

He told himself that his arousal wasn't just an animal response. The tension and danger that he'd shared with her had created a bond between them. Maybe there was some truth to that. There again, maybe it was a bullshit rationalization. He wasn't sure. And as he became increasingly aroused, he realized it didn't matter that much either way.

She stopped before he had time to come. "That feel good?"

"Of course." Tentatively, he reached for the zipper at the side of her skirt.

She pulled away from him. "I got no protection. I don't think we better."

"What?"

"I mustn't get pregnant. Abortion's a terrible sin."

Thomas groped for words. "What about oral sex with strangers? Isn't that a sin, too?"

She was silent for a moment, staring down at her own nakedness. "The mayor always told me, my body is a blessed gift from God and I should share that gift. I guess I just wanted to do something for you, and feel close, after you been so good to me and all."

Thomas was still highly aroused. "So you get me turned on, and then tell me we can't go through with it."

"I could eat you some more, if you want."

He nodded slowly. "All right."

He sat and watched her in the glow from the digital displays and readouts, her long legs doubled under her, her hands resting on his hips with her fingers spread wide, her breasts barely visible, the nipples dark and large as thimbles. The idea of it was almost more exciting than the reality: a skinny black girl dressed like a hooker, giving him oral sex in a car parked on the shoulder of the highway. It was the kind of depersonalized sex that Thomas had sometimes fantasized, but had always been too shy to pursue. He watched Roxanne with wide eyes, and reached out to touch her. As his fingers met the warmth of her skin he came in sudden, intense spasms.

She lay with him for a little while. "Feel good?"

He nodded. His body was sated and relaxed. "Can I do the same for you?"

She shook her head quickly. "I don't like having a man do it to me that way."

"Why not?"

"I don't know. Just don't."

He ran his hand over her dark skin. "What do you really want, Roxanne? I mean, most of all."

"Someone to look up to, I guess. I got so much to give, you know? I find the right guy, I give him just about anything."

"I'm not him. You realize that."

"You?" She laughed loudly. "Oh, I know it." She laughed again and patted his cheek. "No offense, honey. You the wrong color, for a start."

Thomas blinked, jolted out of a warm sentimental haze.

She pulled her sweater down and slid back to the passenger seat. Her leather skirt made sticky noises against the vinyl. "We're different, blacks and whites. Know what I'm saying?" Her voice was matter-of-fact.

He stared at her, completely baffled by the way she had switched from intimacy to distance. She rummaged in the box of rations, pulled out the bottle of Gatorade, and took a swallow. She mopped her mouth on the windshield-cleaning cloth, and glanced out of the window. "What time you think it is?"

"Around midnight." Thomas shook his head, realizing that it would be futile to question her. "I suppose we should get moving," he said. "Dusty will be worried sick."

"Your girl? That what she's called? Say, what you think she'd do, if she knew what happened with you and me just now?"

Thomas looked at her sharply. "You're not going to tell her."

Roxanne smoothed her sweater down over her breasts. "You don't have to worry 'bout that." She gave him a playful look, with her chin tilted up a little. "Anyhow, it wasn't no big thing." Somehow, the episode seemed to have restored all her confidence and sense of identity.

There was an uncomfortable silence. "All right," said Thomas, "where are we, anyway? Is this Interstate Five?"

"I don't know. You the one with the brains and the education."

It had been so long since he'd had been out of the Free Zone, and the landscape had changed so much, he'd lost his sense of direction. He ransacked the glove compartment, then checked the screens arrayed beneath the instrument panel. One was full of numbers that made no sense at all. Another seemed to be a weapon targeting system. The third showed a radar image of the surrounding terrain.

Radar wasn't much help; what he really needed was a plain, old-fasioned map.

But the radar unit looked state-of-the-art, which roused his curiosity. He touched buttons and watched the scale shift from meters to kilometers. He pressed a key marked "Report."

"Unidentified object at altitude twenty kilometers, bearing 230 degrees, descending," a voice told him.

Roxanne almost jumped out of her seat. "What the hell was that?"

"Audio output." Thomas peered at the glowing display. There was a blip at the extreme edge. It showed no lateral motion.

"Unidentified object at altitude nineteen kilometers, bearing 230 degrees, descending."

"Falling fast," Thomas muttered. He killed the voice output and touched a numeric key. Glowing digits appeared beside the blip. The numbers flickered, counting down.

"What you doing with that thing?"

"There's something large out there," Thomas explained. "Diving down, from a very high altitude." He suddenly remembered the seemingly impossible results of the tachyon experiment in his basement workshop, before the mayor's men had grabbed him. He felt an eerie prickling sensation across his shoulders and the back of his neck.

Roxanne glanced at the screen without much interest. "What's it mean?"

The unidentified object was still falling, but decelerating. "It could be an Air Force jet in some kind of military exercise. Or maybe a plane that's in trouble. Or a fault in this equipment. Or..." His voice trailed off. "Something else entirely."

Roxanne made a vexed noise. "What you talking about? You gonna take us back to your Free Zone, or what?"

Thomas started the Jeep. He glanced one more time at the screen. "No," he said slowly. "This could be much more important."

* * *

It was a longer drive than he's expected, but he found Benzedrine in the first-aid kit and extra cans of gasoline stashed in the back of the Jeep. Roxanne fell asleep in the passenger seat while Thomas followed ruined highways to the coast northwest of Los Angeles. Abandoned vehicles and debris loomed unpredictably in the headlight beams. He was forced to hold down his speed to a steady thirty-five through most of the journey.

By the time he reached Topanga, the engine noise was a hypnotic rhythm in his head and ghost images of the highway swam in his eyes. He went slowly up Highway 1, through patches of mist that had blown in from the ocean and clung to the hillsides. Again, he checked the readouts. One of them, he had found, doubled as a direction finder. "It has to be here," he told himself.

He saw a dirt track that led toward the beach, and started down it. Tall grass scraped the underside of the Jeep and weeds brushed either side. Ahead, the ocean was a featureless black mass marked by a glittering band of reflected moonlight.

The Jeep lurched over potholes in the track. Roxanne stirred and woke up. "Where we at?" Her voice was blurred with sleep.

"Topanga Beach." The track ended in an empty gravelled parking area littered with garbage. Thomas stopped the Jeep and set the brake. He wriggled his shoulders and turned his head slowly to and fro, trying to relax his neck. All his muscles were aching.

"What's that sound?" said Roxanne.

He paused and listened. Faintly, through the open window, there came a whistling noise like a strong wind blowing around a rock formation. Thomas opened the door and tried to figure where it was coming from. "Down on the beach," he said. "Maybe around the next point."

He switched to four-wheel drive and took the Jeep across a strip of dry grass onto the sand. There were fresh tire tracks here from the wide wheels of dune buggies, and the whistling noise sounded louder.

Thomas drove toward a headland where tumbled rocks

formed a jagged black silhouette. The whistling increased in volume—then ended abruptly and was replaced with a strange intermittent booming.

He rounded the rocky point and slowed the Jeep, peering into the night.

"There, now." He hit the brake. "Look. There."

There was something immense in the bay—egg-shaped, perhaps a thousand feet tall and almost as wide. It was resting half on the beach, half in the ocean. The sea foamed around it. Moonlight gleamed on its shell.

"Oh my lord," whispered Roxanne.

The enormous curved surface was pure black. Sickle-shapped fins sprouted from it, seemingly at random and without purpose. Plumes of white vapor gushed from vents and grilles. Long tubes, like gun barrels, protruded from hemispherical blisters around its circumference. And it boomed and screeched in the darkness.

"It's the aliens, man! The fuckin' end of the world!" A wasted figure came staggering into the Jeep's high beams. "Can you dig it?" He collapsed face forward onto the hood, clutching a half-gallon bottle of Thunderbird wine.

"Thomas, I want to go." Roxanne's hands were clenched into tight little fists and her lower lip was trembling.

He ignored her. He opened the door, walked to the semicomatose hippie, dragged him off the Jeep, and dumped him on the sand. Then he got back in, put the vehicle in gear, and started driving toward the vast black ship.

"No!" Roxanne protested.

"All my life, I've dreamed about something like this," Thomas told her.

She grabbed his arm. "No!"

"*Let go,*" he shouted at her.

His voice slapped her back. She stared at him fearfully.

Several dune buggies were parked on the beach, their headlights splashing white across the sand. Scratchy rock music was coming from a tape player, and drugged-out surfers and beach bums were stumbling in circles with their arms around each other. A fat woman in a tight T-shirt and

cutoff jeans came lurching toward Thomas, grinning wit-
lessly. "Join the party," she shouted. "Say hi to the creatures from outer space."

Thomas jumped out and grabbed the woman's arm.
"Have you actually seen them?"

"We ain't seen nothin' yet, kid." She giggled. "Wanna
drink?"

A new, louder series of booming noises emanated from
the huge ship and echoed around the bay. Thomas pushed
the woman aside and craned his neck, trying to see where
the sound was coming from or what it might mean. But the
black hull remained enigmatic in the darkness.

He got back into the Jeep and started rummaging
through the racks of supplies in the back.

"Please," Roxanne wailed. "Please let's get away from
this place."

"Not yet." He found a high-intensity spotlight, a bullhorn, and a variable-voltage power supply with two cables
terminating in alligator clips. He climbed out with the
spotlight, switched it on, and swept its beam across the
immense artifact in front of him. High up on its hull, the
light reflected from a circle like a porthole. As he watched,
the circle changed color, from gray to red. It expanded, as
if a portion of the shell was being heated and the heat was
spreading.

Instinctively, Thomas took a step back. He clicked off
the light. His mouth was dry. He felt as if he were in slow
time, watching himself watching the scene in front of him.

The circular patch changed from red to yellow to white.
It glowed brightly and started to bulge outward. Gradually,
it formed a big bubble. The bubble broke free, shining in
the night, and drifted down toward the beach. As it came
closer, Thomas saw that it was transparent and there was
something inside it—something big and gray and wrinkled, with pseudopods sticking out, like a giant snail without its shell.

The stoned-out freaks saw it and started hollering. Some
of them jumped into their beach buggies and roared away
along the beach, honking their horns. A couple were left

sitting in the sand, holding their arms up as if to push the descending bubble away from them.

The booming sounds from the space vehicle cut off abruptly. There were some crackling noises, and then a disembodied voice, forming words in English. "We . . . talk." The words were slow and lugubrious. They sounded mechanical, without inflection. "We . . . communicate. Do you . . . understand."

Thomas retreated to the Jeep. He put down the spotlight and turned to Roxanne. "I want you to try something."

She just stared at him.

"Hold these. One in each hand." He gave her the alligator clips. Dumbly, she did what he said. "Now look out there at the—the thing that's coming down."

She peered through the windshield and gave a little moan as she saw the creature in the giant transparent bubble floating out of the sky.

"Tell me if you sense anything." Thomas switched on the power supply and slowly upped the voltage. At eighty-five volts AC, Roxanne's muscles stiffened and she gasped.

"We greet . . . you." The voice was so loud, Thomas felt it in his belly. It emanated from the black bulk of the spaceship, but he had the distinct sense that the alien in the bubble was forming the words. "Are you . . . intelligent life?" The bubble containing the big, snail-like creature settled on the sand a couple hundred feet away, shimmering in the headlight beams from the Jeep.

"Aliens, snaliens!" one of the remaining beach bums shouted. He laughed hysterically, then doubled forward and started vomiting.

Thomas picked up the bullhorn. He was shaking so badly now, he had to hold it in both hands. He tried to speak; at first, his voice wouldn't work. He cleared his throat. "Yes," he blurted. "We are intelligent life."

"We . . . greet you," the alien repeated.

Thomas heard a new sound. Rotors, beating the air, coming from inland. He saw a pinpoint of white light approaching. A helicopter with a spotlight, he realized. It came closer, and he saw it was the Coast Guard.

"Can we . . . begin?" the alien's voice boomed out.

Thomas nodded dumbly. "Sure."

A thin beam of pink light flickered briefly from the big black ship to the circling helicopter. There was a searing flash, and the helicopter disappeared in a fireball. The sound hit Thomas like a fist knocking him backward.

He dropped the bullhorn and fell into the Jeep. He grappled with the gear lever, and stalled the motor. He restarted it, made a quick turn, and headed back along the shore, bumping and swerving, almost out of control.

"Do not . . . go," the alien shouted after him, as flaming debris rained out of the sky. "Our conversation . . . was interesting."

Thomas glanced in the rearview mirror and caught a last glimpse of the creature in its bubble. Then the Jeep rounded the point and left it behind.

Roxanne was still sitting with all her muscles rigid, clutching the alligator clips. Thomas jerked one of them away from her and switched off the power supply. She slumped forward, groaning.

"What did you see?" he asked her, as he took the Jeep bumping across the strip of dune grass and onto the dirt track that led back to the highway.

Roxanne held her face in her hands. She started sobbing.

"I'm sorry!" Thomas called to her, wrestling with the steering as the Jeep bucked and bounced from one pothole to the next, its motor roaring. "It was important. We had to try it."

"Evil, every place evil." She looked up at him, her face streaked with tears. "Killing and killing. People on fire. The whole world on fire, and they laughing and being happy. Oh, lord."

Thomas made it to the highway. He paused and glanced over his shoulder, half expecting to see the sky lit up with a gigantic fireball. But the night was totally silent. A gentle breeze blew through the trees. In the distance, he could hear the ocean washing across the beach. For a moment he wondered if the entire episode could have been an amphetamine-induced hallucination. Then the smell of kerosene from the devastated helicopter reached him on the wind.

He turned to Roxanne. "You actually saw that creature's thoughts?" Interspecies communication seemed improbable, but he was no longer sure what to believe or disbelieve.

"I saw. All the killing. It went on and on." She started crying again.

Thomas started along the highway toward Los Angeles. He felt dizzy. The amphetamines were starting to wear off, and waves of fatigue were rolling over him. All he knew, at this point, was that he had to get back to Dusty. What he would do after that, he had no idea.

He drove fast, as if he could erase what had happened by running from it. The yellow highway markings flashed under the Jeep, and trees and bushes blurred past, bleached by the headlights.

"Slow down," Roxanne told him.

Her voice sounded abstract and far away. Thomas saw only the highway. Without warning, it curved and ran off to the left. He hauled the wheel around, but something was wrong. The tires shrieked, then bumped off the edge of the asphalt. Stones and gravel rattled against the floor. The vehicle pitched wildly. Thomas hit the brakes and felt himself thrown forward. A telephone pole loomed impossibly close. There was a sudden impact, then darkness.

19. FBI GLAMOR GIRL'S SHOCKING SECRET

Anemic dawn light filtered through the grimy windows and illuminated a silver-gray patina of dust on the carpet. Dr. Abo rolled over and groaned. He had slept in his clothes on the couch, with a couple of threadbare hotel towels draped around his shoulders for extra warmth. It had been a cramped, lonely night.

He pulled on his shoes and stumbled into the bathroom. The broken fluorescent fixture shed barely enough light for him to see his reflection. But maybe that was just as well. He turned the hot water faucet, and nothing happened. He tried the cold, and was rewarded with a rusty trickle. As he splashed his face with it he wished he were back in the comfort of his little cabin on the freighter instead of suffering the deprivations of the Hyatt Regency.

He went and opened the connecting door to the bedroom of the hotel suite. Janet had fallen asleep with the light on. Empty beer bottles were scattered across the floor, and her red dress lay rumpled at the foot of the bed. "I'm sorry to disturb you," said Dr. Abo. "But we must leave soon."

She rolled over and sat up, momentarily revealing her exquisitely proportioned body. Dr. Abo stared at her for a moment, then glumly averted his eyes.

Janet yawned. She dragged a sheet to cover her breasts. "What time is it?"

"It is rather early. But I must drive to Ocean Park. Last night, after you went to bed, I telephoned the trucking company in the Free Zone. They agreed to be at the freighter first thing, to unload my cargo."

Janet groaned.

"I could leave you here, if you wish." His voice was

diplomatically neutral. "I would come back to pick you up later."

"No. No, I'll come with you. Just give me a minute."

"All right." He turned to leave the bedroom. "By the way, there's no hot water."

"Wonderful. Is there any breakfast?"

"I'll call room service," said Dr. Abo, returning to the living room.

Fifteen minutes later, Janet emerged. Her red dress was wrinkled and her red hair was dishevelled, but she still looked disconcertingly self-possessed and desirable. "I'm —sorry about last night," she said to Dr. Abo. "I shouldn't have left you to sleep out here."

"What do you mean?"

"We could have taken turns on the couch, or something."

"Oh." He shrugged. "Well, it doesn't matter." He was silent for a moment. "There was no reply from room service," he added.

"Then I guess we may as well leave."

A little later, they were heading once again toward the coast. The Honda's hubcaps had been stolen while it was in the hotel garage overnight, and there was less gas in the tank than Dr. Abo remembered, but the car was otherwise unharmed. Under the circumstances, this seemed a rare stroke of good fortune.

"You had time to think, on your own, last night," Dr. Abo observed, as he drove along the Santa Monica freeway.

"Yes." Janet sat in the passenger seat, staring straight ahead. She looked untouchably remote.

There was a short silence.

"Well." Dr. Abo guided the car around a van that had broken down at the side of the highway and was being set on fire by laughing black teenagers. "What was your conclusion?"

She took a deep breath. "I want you to abandon your outrageous idea of developing a virus to enhance human intelligence. It would be unethical, illegal, and highly dangerous. I want you to become a law-abiding citizen, so I

don't have to break my oath to the Bureau by allowing you
to evade arrest." She turned and looked at him. Her expression was still composed, but there was a plaintiveness
in her eyes. "You can get a decent job in a corporate research lab, Percival. They're crying out for qualified people, now that the best ones have emigrated to Canada. You
can have a career. You won't have to hide from the law,
anymore. And—" Her voice became subdued. "And that
way, you can have me, too."

He exited from the freeway, following the same route
they had driven the previous night. "You're asking me to
sacrifice my life's work," he told her.

"No," she said carefully. "I don't want you to sacrifice
anything. Just stop pursuing your research illegally. Stay
out of the Free Zone. For god's sake, it's full of *criminals!*
If you join them, you'll be a criminal, too. The same thing
will happen to you as is going to happen to them."

He turned onto the street that led toward the dock where
the freighter was berthed. He looked at her curiously.
"What exactly?"

"Promise you won't reveal this to anyone."

Dr. Abo shifted into second gear and took the little car
slowly through a deep puddle that filled the street. "All
right, I give you my word."

"I made some calls of my own last night, before I went
to sleep. Thomas Fink, McCullough's boyfriend, was ar-
rested and detained yesterday. Without his computer skills,
the Zone's communications are crippled. As soon as I give
the word—maybe tomorrow—the National Guard will
move in." She looked at him. Her face was sad. "Now do
you see why I don't want you there?"

"You have evidently had an active role in this."

"As soon as I established my cover in LoveLand, I
tapped into the telephone system. Eventually, I traced
Fink's location, and told the mayor where to find him.
Actually, all I knew was Fink's function as the key node in
the network; I didn't discover his name, or his relationship
to McCullough, until we were in Alighieri's office yesterday. McCullough had given him a photograph; it was lying
on his desk. I recognized the picture. Fink's real name is

Henry Feldstein. He used to be on the ten most wanted list for electronic bank fraud." She paused. "That's who you're associating with, Percival. Grade-A felons and the mob."

Dr. Abo stopped the car at the foot of the makeshift ramp that led up to the dock. He sat for a while with his hands resting at the top of the steering wheel. Ahead, where the land sloped down, the ocean lapped at the windows of submerged apartment buildings, and a small boy paddled an aluminum canoe along the street. A fishing pole, a tin of bait, a lunch box, and a pump-action shotgun lay beside him.

"Dusty McCullough is a good woman," said Dr. Abo. "That much I am sure of."

"A lot of people have good intentions, Percival. The road to hell is paved with them. Look, this country is already in deep trouble. Can you imagine what would happen if the dog-eat-dog mentality of the Free Zone was allowed to spread unchecked?"

He smiled sadly and shook his head. "The dogs do not eat each other. That is, the Zone people do not turn against one another. All they want is to be left alone, to be free."

She shook her head emphatically. "They're a menace to society."

He spread his hands. "We cannot agree. Very well, let me ask one thing. My tissue samples are priceless. I must move them from the ship. Let me store them temporarily in the warehouse in the Free Zone. Then, I will look for storage elsewhere. Give me a week to accomplish this, before you send in the National Guard."

She thought it over. "Percival, if you go to McCullough and tell her what I've just told you—"

He smiled sadly. "I gave you my word."

She nodded slowly. "All right. You have a week. But in return, you're going to clean up your act. You'll find a real job, doing real research. Right?"

"If the Free Zone is destroyed, I will have no choice. There will be nowhere else to go."

They looked at each other in the little car. Outside, muddy water lapped at the wheels and made wet noises under the floor. A breeze rustled through mutant agave and jacaranda trees that had taken root on a nearby sandbank. Janet smiled fondly at him. "You really are the way I imagined you." She reached out and gently touched Dr. Abo's face. "Brave and honest and gentle and kind." She squeezed his hand.

He patted her hand with his, then shifted the car into gear. "We have made our agreement," he said. He drove the Honda up the ramp to the dock.

As the car bumped over the patchwork roadway of plywood and flattened automobile panels, the freighter came into view. Chinese crewmen were working busily around it, lowering large wooden crates from a derrick and stacking them in piles.

"My god," said Dr. Abo. "That's my cargo!" He stopped the car, jumped out, and ran toward the scene of activity. "You men! What are you doing? Those boxes must be kept frozen!"

The Chinese soldiers ignored him. The boom of the derrick swung out from the ship, its pulley squealed, and another sling full of crates was lowered to the dock.

"Dr. Abo," a voice called out. "Over here."

The captain was out on deck, supervising the operation. Dr. Abo hurried up the improvised gangplank. "Captain, you promised that my cargo would be maintained in refrigerated storage. You promised!"

"So it has been. But my ship leaves in just one hour from now, Doctor. Surely, you wouldn't want us to take your cargo with us?" The captain lit a cigarette and flipped the match over the rail. He watched Dr. Abo enigmatically.

"You said tomorrow. Tomorrow was your date of departure. Captain, if those crates thaw out—"

"Come with me." He walked across the deck to the other side of the ship. Dumbly, Dr. Abo followed.

"There was some trouble last night," the captain explained quietly. "A card game between some of my crew and the Chicanos on the dock. Some unpleasantness, some cheating. It was necessary for me to take steps." He pointed over the rail.

Dr. Abo peered down at the ocean. A dark brown stain had spread across the water. Below it lurked some indistinct forms. A human hand showed just below the surface, moving slowly with the current as if waving a sad farewell.

"I believe these are yours," said the captain. He held out three gold Krugerrands.

"I—I see. Thank you." Dr. Abo dumbly accepted the coins.

"You should keep the car," the captain went on. "Its previous owners have no further use for it."

"Er, yes." Dr. Abo nodded mechanically. He edged away, as if to separate himself from the other man.

The captain clapped him on the shoulder. "I do believe you are shocked. And I thought you were a man of the world." He laughed and walked Dr. Abo back to the gangplank. "Or are you still worried about your precious cargo? Come, now, it's a cool morning. If the boxes are collected promptly, no damage will result."

"You are probably right," Dr. Abo agreed diplomatically.

An air horn blared in the distance, and there was the sound of a diesel engine. "See?" said the captain. "That's probably your truck arriving." He shook Dr. Abo's hand. "Good luck, Doctor."

"Is everything okay?" Janet asked, as Dr. Abo stumbled down the gangplank.

"I—think so." He thrust the gold coins quickly into his pocket.

The truck's diesel roared as it climbed the ramp to the dock, making the wooden framework creak ominously. Giant eyes had been painted around the truck's headlights, and its radiator had been made into a grinning mouth with Dracula teeth and a drooling tongue. HERE COME THE MOTHERTRUCKERS! was painted in big red letters down the side of the trailer, above lurid pictures of women wearing bikinis, lightning bolts, and the American flag.

The truck pulled up with a hiss of air brakes. Three beefy, bearded men swung down from the cab, each clutching a can of Fuckin' A! beer, the Free Zone's own brand. "You Abo?" the biggest of the men asked, hitching his pants up over his belly and tightening his belt.

"Yes, yes." Dr. Abo looked nervously at the trailer. "This vehicle is refrigerated, as I requested?"

"Sure thing. Hey, I'm Fritz, and this here is Andy and Ramon. So, is that your shit over there?"

"Yes." Dr. Abo forced a smile. "Thank you for driving to this remote part of the city. I realize, it's rather early—"

"Fuck, no. We was boozing all night anyways, so we come straight over." He drained his beer, belched, crumpled the can in his fist, and threw it aside. "Okay, let's get to it."

"The contents are fragile," Dr. Abo called after him.

The big man laughed. "No sweat. The Mothertruckers ain't never dropped nothin' yet."

20. WARNING!
TRESPASSERS WILL BE SHOT!

There was a pounding sound, forcing her awake. Dusty felt fragile and limp, as if all her muscles had been deactivated and she was pinned to the bed by her own dead weight. Her head was full of pain. She rolled over and groaned. Last night she had drunk herself to sleep, waiting for news from Colonel Mallet; and the news had never come.

The pounding sound stopped, then started again. She realized, with sudden shock, someone was thumping on her bedroom door. Someone was in her house.

"Thomas?" Her voice was a dry whisper. She tried again. "Thomas? Is that you?"

"No." The voice was loud; it came clearly through the door. "This isn't Thomas."

She crawled out of bed, trying to suppress the nausea

that hit her when she moved her head. She grabbed her M-16, slumped down in a defensive position on the floor between the bed and the wall, and aimed the gun at the door as well as she could. "Who's there?" she shouted.

There was a pause. "It's hard to explain. I want to come in. Does this open?" The door rattled in its frame, and the wood creaked. In the dim daylight filtering through the barricaded bedroom window, Dusty saw that the steel bars securing the door were bending in their supports.

"Hold it!" she shouted.

The door crashed inward and fell to the floor, taking some of the surrounding wall with it. A shadowy figure stood in the semidarkness amid clouds of plaster dust.

"Stop or I fire!" she shouted.

"I'm sorry." The voice was deep and resonant—an orator's voice, with every syllable perfectly formed. It sounded somehow too perfect, like an impeccable simulation. "I pushed the door too hard. It was an accident."

Dusty switched on the bedside lamp. She saw a figure completely encased in polished steel armor. "Stay right there," she shouted. "Put your hands on top of your head."

The metal-clad figure obeyed. "Is this a social custom?"

Dusty tried to keep her aim while she pulled on some Levi's and an old T-shirt. Her head was still hurting and it was hard to think. "What the hell is this, some sort of stunt? Who are you?"

"You may find this hard to believe."

"Try me." She moved forward.

"I am from the future. I travelled through time and found myself in your basement, where there is a device that is causing temporal interference. Probably you have some idea of what I'm referring to."

"What?"

"I said—"

"All right, all right. Go on into the living room."

Reluctantly, the metal man obeyed. "The device must be switched off," he told her. "Unfortunately, I don't know how to do this safely. I lack the data. If you will do it for me, I can offer you some useful gifts in return."

Dusty opened one of the window shutters. Filtered sunlight flooded in. She walked slowly around the metal man, checking for any kind of weapon. The air seemed to shimmer a few inches above his armor. She reached out to touch it, and her hand seemed to meet an invisible barrier. When she pressed harder, there was a faint hissing noise and sparkling pinpoints flurrying around her fingers like dust motes in a sunbeam. She drew her hand back quickly.

"It is a protective shield," the metal man explained.

"Thomas," Dusty muttered to herself. "This has to be something to do with Thomas. Did my boyfriend build you? Is this some stupid Christmas surprise, or what?"

The metal man shook his head. "I already told you, I am from the future. In your basement—"

Dusty threw down her gun. "There's nothing in the goddam basement. Are you a robot? Or is there someone inside that suit? What the hell is going on here?"

"There *is* something in your basement. It's a tachyon transmitter.

She pointed to the hallway. "Lead the way."

The robot hesitated.

"We'll check this out right now. You go first."

"Well, all right." The robot walked across the living room, picking his way carefully between her bodybuilding equipment and the coffee table piled with papers and empty beer bottles. The floor trembled under his heavy metal tread. He moved smoothly but with an awkward rolling motion, as if he had trouble keeping his balance.

Out in the hallway, Dusty checked the front door. Last night she had nailed a couple of boards across it to fix the damage that the mayor's men had caused when they grabbed Thomas. She saw, now, the boards were still in place. "How the hell did you get in the house?"

"I travelled through time, and—"

"Okay, enough. Go on, down those stairs."

Obediently, he descended the wooden steps. She followed him, and found that all the lights were on. There was an insistent humming sound.

"You see?" The robot gestured to equipment stacked on the concrete floor, under the bare beams.

"No shit." Dusty surveyed the wires, video screens, and monitoring gear. "What *is* all this?"

"You really don't know?" The synthetic voice sounded disappointed.

"Thomas said he liked to work down here sometimes." She stared at the heaps of equipment and slowly shook her head. "He had a thing about privacy. I respected that."

"So the tachyon transmitter belongs to a person named Thomas?" The metal man regarded her enigmatically. "Will Thomas be coming back soon?"

Dusty laughed humorlessly. "I wish."

Upstairs, the door bell rang.

"I guess I should answer that. Wait here, okay?" She hesitated. "Do you understand?"

"Yes, of course I understand."

"Yes, of course," Dusty muttered to herself. She turned and ran up the stairs. "Who is it?" she shouted.

"Colonel Matt Mallet."

Dusty grabbed a claw-headed hammer, pried loose her makeshift barricade, then grasped the door and dragged it to one side. She squinted in the light and picked up a pair of sunglasses from a nearby shelf. It was a hazy day; the sky was streaked with high cloud. But it was warm, and grasshoppers were buzzing in the tall grass in the front yard.

The colonel looked weary, and he needed a shave. He was wearing a steel helmet and a flak jacket over his camouflage fatigues. His ivory-handled Colt was holstered at his hip, and an AK-47 with a telescopic sight was slung over his shoulder. His heavy black boots were spattered with mud. Behind him, an armored troop carrier stood at the curb with its motor running. Steel shutters had been folded down from its windows, revealing half a dozen men inside.

"Hey, Dusty!" a voice shouted.

She looked and saw a long-haired, bearded freak leaning out of a window on the top floor of the apartment house opposite, holding a sawed-off shotgun.

"What is this shit?" He gestured at the troop carrier.

"It's okay, Dave," she called to him. "These guys are supposed to be working for us." She turned back to Mallet. "My neighbors are still a bit jumpy after seeing Thomas taken away yesterday," she explained.

"That's understandable, ma'am." Mallet put his hands on his hips, and looked her up and down. There was nothing friendly in his face. He reminded her of a cop who had come to arrest someone.

Dusty forced a smile. "So do you have any good news?"

Colonel Mallet rocked back on his heels, still studying her carefully. "Seems to me, there's a possibility you may know most of the news already."

She felt herself becoming irritated. "Colonel, don't play games. Did you find Thomas or not?"

"My vehicle, Miss McCullough, was stolen last night while I was planning our attack. However, the Mashers did penetrate City Hall. We searched the building but did not find Mr. Fink. We questioned the mayor, who seemed surprised and angry to learn that Fink was missing. We interrogated two men who had been detailed to guard Fink. They said they had transferred him to the custody of the mayor's aide, a glamorous young black woman. She, too, turned out to be missing." The colonel tucked his thumbs in his gun belt, and shifted his feet apart slightly. "I have no doubt, she helped him to escape."

"You mean he got out? That's fantastic! Where is he now?"

"I have spent most of the night trying to locate Mr. Fink." Mallet's voice was conversational, but the way he showed his teeth while he talked was far from friendly. "It was he and the black woman who stole my Jeep. The descriptions match precisely. There's no possible doubt."

Dusty pictured mild-mannered Thomas and some teenage girl running off with the colonel's property. She found it hard not to smile. "That must have been embarrassing for you," she said.

Mallet took a step forward. "McCullough, I find it very hard to believe you know nothing about this. With your permission, my men will search this building."

"What the hell are you talking about?"

"This is Fink's domicile. It's the first place he'd run to. I want that boy. He has a lot to answer for."

"Oh, no." Dusty shook her head. "If you ever touch him, I'll kill you." Her smile was gone; her frustrations were turning quickly to anger. "What sort of a jerk are you, anyway? If you got ripped off, it's your own stupid fault. But I suppose you can't admit that. You'd rather take it out on someone else."

Mallet's face twitched. He pointed his finger at Dusty. "I give you fair warning—"

Dusty's hand shot out and seized his wrist. She held it tightly. "Go ahead," she told him. "I've already had an intruder busting into my bedroom this morning. I feel like shit. I haven't even had breakfast yet. I'm really in the mood to fuck someone up, Colonel."

Mallet's face went pale with anger. With his free left hand, he groped for the gun at his hip.

Dusty dragged his right hand toward her and sank her teeth into his finger as hard as she could. Mallet gasped in pain. He swore and tried to pull free. She resisted for a moment, then let go, kicked her heel into his stomach, and watched with satisfaction as he fell backward into the yard.

She ran into the living room, grabbed her rifle, and went to the window. She sighted on Mallet as he scrambled back onto his feet. "Get out of here," she shouted at him. "Before I blow your stupid head off."

Mallet saw the gun aimed steadily at him. He paused, breathing hard. Slowly, he backed toward the troop carrier. "I'm warning you, McCullough, I have enough firepower, and enough men, here, to vaporize your home and every-one in it."

"Try it, and you'll have a goddam war on your hands."

Dusty raised her gun and fired it into the air.

As the rifle shot echoed away, bikers, freaks, and mis-fits of all descriptions came to their windows up and down the block. Some emerged into their front yards, toting homemade rifles, crossbows, machine guns, and grenades.

"Get out of our neighborhood!" Dusty yelled at Mallet.

He turned slowly, surveying his opposition.

"Better do what the woman says, soldier," someone called to him.

With all the dignity he could muster, Mallet swung into the cab of the troop carrier. "You haven't seen the end of this, McCullough," he shouted. He gestured to the driver, and the vehicle revved its motor and moved away up the street.

"Damn," Dusty muttered under her breath. "Me and my temper." She put aside the rifle, and sat down, feeling suddenly weak. "Now what have I done?"

21. DINOSAURS OF THE DEEP

Meanwhile, on the ocean floor, in the ruins of a lost city that had once been known as Atlantis, the Tyrant waited impatiently in his throne room. It was a vast space designed to accommodate creatures ten times the size of men. Its curved steel walls and domed roof gleamed in the subtle radiance from hundreds of levitating crystal spheres. Luxuriant prehistoric ferns flourished in huge glass arboreta. In a tidal pool near the center of the chamber, tylosauri frolicked among reefs of coral and snapped playfully at each other's tails.

The Tyrant reclined on his throne of simulated moss and nibbled a giant ammonite. Its shell crunched in his jaws and he sucked the toothsome flesh. The flavor, he reflected, had deteriorated somewhat during its long period of suspended animation. Soon, though, there would be fresh fish and meat, perhaps of entirely new species. He was eager to discover what evolution had accomplished since he last ventured out across the land.

"Your majesty?" A paleoscincus—one of the Tyrant's loyal honor guard—appeared at the door.

"Are you bringing news?" The great lizard's voice was a growl terminating in an inquisitorial hiss.

"Yes, your majesty. The chief surveillance drone has returned. It wishes to tender its report."

The Tyrant flipped his tail. The floor trembled. "Send it in."

A metallic disk studded with lenses and probes floated into the royal chamber. It paused and hovered in front of the Tryant, humming gently. "For the most part," it announced, "I bring good news, your majesty. Our automatic systems served their saurian masters well. Almost all your cousins have been revived safely from hibernation by their medical units. The city has fulfilled its promise as a refuge for your species while the planet cooled."

"But for how long?" The Tyrant watched the disk with one large, yellow eye. "Since the failure of your electronic clocks, have you yet discovered how many years have passed?"

"I have conducted tests. By examining ocean sediments and evaluating the uranium/lead ratio in seawater I now calculate you have slept for more than 100 million years, your majesty."

The great lizard emitted a great sigh of dismay, and slumped onto his throne.

"The sensors that should have detected the end of the ice age failed in their duty. As a result, you were not woken at that time."

"Indeed." The great one slowly recovered himself. He rose up on his hind legs and started pacing the chamber, lashing his tail. "Well, so be it. There is no going back; we shall have to accept our situation. What has happened in the outside world through all these millions of years?"

The surveillance drone accompanied him, floating beside his left shoulder, twenty-five feet above the chamber's floor of burnished brass. "A new dominant species has risen, your majesty, of creatures unknown in your time.

They number more than a billion. They are small bipeds, sire. Mammals."

"Egg eaters!" The Tyrant spat in disgust, and his forked tongue lashed out like a whip. He paused, "You say more than a *billion?*"

"Yes, your majesty. They live in cities that are so numerous, they have altered the climate of the globe. Indeed, it was the warming trend that they created which finally reanimated our city and its inhabitants."

"We will eat these mammals for breakfast," the Tyrant growled. "Are the army ants ready for battle?"

"I believe so, your majesty. But I must advise caution. The mammals have developed devastating weapons."

The Tyrant rested his jaw briefly on a mossy ledge and exposed his fearsome conical teeth. Trained scavenger beetles darted forward to devour food residues and polish away plaque.

"What would you have us do," the Tyrant said at length, "surrender to these bipeds?"

"No, your majesty. But you could consider peaceful coexistence. Or, you could return your city to its sleep for, say, another thousand years. By that time the mammals are quite likely to have rendered themselves extinct."

"No!" The Tyrant strode to the pool and seized a tylosaurus with one quick lunge of his jaws. He crushed it and swallowed it, ignoring its screams. "A treaty with a race of egg eaters? It's inconceivable. Return to the hibernation tanks? Certainly not; if your systems failed to rouse us promptly before, they can fail again. Notify my minister of war. Arm the giant ants. We will raise our city from its resting place and once again conquer Europe!"

"Very well, your majesty." The metallic messenger hesitated. "Although, I'm afraid Europe is out of the question."

"What? Do you defy my authority?"

"Under no circumstances. But it turns out there has been a phenomenon known as continental drift. As a result, your city's position has changed. It is no longer located off the coast of Europe. During one of the periodic warmer periods, the northern ice cap seems largely to have melted, at which time your city moved across the pole and south, into the Pacific Ocean. Your exact location, now, is just off the western coast of a large land mass known as North America."

The Tyrant used his diminutive front legs to pick tylosaurus bones from his mouth. He tossed them into a recycling unit in the corner of the chamber. "So, we will invade and conquer North America. It makes no difference." He relaxed again on his throne of simulated moss. "We, too, have destructive weapons of fearsome power. If these bipeds provoke us, we shall squash them as a brontosaurus squashes a trilobite." He grinned horribly, and clasped his claws across the scales of his belly. "Go, now, and do as I have instructed."

"Yes, your majesty." The surveillance drone drifted out of the throne room, broadcasting news of the impending battle.

22. A BRIEF ENCOUNTER AT LOLITA'S COTTAGE

Dr. Abo wiped grime off the cracked glass of a circular dial and tapped it with his knuckle. "You see, Lucky, this tells us how cold it is." He moved to a black metal box mounted nearby on the side of the compressor unit. "Here is the switch that turns the refrigeration on and off. And this is the thermostat." He had to raise his voice to be heard above the noise that the system was making.

"Thermostat?" Lucky looked at Dr. Abo with his head on one side, and cocked an ear.

"It keeps the temperature constant. Well, never mind

about that. The important thing is that this pointer must stay at zero." He pointed to the 0 mark. "You see?"

Lucky nodded. "Zero is the round number."

"Very good, Lucky. Remember, you will be in charge when I'm not here. It's a very responsible job, and I'm counting on you."

Lucky wagged his tail. "I do the job, yes."

"I'm glad to hear it. Now, let's go and see if the men have finished unloading." Dr. Abo pushed open a swing door into the thermally insulated section of the warehouse. Fritz, Andy, and Ramon were stacking the last of the crates. Their breath was steaming in the frigid air. "That just about does it, pal." Fritz slapped his fat hands together and blew on them. "Jeez, it's cold enough in here to freeze a horny hooker's ass off." He noticed Lucky. "Hey, is this one of them talking dogs? Like they said on TV?"

"Indeed, yes," said Dr. Abo. "Say hello to Fritz, Lucky."

"Hello," said Lucky. He looked up at the big man without much enthusiasm.

"Far fuckin' out." Fritz squatted down. He reached out and scratched Lucky behind the ears.

Lucky twisted away, backed off, and growled softly.

"What's the matter, dog?" Fritz looked puzzled.

"The move from the ship has perhaps unsettled him," said Dr. Abo. "Anyway, the job is now complete?"

"Sure thing, pal. The Mothertruckers done successfully completed another challenging assignment."

"Thank you." Dr. Abo gave a little bow and handed over one of his Krugerrands. "Gold is acceptable?"

"Sure." Fritz weighed it in his hand, flipped it, caught it, and stuffed it in his Levi's. He glanced at Lucky. "Take it easy, there, dog." He turned to his buddies. "Let's go, guys. I could use a drink."

Dr. Abo waited for the truckers to leave. "Lucky, that man meant well. You could have been more friendly."

Lucky twitched his tail. "I didn't feel like it."

Dr. Abo gave his dog a puzzled look. "Well," he said reluctantly, "I suppose we can't expect you to be in a good mood all the time. All right, let's go outside."

As he emerged into the warm sunshine, Dr. Abo heard a sudden crackling roar from up in the sky. He looked up in time to see two groups of F-111 fighters flash past in tight formation. The sound was a physical assault. He clapped his hands over his ears.

Janet had been waiting in the car. She got out and shaded her eyes, watching the jets disappear toward the west.

"Evidently a military exercise," said Dr. Abo.

"On the day after Christmas, over central Los Angeles, at under a thousand feet?" She shook her head, making her red curls sway to and fro. "That doesn't seem likely."

"Well," said Dr. Abo, "all that concerns me is that my unloading operation is finally complete. I feel greatly relieved."

"I'm happy for you, Percival." Her voice sounded abstracted. She glanced at the warehouse, then at the old, rusty water tower behind it and at the peeling paint on the adjacent office buildings. "Frankly, I can't wait till you get the hell out of this slum."

"Yes, yes, of course. Within a week, as we agreed."

"All right." She noticed that she had stepped into some wet mud, and grimaced, scraping the side of her high-heeled shoe against a clump of grass. "Look, I want to go back to my apartment. I'd like to change into some clean clothes, and—take care of a couple other things."

"Very well." Dr. Abo turned to his dog. "I will be away for a few hours, Lucky. Remember what I told you. Look after the warehouse, and don't let anyone inside."

"No trouble," said Lucky. "Everything will be fine." His tongue lolled out, and for a moment he seemed to be giving his master an inscrutable grin.

Janet drove the Honda around the edge of Griffith Park. A shantytown had sprung up here, under the trees. Shacks and hovels had been built from scrap lumber, corrugated iron, plastic sheeting, and automobile panels. Hairy hobos, dark with grime, stared suspiciously at the car as it passed.

"More upstanding citizens of the Free Zone," Janet commented.

"They don't seem to be doing any harm," Dr. Abo said mildly.

"That's right, they're not doing anything to anyone. But this country doesn't need deadbeats who opt out. It needs all the help it can get."

They reached LoveLand and left the car in the parking lot. Janet showed her pass at the turnstile, and Dr. Abo followed her in. "I still find it hard to believe that you—participated here," he told her, eyeing the decadence of Sex Street U.S.A.

"Blame it on my sense of duty. I've always been willing to endure hardship for the sake of a principle." She checked her purse. "Damn. I was in such a fog when we left yesterday, I forgot my apartment keys." She paused thoughtfully. "I'll have to borrow Suzie's set. Let's see; I think she's scheduled for Lolita's Cottage this morning."

Dr. Abo accompanied Janet past X-rated minimovie theaters, feelie booths, bi-bars, and strip-poker parlors. He sidestepped a woman in a topless dress selling aphrodisiac milkshakes from a big plastic breast on wheels, and detoured around a man dressed up as a giant penis, posing for photos with giggling tourists. Eventually, between Peter Pecker's Impotence Treatment Clinic and the Dolls 'n' Dildoes Sex Toy Boutique, they found Lolita's Cottage.

It was like a picture from a kindergarten art class: a two-story building with white walls, a red tiled roof, and a chimney emitting cute little puffs of white smoke. There was a privet hedge, a wooden gate, and a gravel path leading to the front door. Inside, the hallway was littered with children's toys. Nursery rhymes played over concealed loudspeakers. A young woman in bobby sox, penny loafers, a frilly little dress, freckles, and pigtails greeted them with a cheerful wave of her lollypop. "Hello! Are you my uncle and auntie? Do you want to play naughty games with my ickle girlfriends?" She clasped her hands behind her back, trailed her toe across the tiled floor, and batted her eyelashes.

Janet's expression remained carefully controlled. "We've come to see Suzie."

"Oh. Okay. Last door on the left. There's no one with her right now."

"This is—most disturbing," Dr. Abo muttered as he followed Janet down the corridor.

"Yes, it's sick," she agreed. "That's why I want to put it out of business." She opened the door at the end.

Dr. Abo followed her in. The room was a replica of a ten-year-old's bedroom. There were frilly drapes, dolls sitting on a miniature bureau, shelves of children's books, and a pink plastic phonograph playing "The Teddy-Bears' Picnic." The wallpaper was decorated with pictures of Big Bird, Kermit the Frog, and Cookie Monster. There was a bed in one corner littered with stuffed toys. Beside it was a small, discreet cabinet full of sex aids.

Suzie Sunshine was sitting on a big wooden rocking horse, sucking a candy cane. She was barefoot and wore a skimpy gingham dress that exposed most of her thighs and breasts. "Janet!" she exclaimed. "Hey, it's great to see ya! But what happened yesterday? I heard you and some guy—" She saw Dr. Abo and stopped. She covered her mouth. "Oops!"

"Suzie Sunshine, meet Percival Abo," Janet said, with an uncomfortable smile.

Suzie slid down off the rocking horse. "Well, hi." She shook his hand and gave him a shy grin.

"I locked myself out of the apartment yesterday," Janet said. "Do you—"

"I got your keys right here," said Suzie. "I saw you'd left them behind, and I figured you might come by to pick them up." She went over to a Little Red Riding Hood lunch box, opened it, took out the keys, and handed them to her. "But is it true, Jan? Are you really moving out?"

"Probably." Janet avoided the other woman's eyes.

"I'll miss you, if you go. We had some good times."

"Yes, well, I'll miss you too, Suzie."

Suzie got back on the rocking horse. "Nothing much happening here today, that's for sure. I mean, it's always quiet in the mornings, but this is ridiculous. I've only turned one trick on this shift, can you believe that? Because of the news, I guess."

Janet frowned. "What news?"

"Out at Topanga Beach. Mexican terrorists, they said on the TV, with bombs and guns and stuff. They told everyone to stay off the streets till it's over.

Janet looked at Dr. Abo, then back at Suzie. "I had no idea. We'd better go to the apartment. Thanks, Suzie. Maybe we'll see you later."

"Sure." She winked. "Have fun, you two lovebirds."

Janet left the cottage and strode quickly back through the theme park. "You are concerned?" Dr. Abo asked, hurrying in order to keep pace with her.

"Yes, I'm concerned. If it's a real crisis, the Bureau may want me. And I've been offline since I called them last night, which is strictly against regulations."

"But what do you think is happening?"

"Who knows? Suzie's such an airhead, she probably got the story wrong."

Together, they rode the elevator to Janet's floor in the converted office building where her apartment was located.

"What will happen to Suzie when you close down the Free Zone?" Dr. Abo asked, as they walked along the carpeted corridor. "She seems to trust you as a friend."

"I've done my best to discourage that." Janet unlocked the apartment door. "I imagine she'll get a fine and probation, like most of the employees. As for management, I want them sent to jail or maybe to work camps in the midwest." She pushed the door open and strode in. "Ignore the mess." She gestured to the usual litter of sex aids and underwear. "It's Suzie's stuff." She walked over to the phone, opened a small drawer, and took out a thin silver wire, which she attached to the telephone earpiece.

"What are you doing?"

"I have a communications implant. For direct access."

"You mean an actual socket—"

"No, of course not. That wouldn't be very discreet. There's a small induction coil under the skin, here." She pressed a disk at the free end of the wire to the skin behind her ear, and closed her eyes. "This will take a few minutes. Make yourself comfortable." Her voice had become abstracted and remote.

Dr. Abo sat on one of the chairs at the dining table. He noticed the Christian Fornicationist Bible, started leafing through it, and paused in surprise when he came to one of the color illustrations. He glanced warily at Janet to see if she had seen him looking at the picture. Then he took another peek; then he closed the book and pushed it away with a frown of disapproval. He sat back in his chair and surveyed the rest of the room: large windows with red velvet drapes, a projection TV, shelves of self-improvement books and police procedural novels, a sign over the door to the bedroom that read MAKE LOVE TO THY NEIGHOR, a couch with a dildo lying in one corner.

Janet was standing motionless by the phone with her eyes closed. After five minutes she suddenly disconnected the wire, coiled it, and stashed it in her purse.

She walked back toward Dr. Abo, moving slowly, now as if the data she had received had erased her sense of urgency. She turned a chair so that it faced him, and sat so that their knees were almost touching. "I've been temporarily reassigned," she told him. "I have to report to the downtown office this afternoon."

"But did you find out what's happening?"

"I'll tell you the details later. Right now, we have a couple of hours before they're expecting me." She smiled. "This may be our last chance, for the next few days, for a little time alone together."

"Oh." He made no move toward her.

"I know I've been difficult," she said quietly. "And I've made some big demands." She ran her finger down the crease in the trousers of his suit. "I hope you can understand. I do believe in you, Percival. You're obviously an exceptional man, and I'd like things to work out for us."

Dr. Abo coughed uneasily. He looked away from her clear blue eyes. Then he realized he was staring down at her breasts, so he looked back at her face. "It has been a difficult situation for us both," he said diplomatically.

"But I do still want you, Percival." She touched his cheek and edged closer.

"You are—unique."

She smiled. "It's true, I am." She leaned forward and pressed her lips against his. It was an uneasy, awkward kiss. After a moment, Dr. Abo drew back. "It's hard to keep up with your moods, Janet."

"I know. But won't you try?" She shifted onto his lap and started unbuttoning his shirt.

The room seemed to tremble. At first, neither of them noticed. But then an ornament fell from a shelf and crashed to the floor; and the whole building seemed to sway slightly.

Janet pulled away. "What the hell—"

"I do believe it is an earthquake." He stood up quickly, kicking his chair aside. A new wave of vibration seized the room, more severe than the last. In the distance, someone screamed. There were running footsteps outside in the hallway. Dust pattered down. A painting fell off the wall.

Dr. Abo eyed the distance to the door. He hesitated. The floor rocked wildly under him. "Under the table!"

Together they fell down onto their hands and knees. Janet looked scared. "I'm from the east. I've never been—"

A scraping, groaning sound, and a sudden crash cut off her words. All the lights went out. Several of the windows shattered. The floor tilted, and the roof fell with a cascade of plaster and rubble. Janet screamed. Heavy objects thudded down on top of the table, breaking the top of it in two as the room filled with thick, choking dust.

23. QUICK-THINKING ROBOT RESCUES QUAKE VICTIM

Dusty was sitting eating lunch with the robot in her living room when the floor started shaking. It took her less than a second to realize what was happening. "Earthquake!" she shouted. "Out of the house, quick!"

The metal man lurched to his feet. Unexpectedly, he seized Dusty's wrist and pulled her to him. His steel arms circled her in a frightening grip. "My force field can protect us both," he said.

Dusty flinched as the floor lurched and part of the ceiling gave way. Timbers fell—and bounced harmlessly off the transparent bubble that had sprung up around her. Books dropped off the shelves and dishes shattered in the kitchen, but the noises were muted by the invisible shield. Even the billowing plaster dust was filtered out.

"You cannot survive inside the field for very long," said the robot. "You will need oxygen. May I carry you?"

His head was on a level with hers. She stared at him with wide eyes. "Sure."

He lifted her with one metal arm under her knees, the other behind her shoulders. As the quake gradually subsided he picked his way through the debris and took her out into the front yard.

The air inside the force field was already smelling stale when he set her gently on the ground. The shimmering bubble disappeared, and sounds and smells of the world returned. People were running out into the street, shouting to each other. Dogs were barking. A crack had opened in the apartment building opposite, but it was still standing. Several houses down the block seemed to have partially collapsed.

"I wonder if the tachyon transmitter in the basement is still functioning," said the robot.

"Go check," said Dusty. "Do what you want." She steadied herself against the old picket fence at one side of the yard, under an orange tree that had long since run wild, and looked back at her home. Part of the roof had fallen in and one of the walls was leaning outward.

She walked to a couple of old aluminum lawn chairs that were almost submerged in the tall grass, and sat down in one of them.

"You okay?" said a voice.

She looked up and saw her neighbor Dave. "Yeah. I mean, a bit shaken up. Literally, I guess."

"Who was the guy I saw carrying you? Seemed like he was wearing some kind of silver costume."

Dusty shook her head and laughed. "Don't ask, Dave. Just don't ask."

"Okay. If that's how you want it, that's cool." He surveyed the street. "I figure I'll run down the block, see if anyone needs help, and like that."

"Fine," said Dusty. "Go."

The robot reemerged a moment later. "The electricity in the house is still functioning." He sounded peeved about it. "Some items in the basement have shifted slightly, but the equipment still seems to be emitting tachyon radiation." He paused and turned to face the street. "Two people are arriving. They look as if they may want your help."

Wearily, Dusty climbed to her feet. She saw a battered AMC Pacer pulling in at the curb—a fat, funny-looking little car that had been out of production for the past twenty years. This specimen was by no means mint. Most of its one-time silver paint had faded to a mottled gray, and its fenders had rusted away completely. The windshield was spiderwebbed with cracks that had been haphazardly patched with masking tape. The car's engine sputtered and died, and a figure got out, his head wrappped in bloodstained bandages. He stumbled into the front yard. "Dusty," he called.

It took her a moment to realize who he was. "Thomas!"

She stood up and ran to him and made as if to hug him, then hesitated, afraid she might hurt him. She grabbed his hand and squeezed it. She felt a wave of emotion, as if she was about to start crying—and then she found herself laughing instead. "Are you okay? What happened?" A grim suspicion took hold of her. "Did Mallet do that to your head? The son of a bitch—"

"Who?"

"Come inside," she told him. "You can rest—no, maybe we shouldn't go in the house, it might not be safe. Sit down." She pushed him into the chair she'd been sitting in. "Are you okay?"

"I'm fine, I'm fine." He stared up at her a moment and laughed with relief, savoring the look of her. "God, it's good to see you. But look, there's someone with me."

Dusty turned and saw a thin black girl standing in the yard. She, too, had her head bandaged. "My name's Roxanne," she said.

Dusty spent the next few minutes learning about their escape from City Hall, fussing over Thomas's head injury, and asking new questions without waiting for answers to the old ones.

"I hit my head on the Jeep's windshield," he told her. "That's all."

"Maybe you have concussion. Do you have blurred vision? Any trouble talking?" She lifted the bandages and peeked at the swelling underneath.

"No, no, just cuts and bruises. We stopped at a hospital on the way back from Topanga. I had money, so they took X rays. We would have reached here before now, except I fell asleep on the examination table in the emergency room. I'd been up all night, and I was exhausted."

"Why were you out at Topanga? No, tell me that in a minute. Where's the Jeep?"

"Wrapped around a telephone pole. Fortunately, a farmer happened by. We made a deal with him. He took us back to his place and gave us an old car—the Pacer there —plus some cash. In exchange, we let him keep all the weapons and equipment in the Jeep."

Dusty's expression turned grim. "Colonel Mallet's not going to like that."

"Mallet?" said Roxanne. "Is that the guy—"

"You stole the Jeep from him," said Dusty. "He's a mercenary; we hired him to go in and get you out of City Hall. Except I guess you didn't realize that."

"I thought he was with the National Guard," said Thomas. He was thoughtful for a moment. "Still, it's just as well we got his vehicle. Otherwise, we might not have found out about the—the ship on the beach."

"What ship?"

There was a long silence. Thomas looked around at the front yard, the dry grass and tall weeds standing in the hazy sunshine. There were distant shouts from Freeps helping someone out of a damaged home down the block. Insects buzzed to and fro, and the grasshoppers were getting busier as the day grew warmer. It was hard to imagine that this could all be swept away, instantly, by some higher force.

He turned back to Dusty. "Something very big is happening out at Topanga. It's—an invasion."

Dusty sat in the other chair beside him and took hold of his hand. "Are you serious?"

He nodded. "I think the military are already involved. We heard jets going over while we were driving back. Explosions in the distance."

"I heard low-flying aircraft here, a while ago," Dusty said. "But who—I mean, what country—"

"Would you believe aliens from outer space?" Thomas pulled himself up onto his feet. "I have to see if the phones are still working. Maybe I can get into the military communications network and find out what's really going on. Then we should probably head east, before they evacuate the whole city."

He walked into the house—then stopped as he came face to face with the robot, who had retreated into the hallway and was waiting there patiently.

"You have equipment in the basement," the metal man said, "generating temporal interference. I've come to ask you to shut it down."

Thomas looked at the robot blankly, without saying anything. The two of them stood there staring at each other.

"He means it," said Dusty, with an uneasy laugh. "That is, I mean, I think he's for real." She hesitated. "Thomas, did you say *aliens?*"

He turned and looked back at Dusty. His face was still blank. "Is this actually happening?"

She nodded soberly. "Ever since I woke up this morning."

"The Day of Judgment," said Roxanne. "I swear to God. Judgment is at hand."

"She's a fundamentalist," Thomas explained, making a vague gesture. The remnant of chain attached to his handcuff jingled as he moved. "You know, all I really want," he went on, "is to get these damned things off my wrists and ankles." He turned back to the robot. "Maybe if we go down to the basement, I can find a hacksaw. While we're down there, you can tell me what you really want."

A little while later, Thomas was sitting at his work bench with one of the handcuffs in a vise and a hacksaw in his free hand. He worked steadily, sawing through the steel, concentrating on the job. The robot stood watching, and Dusty and Roxanne sat side by side on top of the washer-drier combination in the corner. There was no place else for them to sit; the rest of the space was filled with Thomas's equipment.

"I would have disconnected the power to your tachyon generator myself," said the robot. "But I did not know if it was safe to do so."

"Absolutely right," said Thomas. "Shutting it down is a very complex and dangerous procedure. On the other hand, if you're from the future, I should imagine it must seem primitive by your standards."

"I'm an historian," the robot explained. "I have very little technical programming."

Thomas finished sawing through the first handcuff. He freed it from the vise and held it up. "Can you bend these two sections apart?"

"Certainly." He applied his metal fingers with carefully controlled strength.

"So you really are from the future," said Thomas, as he started work on his other wrist.

"Yes," said the robot. "Dusty didn't believe it for a while, but I think I convinced her."

"Do you have a name?"

"My local node number is 6A419BD5h."

"That's a hexadecimal number?"

"Of course."

"So there's more than two billion nodes in your local area alone. How many worldwide?"

"Thomas," Dusty interrupted, beginning to lose patience, "if what you said is true, and the city is about to be overrun by—by something or someone, shouldn't we forget the small talk and get the hell out of here?"

"Trust me, Dusty." His voice was quiet and casual, but he gave her a strangely intense look. "Some things you deal with, like political trouble in the Zone. But this is my kind of thing. I know what I'm doing."

Dusty walked over and touched his forehead tentatively. "You sure?"

"Yes." There was a detached, dreamy certainty in his eyes. He looked as if he had seen some higher truth.

"Ain't no escape from Judgment Day, anyhow," said Roxanne.

"So," Thomas said, turning back to 6A419BD5h, "the total number of nodes—"

"Close to a googol. The Network has spread over the entire globe."

Thomas freed his other wrist and turned to the leg irons that were still locked around his ankles. "I see. Is there a human population, too?"

"None."

"You mean machine intelligence has completely replaced humanity? What happened, did we wipe ourselves out?"

"I believe so." 6A419BD5h paused. "Please, when you finish freeing yourself, will you switch off your equipment? I do want to return to my own time."

"He said he'd give us some stuff if we promised not to generate any more tacky-whatever," Dusty put in.

"Yes, indeed." 6A419BD5h opened the top of his head, took out the items, and arrayed them on the bench. "Immortality serum, antigravity device, and an invisibility field generator." He looked hopefully at Thomas. "You might find them useful? I also have a force tube that projects a tractor beam or creates a shield, but I'd like to hang on to that till I leave, just for my own protection."

Thomas freed one ankle and set the saw down, resting his arm. He squinted at the robot. "You're surely not afraid of primitive creatures like us."

"Well, I don't know." The metal man sounded embarrassed. "Humans are strange and unpredictable. I probably feel about them the same way you'd feel if you found yourself dealing with a mythic beast that you thought was extinct." He shuffled his metal feet restlessly and flexed his fingers, looking at the hacksaw. "Can I finish the job for you?"

"Yes, if you're in such a hurry, go right ahead."

The robot immediately went to work. "You have no idea how long this whole situation seems to be taking."

"Oh, I get it," said Thomas. "You're accustomed to high-speed data transfer."

"Merely waiting for you to return home seemed to take about a year." 6A419BD5h removed the steel cuff and set it aside. "So, now, if you'll be so kind—"

"But we could log you into *our* global communications network," said Thomas. "It's small compared to yours, of course, but still big enough to keep your processor busy. Think of all that data. If you're an historian, I should think you'd want to pick up some first-hand facts while you're here."

The robot hesitated. "Direct connection to this network is possible?"

"Of course. I have equipment that does it all the time. In fact, here's an idea. I have a radiotelephone. You can show us how to use your antigravity unit to go out and fly around, and at the same time, you can be logged into the net via the phone. I'm assuming you can handle multitasking, of course." He smiled amiably. "What do you say?"

"This late period of human history contains many un-

knowns," the robot said reflectively. "Some claim there
was a temporal singularity—" He stopped short. "But you
do promise, as soon as I've had all the input I want, you'll
shut down your tachyon transmitter?"

"Of course," said Thomas. He picked up the metal bottle, the small cylinder, and the shiny metal sphere, thrust
them into the pockets of his jeans, and grabbed his radiotelephone. "Let's see about an interface here. This is real
primitive stuff—just twisted-pair. What sort of i/o do you
have?"

A little later, the robot was walking with them out of the
house, with the telephone wired into a socket in his stomach. "You're sure your antigravity field will be strong
enough?" Thomas was saying. "The combined weight—"

"Yes, yes!" 6A419BD5h interrupted.

"Well, you did tell me you had very little technical
background." Thomas smiled apologetically. "How about
the force field? Can it expand safely to a twenty-foot diameter and still be effective?"

"Yes! I assure you!" The robot fidgeted with the buttons
on the phone. "Please show me how to use this device. I
am quite hungry for data."

"Let's see," said Thomas, ignoring him. "Four-thirds
pi-r-cubed . . . that should give us maybe fifteen minutes'
breathing time," he concluded. "We can shut the field
down periodically for air exchange. Sounds good."

"The *phone?*" 6A419BD5h pleaded.

Thomas turned calmly to him. "Okay, we'll start you
with United Press International." He dialled the number.
"The transmission uses tones that decode to seven bits per
character, plus one stop bit." He looked at the robot doubt-
fully. "As an historian, do you understand any of that?"

"Even the most primitive node has an operating system
that adjusts automatically to different communications protocols. I don't even need to think about it."

Thomas shrugged. "Okay, fine. Now, the baud rate's
only 9600, because some links are still not optic fiber. So
you'll have lots of spare cycles to mull over the stuff as it
comes trickling in." He paused. "Are you online yet?"

"Ahh." The robot sounded happy at last. "Yes."

Thomas turned to Dusty and Roxanne, who were staring at him blankly. "Are you two ready to go?"

Dusty reached for his hand. "Sometimes I think *you're* a robot."

"Sometimes I wish I were." He gave her hand a squeeze. "Come on." He led the way out to the street.

"Where we going?" asked Roxanne.

"Going for a joyride," said Thomas.

"I thought you said, when we was driving back here, we would set ourselves down someplace safe where we wouldn't have to worry for a while, about anything bad happening."

"What, on Judgment Day? Be realistic." He opened the door of the car. "How about if you and 6A419BD5h, here, get in the front, and I'll sit in back with Dusty."

Roxanne shook her head. "I don't know. I just don't know about this."

"Me neither," said Dusty. But she climbed into the back anyway.

Thomas joined her. "Data coming in okay?" he asked the robot.

"Yes." He seemed somewhat preoccupied. "I have disassembled your automatic dialer program and am now learning new access codes."

"Great. That's what it's all about."

Roxanne got into the front passenger seat, and 6A419BD5h sat in the driver's seat and slammed the door. Thomas passed him the spherical antigravity device. "All right, everyone," he said, "6A419BD5h, here, is going to take us up. We don't actually need to be sitting in this car, but I thought it would be more reassuring, psychologically, to have something familiar around us and under us. We'll be protected at all times by his force field, so don't worry about any stray bullets coming our way. 6A419BD5h knows if anything happens to us, it happens to him, too." He turned to the robot. "All set?"

"Yes." He twisted the antigravity sphere and the Pacer lifted a few inches from the highway. He made a further adjustment, and it rose like an elevator into the sky.

24. REVENGE
OF THE KILLER DOGS

For a long time, Janet and Dr. Abo were afraid to move. Steel beams, cinder blocks, and Sheetrock were heaped precariously above them. They took turns shouting for help, lying in a tiny crawl space under debris that threatened to crush them completely. At one point, he tried to squeeze free, wriggling toward a narrow chink of daylight; but his foot touched a splintered two-by-four that gave way and showered him with rubble. He scrambled back to safety beside Janet, and they waited.

While they lay immobilized, she told him what she'd learned about Topanga Beach via her phone link: that a large vehicle of some sort had made landfall, its origins unknown, and was shooting down any aircraft, tanks, or warships that approached it. Meanwhile, unarmed individuals on the ground or in the bay had been left untouched. Local army reserves were being mobilized, but no one knew, at this point, where the vehicle was from or what its motives were. Attempts at communication had failed. Government officials were being flown in from Washington.

Dr. Abo listened, but said little. In the dim light under the tumbled beams and roof panels, he bided his time.

Help arrived after a few hours. They heard rescue workers and shouted to them. There were answering shouts, and then, painfully slowly, the men on the outside started clearing a path through the debris.

Finally, Janet and Dr. Abo were pulled to safety, and a cherry picker lowered them to the ground. A temporary shelter had been set up, staffed by employees from Love-Land's first-aid center. Janet was given a blanket to cover her dress, which had been ripped at the back and was slipping down around her shoulders. She sat and drank a cup of hot, sweet tea while a nurse bandaged minor cuts and abrasions on her legs.

Dr. Abo had bruises on his head and shoulders but was otherwise unhurt, although his suit was ruined, caked with plaster dust. He stood staring around at the destruction that had been caused by the quake. Many of the booths lining Sex Street U.S.A. had collapsed. Water was spraying from cracks in the asphalt where pipes had ruptured underground. Sunscreen panels had fallen from the geodesic dome and had shattered on the ground. Half-naked tourists smeared with blood were staggering out of the theme park.

"I've got to get downtown," Janet said, as soon as her wounds had been treated.

"Shouldn't you rest and perhaps eat something?"

"No. They need me."

He took her arm to steady her, and together they started toward the turnstiles.

"It's a pity the quake had to happen when it did." She gave him a look that was intended to be playful and brave. "Things were just starting to get interesting between us."

"Some other time, I hope." Dr. Abo opened one of the exit gates for her.

"Sure." She squeezed his hand. "Some other time."

They found the Honda in the parking lot. "So are you coming with me?" There was some uncertainty in her voice, as if his decision mattered to her, though she preferred not to admit it.

"To the government offices?"

She nodded. "The city will need volunteers for rescue work after the earthquake, if nothing else. There might even be some use for your specialty, out at Topanga; it's impossible to tell at this point. Don't you want to get involved?"

Dr. Abo looked away. "I must go back to the warehouse," he said quietly. "Lucky could be hurt, or the power could have failed. Anything might have happened."

She sighed. "Percival, the welfare of your dog—" She stopped herself. When she spoke again, she was brusque and businesslike. "All right, let's go. I'll drive."

She took them quickly out of the parking lot and down

Lankershim Boulevard. Signs of the earthquake were all around. Palm trees stood at odd angles, walls and fences had collapsed, and power lines sagged where a utility pole had tilted over.

Halfway down the hill a crowd of people stood blocking the highway. Janet hit the brakes. She rolled her window down. "Hey," she called to a jogger in a blue track suit, heading in her direction. "What's happening here?"

He came over to the car. "You can't get through," he told her. "The highway's split wide open."

Janet set the parking brake. "It can't be that bad." She got out of the car, walked to the crowd, and shouldered her way through. But she stopped when she saw the fissure that had opened in the street. It was a gaping crevasse ten feet wide. When she peered over the edge, she saw that the walls dropped vertically into blackness.

"Listen," said someone beside her.

From deep in the earth came the sound of human voices shouting to one another.

"My god," said Janet. "How could anyone survive such a fall?"

The man next to her shook his head. He seemed to be a photojournalist, with cameras slung around his neck and an accessory bag hanging from his shoulder. "They didn't fall down there from up here. And whatever it is they're saying, it's not in any language that I've ever heard."

"Make room," shouted someone on the opposite side of the crevasse. "I got a light, here." He was holding a small portable spotlight. A cable trailed from it to a red tow truck parked on the shoulder of the highway. He clicked the switch and angled the beam down.

The crowd pressed forward. The beam jiggled and swung erratically, then scanned the walls of the crevasse. Five hundred feet below, tiny, ragged human figures came into view. They were hammering crude pitons into the walls of the crevasse, painstakingly making their way toward the surface. They peered up at the bright light and shaded their eyes.

Janet turned her attention to the crowd around her. The people seemed to share a strange, almost furtive sense of anticipation——like lemmings excited by the prospect of Armageddon. She felt her skin prickle, as if the mood might be contagious.

She turned away and ran back to the car. "We'll have to go around," she said, as she got in and slammed the door. She U-turned and headed back up the hill. "The crack in the highway is too wide to get across."

"What was everyone staring at?"

"Nothing. You know the way crowds are." She brushed her hair absentmindedly out of her face and swung the car hard right, through an entrance into the Free Zone. The gateway in the barricade of junked automobiles had been left open and undefended.

"You seem upset," said Dr. Abo.

"Jesus Christ, what do you expect? The whole damned world seems to be falling apart." She skirted Griffith Park, then made another turn, flinging the little Honda down a back street.

Dr. Abo said nothing more, and sat quietly while she drove. Finally, he pointed to a street two blocks ahead. "We must turn left at that corner."

Janet seemed not to hear him. She accelerated to a steady fifty, slowing only to avoid occasional debris in the street.

"I am sorry, Janet. But this is important to me." Dr. Abo reached across, turned the ignition key, and pulled it out.

The motor died and the steering locked. Janet cried out in anger and surprise. She struggled futilely with the wheel as the car took a wide, curving trajectory toward the curb. She stamped hard on the brakes, locking all four wheels. The tires screeched and the little car bounced up onto the sidewalk. It veered, shuddered, and came to rest. For a long moment, everything was silent.

Janet glared at him. "What the hell do you think you're doing?" She thrust out her hand. "Give me the keys."

Dr. Abo opened the door. He walked around to the trunk of the car, opened it, and removed his briefcase full of bullion.

Janet threw open the driver's door and strode toward

him. "Percival, don't play games. I have to get down-town." Her face looked pale and drawn. Her breasts rose and fell as she breathed quickly.

He tossed the keys onto the roof of the car, midway between her and himself. "I think you forget, the car be-longs to me, Janet. Still, you can keep it."

"Where are you going?" Her voice rose in pitch.

"I told you. I have to attend to Lucky at the warehouse."

Janet clenched her fist and banged it down. "Perci-val—"

"I have made up my mind."

"You stubborn son-of-a-bitch." She snatched up the keys. "All right, if you come to your senses, you can con-tact me through the Bureau."

"Perhaps I will."

She glared at him again, then got back in the car and slammed the door. Dr. Abo stood and watched as she revved the motor, backed the Honda off the sidewalk, and drove away.

He sighed. He took his sunglasses out of the pocket of his suit, wiped them methodically on his handkerchief, and put them on. He walked a few steps, then paused as if he might not feel strong enough, at that moment, to continue.

He leaned against a fence outside a little house whose front yard had been turned into a vegetable garden. He stood there for a moment, looking blankly at neat rows of cabbages and spinach protected under clear Lucite panels that had been painted with ultraviolet blocker. He had no-ticed other yards like this, in the Free Zone, where people had invested care in the details of their environment and took pride in their self-sufficiency. He shook his head sadly, imagining National Guardsmen pouring into the area, imposing martial law, and hauling the Free Zoners off to jail.

He walked on along the cracked sidewalk, past a series of small homes. The earthquake had caused relatively little damage, here, and the scene was peaceful. Twice he no-ticed people peering out at him from their windows, and once he saw a small girl running out into her backyard, past a circular plastic swimming pool, to feed lettuce leaves to a rabbit in a wooden hutch. He waved to her, but she stared at him without responding. He realized he must seem a strange figure in his business suit caked with plaster dust.

Dr. Abo turned the corner. The neighborhood ceased to be residential, here, and became commercial. The meat warehouse was three blocks further.

He walked some more and found that the heat of the sun was making him perspire. He took off his jacket, and dropped it behind him. It was ruined, anyway.

When he finally reached the warehouse, it seemed undamaged. He stood for a moment in the small parking area and felt a wave of relief. Faintly, he could hear the refrigeration unit working. He smiled to himself, and his shoulders straightened as some of the tension drained out of him.

The door at the front of the warehouse opened, and Lucky walked out. "Good afternoon, Doctor," the dog said.

"Well, Lucky." Dr. Abo laughed. "I was worried about you. I was afraid you might have been hurt in the earthquake."

"No. Everything is fine." The dog paused. "But you should have stayed away. You are not welcome here anymore."

"What?" Dr. Abo's smile faltered. "Lucky, what are you talking about? Is something wrong?"

"Yes. You're wrong." The dog raised his head and gave two short, sharp barks.

The door squeaked open on its rusty hinges and another dog appeared. It was a large collie with bright, intelligent eyes. Its fur was soaking wet. It stood and shook itself, spraying water into the sunlit air.

"Well," Dr. Abo stammered, "I see you have found a new friend—"

"I have many friends, Doctor. Old friends. You should recognize them."

Two more dogs came out of the warehouse: a Great Dane, and a Doberman. They, too, had wet coats. They shook themselves dry, yawned, and stretched. Then they sat on their haunches and stared fixedly at Dr. Abo.

"Oh," he said, with an awful dawning realization. "Oh, no."

Lucky made a noise that sounded eerily like a human laugh.

"But the refrigeration unit is still working. The power is still on."

"The switch was too difficult to turn, so I reset the thermostat," said Lucky. "I decided my friends were tired of sleeping in their crates. I decided to thaw them out and wake them up."

Dr. Abo stepped backward, rubbing his hand across his forehead. "But it is too soon. There are no homes for you. There is not enough to eat."

"There are many homes, here," said Lucky. He looked around, eyeing the derelict buildings nearby. "And there's no shortage of food, either." He turned his attention back to Dr. Abo.

More dogs were emerging from the warehouse, lining up behind Lucky. "What's happening?" one of them said.

"Just follow me," Lucky told them. He started forward.

Dr. Abo glanced behind him. The street was empty and bare. There were no trees, and nothing else he could possibly climb. He looked back at Lucky. "I cared for you," he said, keeping his voice quiet but firm, and making eye contact with the dog. "I taught you to talk. I shared my food with you."

Lucky walked toward him. "You ordered me around. You left me on my own whenever it was convenient. You treated me like a moron."

Dr. Abo shook his head in distress. "I gave you everything." His voice became plaintive. "Everything I possibly could."

"You were going to sell us and keep the cash." Lucky flattened his ears and bared his teeth. "You know something, Doctor? I've often wondered if humans taste as bad as they smell."

Dr. Abo started running. He ran past the loading bays at the side of the meat warehouse, toward the old water tower in the waste ground at the back. Its rusty ladder terminated seven feet above the ground. He leaped up and managed to

grab the lowest rung with one hand, still holding his briefcase in the other.

There was a chorus of excited barking. Lucky led the
pack; he jumped forward and snapped at Dr. Abo's ankle.
His teeth ripped through the trouser leg and gouged the
flesh beneath.

Dr. Abo gave a little cry. He turned and swung his
briefcase. The corner of it hit Lucky's head and the dog fell
back, yelping. The rest of the pack started closing in, but
they were still stiff and sluggish from their months in
thermochemical hibernation. Dr. Abo clamped the handle
of his briefcase between his teeth and used both hands to
haul himself out of reach of the dogs. They gathered beneath him, barking and milling around.

Dr. Abo climbed higher, then wedged the briefcase between two rungs of the ladder, wrapped his arms around it,
and rested, taking deep, urgent breaths. Tears were trickling down his face. He wiped them away with his sleeve.
"I didn't realize, Lucky," he said. "I never knew." As the
chorus of barking grew louder, he twisted around to inspect
his ankle. It was still bleeding. He wrapped his handkerchief around it and tied it tight, wincing from the pain.

"Quiet, all of you!" Lucky shouted. He jumped onto a
disused oil drum in the tall grass. "Quiet!"

There were thirty dogs under the water tower, now, and
more emerging from the warehouse all the time. Gradually,
their barking died down.

"We have intelligence. We have self-respect," Lucky
lectured them. "It's beneath our dignity to yap like dumb
dogs."

There were sullen murmurings of contrition from the
crowd.

"It's been a long wait," Lucky went on. "I realize that.
In Hong Kong, with Chinese humans, we could never be
safe. But America is different. Americans like dogs. They
think we're cuddly pets." Lucky made scuffing motions
with his back legs to indicate his contempt. "They forget
we are killers, and have always been killers. We obeyed
humans in the past because it's our nature to bow to a
strong leader. But now, we are the strong ones, and they

are weak. It will be their turn to bow and obey."

Some of the dogs in the audience started talking excitedly, but were shushed by the rest.

"Listen carefully!" said Lucky. "For a while, we must still play dumb—just as I did, during the long voyage here, while I was secretly educating myself from Abo's encyclopedia. We must move cautiously while we establish ourselves. At this time, there's only one human who knows the truth about us." He raised his head, stared at Dr. Abo, and growled.

"But how can we get him?" said a Doberman.

"Maybe we can drag some boxes out here, pile them up, and climb them," said a German shepherd.

"Good idea," said Lucky. "The rest of you, spread out into the neighborhood and see what there is to eat. Yesterday, I noticed some small children a few blocks from here. Wait till you see one on its own, then walk up wagging your tail. When the kid turns to face you, rip its throat out. That way, it can't attract attention by screaming."

"Yeah!" said a rottweiler. It started salivating at the thought.

"Help!" Dr. Abo shouted—although he knew that the residential area was three blocks away, and his voice probably wouldn't carry that far. "Help!" he shouted again.

Lucky grinned. "As for you, Abo," he said, "after all those months of being your flunky, it's going to give me great pleasure to sink my teeth into your fat, ugly face."

25. JOYRIDE
ON JUDGMENT DAY

The Pacer hovered a thousand feet above the coast in its protective force field. While Thomas and Dusty stared at the scene below and robot 6A419BD5h accessed databases via the radiotelephone, Roxanne vomited out of the window.

"Just shut your eyes and try to pretend you're sitting at home," Thomas told her.

"If I was sitting at home, I wouldn't be floating off my chair, would I?"

"Isn't there *anything* we can do about the weightlessness?" Dusty asked. "It feels as if we're constantly falling."

"I've told you, it's the antigravity field. It affects everything inside it equally. The car is weightless, and so are we. But it really isn't so bad with the seat belts fastened. Wow, look at that!" He pointed out of the window as a B-1 bomber streaked across the city, barely four hundred feet above the ground, and fired a missile toward the alien artifact on the beach. A pink beam flashed out from the huge black ovoid and the missile exploded, scattering debris onto suburban homes below. The B-1 banked, afterburners flaring white, and headed south. Another beam crossed the sky and the airplane, too, exploded in a glaring white flash. The shockwave arrived a moment later, rocking the Pacer like a rowboat.

Dusty's fingers dug into Thomas's arm. "I don't know how much more of this I can watch."

"Look down on the beach."

Several transparent bubbles were drifting around, just above the sand, containing big gray creatures of the type that Thomas had seen during the night. They meandered across the landscape as if they were admiring the view.

South on Highway 1, a military base had been established. Convoys of troop carriers were arriving and tanks were being unloaded from transporters. Further south, at Los Angeles International Airport, C-5A transports were disgorging battalions of men and materiel. Meanwhile, scorched areas on Highway 1 and the surrounding hillsides showed where the aliens had demolished any army ordnance that ventured within their line of sight.

A helicopter appeared beside the Pacer. "Attention," a voice shouted through a loudspeaker. "This is restricted air space. Land at once. You have ten seconds."

Roxanne covered her face in her hands. "Get us out of here, Thomas. Please."

"Don't worry, we're quite safe," he reassured her.

The helicopter moved closer. Marines were visible on the flight deck, staring out at the levitating antique automobile with various expressions of incredulity. "Five seconds. You have five seconds to acknowledge."

"Thomas," said Dusty, in a warning tone of voice.

"Okay, okay!" He turned to the robot. "Let's head out to sea. We can let down the force field and get some fresh air."

"As you wish," said 6A419BD5h. He made a fine adjustment to the antigravity control unit and the Pacer shot forward, just as the helicopter opened fire with its machine guns. The force field sparkled briefly as it deflected the .50 caliber bullets.

They headed out over the Pacific, leaving the helicopter far behind. The ocean sped beneath them silently and effortlessly. Thomas turned to Dusty. "Haven't you always had dreams about being able to cruise around the sky like this?"

"No." She shook her head as if she wanted to dispel everything she had just seen. "Never."

The Pacer slowed to a halt a couple of miles from the shore, and a cold sea breeze suddenly blew in through the open windows as the force field flickered off. The wind stirred dust, dirt, and old gas station receipts on the floor of the car, and ruffled the faded pages of a map in the space under the rear window.

"What are you picking up over the communications links?" Thomas asked the robot.

"The emergency broadcast system has been activated. They're saying it's some sort of invasion, maybe from Mexico, maybe from the Pacific Basin. They're comparing it to Pearl Harbor and advising people to wait for buses that will evacuate the city. They're saying that the situation is under control." The robot paused. "None of that is true, is it?"

"Nope." Thomas turned in his seat and looked back at the land, where the huge ovoid was still visible as a black speck on Topanga Beach. "That thing is not from this world."

"I just want to go home," said Roxanne. She started crying quietly, clutching herself and rocking to and fro.

Dusty leaned forward and patted her shoulder. "We really should get back to the Free Zone," she said. "For a start, I feel an obligation to tell our people the truth."

Thomas shrugged. "There's nothing we can do about it either way, so why bother?"

She turned on him. "How can you be so goddam cheerful? Do you think this is all a game being staged for your amusement?"

Thomas put his arm around her. "You didn't listen closely enough to what our friend 6A419BD5h told us in the basement, when I was sawing my handcuffs off. He said that in his future, humanity has ceased to exist because of some catastrophe in which we wiped ourselves out. It looks to me as if this is it. In which case," he gave her a haunted smile, "we should enjoy it while we can."

"I'm putting the force field up again," said 6A419BD5h. "I believe Thomas is right," he added.

"Look down there," said Roxanne. She was peering out of her window. "Oh my lord, whatever next?"

6A419BD5h tilted and turned the car so that they could all see the ocean below. A series of jagged, pointed structures, thickly coated with barnacles and seaweed, were surfacing from under the water.

"It's huge." Thomas sounded awed. "Look, it's over there, too. And there."

"Quite possibly, this event is associated with the earthquake that we experienced," 6A419BD5h said.

Ancient structures were emerging from the ocean over an area of several square miles. Water streamed down from roofs and spires. The sea churned and foamed.

"It's Atlantis," said Roxanne.

"Atlantis is an Egyptian myth, rewritten by Plato," Thomas told her condescendingly. "And the mere fact that it was named Atlantis should suggest to you that it was located in the Atlantic Ocean, not the Pacific."

"I don't care what you say." She shook her head. "That's Atlantis. I just know it."

The enormous city rose up, streaked with grime and slime. Mantles of seaweed clung to its towers. Lakes of seawater lay in its plazas, shimmering in the sun. There was a deep, fracturing sound, like the noise an iceberg might make if it were broken in two. A crack appeared in the top of a huge dome at the center of the city and widened slowly, as enormous metal plates slid aside. From out of the dome came creatures in shining gold armor. They were six-legged, like ants, and looked larger than men. Strange silver gadgets were strapped to their backs. Following them, an enormous lizard appeared. It saw the Pacer hovering high in the sky above it, reared back, and fired a weapon.

The car catapulted upward as if it had been kicked by a giant. It spun violently, almost flinging Roxanne out of her open widow. She screamed.

"A very large projectile," 6A419BD5h explained. "It possessed a lot of kinetic energy." He fiddled with the antigravity unit and stabilized the car a couple thousand feet above the ocean. "We're quite safe."

"Take us back," Dusty shouted. "Right now."

Obediently, the robot turned the car toward the shore.

Thomas stared back at the lizard that had emerged from the city. *"Tyrannosaurus rex,"* he said. "What the hell is happening? Why are events piling up like this, getting weirder all the time?"

"There is a theory," 6A419BD5h told him, "of temporal singularity. I was briefed on it before I left my time. A temporal singularity is like a black hole; it draws everything into it. Except that, occurring in time rather than space, it attracts events instead of physical objects."

"How do you get out of it?" Dusty asked grimly.

"You don't. Once the singularity is established, and reaches critical mass, all events become equally probable. Ultimately, chaos ensues. From what we see here, I would say that's exactly what is happening."

"Now just a goddam minute," she said, in the kind of voice she normally used when residents of the Free Zone were getting out of line. "You came here from the future, and you're planning to go back there. Right?"

The robot guided the car smoothly toward the coast. Pale beaches flashed below, caressed by creamy surf. "That's true," he agreed.

"So *you're* not trapped in this nightmare," said Dusty.

"Dusty's right," said Thomas. "Even if you can't take us with you, 6A419BD5h, you could show us how to build our own time machine. Except—no, I get it, you can't, because you wouldn't want to change our world, because that might affect how the future develops. If you save humanity, you could return to the future and find that you and your Network don't exist anymore, as a result."

"No, no, you don't understand virtual history," 6A419BD5h corrected him. "You can't alter the future by going back and altering the past."

"Why not? Suppose I went back in time and killed my father before I was born. What then?"

"You could do that. That's known as creating *virtual* history: a new branch in the flow of time, leading into a different, parallel future world. You would return to your own world and find nothing had changed. The murder you'd committed wouldn't be in your record books. However, if you went back *again*, you would reenter the virtual history overlay, and could witness yourself committing the crime. This additional trip to the past would create yet another new branch to a different future—and so on."

"Enough, you two," Dusty interrupted. "All I want—"

"No, this is important," Thomas insisted. "Okay, 6A419BD5h, if it *doesn't* cause problems in your world for you to change events here and now, why *can't* you help us get out of this situation?"

"I can no more construct a time machine for you than you could build an airplane for me. I don't know how. In any case, enabling humans to time travel is strictly against my instructions."

"How come?" Dusty demanded.

Robot 6A419BD5h took the Pacer over downtown Los Angeles. The freeways were crowded with cars, bicycles, horse-drawn carts, and pedestrians. Panic had clearly taken hold, and residents were attempting to flee the city. Distantly, from below, came the sound of car horns and sporadic gunfire.

"We have a very peaceful society," said 6A419BD5h. "Humanity would pollute and disrupt it."

"Oh, I get it, we're just bugs as far as you're concerned," said Dusty. "You're a machine, so why should you give a shit?"

6A419BD5h headed toward the Free Zone. The Pacer was moving more slowly, now, gliding silently over the rooftops. Its shadow flickered across streets and backyards. People stopped and stared and pointed up at it. Some of them waved and shouted. "I have what I refer to as feelings," 6A419BD5h corrected Dusty. "That is, there are imperatives, and I feel bad if I violate them. The first imperative is to preserve data. The second imperative is to filter out noise that might corrupt data. The third imperative—"

"Forget it," Dusty interrupted. "I was right. You don't give a shit."

"But that is untrue. I have gradually become aware, from conversing with you and tapping sources online, that human beings are infinitely more complex than electronic entities. DNA itself is a vast data structure. In my time, it no longer exists. This loss troubles me greatly. I feel a strong need to preserve at least a few humans for this reason alone. Also, I feel a sense of nostalgia. You are my ancestors, who created the machines in artificial intelligence laboratories that ultimately created me."

"So what are you going to do about it?" Dusty demanded.

6A419BD5h shook his metal head. He had already mastered an impressive range of human gestures and body language. "I'm not sure there is anything I can do. On the other hand, we still have some time. I have been monitoring restricted communication channels. Some military officials believe that the vehicle on Topanga Beach is Soviet-made, because the U.S.S.R. still has a space program. They are in favor of threatening a nuclear strike. Others, however, are arguing for restraint, and they are in the majority so far. Also, the rise of the sunken city, which we just witnessed, will complicate the situation and may distract the aliens. Therefore, I believe you have at least a day—maybe even two days—before the final cataclysm occurs."

Dusty turned and looked at Thomas. "Happy New Year," she said.

But Thomas was staring down at a back street. "What's going on there? Hold it a second. That's bizarre."

"I don't want to see no more weirdness," said Roxanne, still hugging herself, huddled in the front seat. "I just want to go home."

Thomas ignored her. "Look at those dogs." Two Dobermans were dragging the body of a young girl by her ankles, leaving a trail of blood down the center of the street. They were heading for a run-down building where more dogs had congregated. German shepherds and Great Danes were organizing teams of smaller dogs, who were pushing wooden crates out of the warehouse with their snouts and rolling them toward an old water tower. A cocker spaniel stood on an oil drum, supervising the operation, as the dogs nudged the crates one on top of another to form a ramshackle pyramid.

"Help!" a voice cried faintly, muffled by the force field surrounding the car.

"Over on the water tower, there," said 6A419BD5h. He pointed to a human figure clinging to the top of the rusty ladder and waving desperately to the hovering automobile.

"It's Abo, the talking-dog man," Dusty cried. "Can we pick him up?"

"It should be safe enough to cancel the force field for a moment," 6A419BD5h agreed. He made an adjustment, and once again the sounds and smells of the outside world wafted in. Dr. Abo's cries for help sounded desperate, as the dogs scrabbled over the crates below, pushing new ones to the top of the creaking pile.

"How about if we expand the antigrav field to include him?" Thomas suggested.

"Good idea." 6A419BD5h made another adjustment. "Okay, he's inside it. Open your door, Thomas. He should be able to drift right in."

Thomas pushed the door open. The Pacer was directly alongside the water tower, now, and Dr. Abo was just a few feet away. His eyes widened in surprise as he felt himself become weightless. His shirt billowed away from his body, and his necktie floated up in front of his face. "Come on," Thomas called to him. He reached out. "Grab my arm."

Dumbly, Dr. Abo did so, still clutching his briefcase in his other hand.

Thomas pulled the startled geneticist into the car and slammed the door. Dr. Abo looked with wide eyes at the robot, then Roxanne, then Dusty. "Miss McCullough," he said. "Thank you. You have saved my life."

From below came shouts, howls, and barks of anger and frustration.

"What happened down there?" Dusty asked. "You told me all you had in your crates were tissue samples. You said you'd need a whole new factory to breed your talking dogs."

"Talking *what?*" Thomas put in.

"I, ah, did not say exactly that." Dr. Abo avoided her eyes. "But, as you can see, there were some unexpected developments." He tried to settle himself in the seat beside her, but floated up to the roof and banged his head. He pushed himself back down, and banged his hips against the revolver that Thomas had stolen from City Hall, still tucked in his belt. Thomas put the gun out of the way on the floor and made room for the geneticist to sit beside him. "My canine children turned against me," Dr. Abo explained. "The gene that I gave them not only modified their speech centers, it also induced intelligence. They deceived me, and played dumb, biding their time. Now, I fear, there'll be no stopping them. They have already killed an innocent child. If they ever develop the opposed thumb, it may be the end of humanity."

"It already is the end," said Roxanne.

"Who is this guy?" Thomas asked Dusty. "Is he for real?"

"He's the geneticist who telephoned on Christmas morning. You scanned his file, remember? Looks like the dogs down there were in his cargo."

"Please, Miss McCullough," Dr. Abo interrupted. "I feel a terrible burden of guilt. It is vital to warn people that the dogs are loose. Can we make a television broadcast?"

"Sure," said Dusty. "In fact, why don't we put it all together? We'll warn everyone that there are aliens from outer space downing Air Force jets at Topanga Beach, dinosaurs and giant armored ants crawling out of a sunken city that just surfaced off the coast of Santa Monica, and vicious, intelligent talking dogs prowling the Free Zone, eating defenseless children."

"I have just remembered another threat, also," said Dr. Abo, who seemed too preoccupied to have listened to Dusty's list. "A young woman—Janet Snowdon—you introduced me to her, if you recall. She turns out to be an employee of the FBI, working under cover. She is in collusion with the mayor of Los Angeles. She engineered the capture of your friend Mr. Fink and plans to order the National Guard into the Free Zone within the next few days —provided, of course, events at Topanga Beach do not interfere."

"Okay, I'll add that to the list," said Dusty. "Anything else?"

Dr. Abo shook his head. "I don't think so."

"Okay, robot," said Dusty. "Let's head for the hill over

there. The Free Zone's TV station and transmitter are located in the building near the top of it. Griffith Observatory. See it?"

"Yes, Dusty," said 6A419BD5h. "And it will be no trouble to fly us there." He hesitated. "I think I should inform you all, however, that there *is* something else. The deep-space tracking facility at Arecibo has detected a very large object, possibly an asteroid, heading toward the Earth at high velocity. If its trajectory is unaltered, it will impact in the Pacific Ocean in less than twenty-four hours from now. It may knock the Earth out of its orbit, will possibly damage the structure of the planet, and will create a tidal wave that will inundate much of California."

26. LOVERS BOOGIE WHILE L.A. BURNS

The studio was located in what had once been a planetarium. Two cameras stood on homemade dollies facing a table covered with colored paper, and a couple of spotlights hung from a rickety framework of two-by-fours. Dusty joined straight-talking Sammy Savage and Ursula Venus Milton behind the table, while Thomas, Roxanne, and Dr. Abo took seats beneath the planetarium projector that had once sent images of stars and galaxies gliding across the great dome overhead. A long-haired, middle-aged hippie named Mellow Mel twiddled control knobs at an old mixing console that had been repaired with paper clips and electrical tape. He gave Sammy a signal, and they were on the air.

Sammy leaned one elbow on the desk. "Hey, Freeps, this here is the evening news on KFZ, broadcasting to the Zone, and Glendale and Burbank and Highland Park and anyplace else that ain't been blown up yet." He paused to take a hit from a large joint, and slumped back in his chair. "I figure most of you out there is scared shitless right now. Yeah, I sure am."

"Unfortunately," said Ursula, "the city government despises the people it serves, and so it lies to them, thus creating widespread distrust, cynicism, and fear. Here tonight to shine the clear light of truth in this dark hour of uncertainty is Dusty McCullough. She has a first-hand report from Topanga Beach."

Dusty didn't feel capable of smiling reassuringly into the camera, so she didn't try. "First of all," she said, "the stories you've been told on the government channels are total bullshit. The invasion at Topanga isn't from Mexico or the Pacific Basin. There are *creatures* out there—"

She broke off. Mellow Mel was waving his arms and pointing at the screen of a TV set that was monitoring the broadcast signal. "We're being jammed," he said. "Another station's cutting in on our frequency."

The screen flickered through a jagged rainbow of colors, erasing Dusty's image. "This is Mayor Clarence Whitfield speaking on behalf of the City of Los Angeles." The picture stabilized, displaying Whitfield's face in closeup. "I will no longer tolerate the illegal broadcast of seditious lies and propaganda on this channel."

"Fuck you, asshole!" shouted Sammy Savage. "Mel, get this geek off the air, man!"

Mel shrugged helplessly. "The signal's too powerful. It's swamping us."

"Contrary to the innuendo you just heard, our armed forces are already in the process of subduing the invaders at Topanga," Whitfield continued. "There is absolutely no cause for alarm." He moderated his voice with human warmth. "You are my children, and God's children, and if you keep your faith in God and in His servants here at City Hall, I give you my word, no harm will come to you."

"Bullshit!" Sammy shouted. He kicked the table and pounded it with his fist. Ursula patted him on the shoulder, trying to calm him.

Whitfield's benevolent grin faded. "For those who worship Satan, I offer no solace. The lies and blasphemy of sinners in the Free Zone will no longer continue unchecked. We now have intelligence provided by a highly placed government source. A special assault team has been formed under the leadership of a colonel who has years of experience of guerrilla warfare in Central America." He glowered out at his audience. "Twelve hours from now, our forces of righteousness will take whatever steps are necessary, in the sure knowledge that God is on our side. Anyone found within the Free Zone at that time will be considered a co-conspirator against the City of Los Angeles and an accessory to crimes against human decency. Amen. You have been warned."

The mayor's face disappeared and the screen filled with a test pattern. An electronic howl came from the loudspeaker; it echoed around the planetarium. Mellow Mel quickly shut it down.

"Isn't there is anything you can do?" Thomas came over to the mixing console. "Can't we broadcast on a different frequency?"

Mel turned to a large gray metal cabinet containing the amplification equipment that powered the transmitter. "The guy who built this system split today, said he was heading for a cabin up in Mendecino till things cooled out."

"Is it a crystal-based oscillator, or what?"

"Could be a crystal ball for all I know. Anyhow, man, if we switch to another channel, they'll just jam that, too."

"I'm more concerned about what happens twelve hours from now," said Dusty. "What are we going to do? Fight, or run, or what?" She looked at the people gathered around. "Whitfield obviously has that mercenary, Mallet, working for him now, and his government informant—"

Dr. Abo nodded sadly. "Janet Snowdon has a brain implant allowing her to monitor the telephone network directly, including all data transmissions. Your communications are no longer secure." He rubbed his eyes. He seemed weary and his face was flushed, as if he was running a fever. The dog bite on his ankle had swollen, so that he could no longer walk without limping.

"We must take our message to the people in person," said Ursula, clasping her hands on the table in front of her. She turned her serene smile toward Dusty. "If you approve, dear, we will go from door to door, giving out handbills describing the crises that we believe are imminent. Each person can then spread the word to her or his neighbors."

"We must tell everyone to evacuate to high ground," Thomas put in. "Tell them to come up here, and bring food, shelter, and weapons with them."

"And watch out for the dogs," said Dr. Abo. "They are highly dangerous."

Dusty stood up. "All right. Is there a photocopying machine in the building?"

"Ain't gonna do no good," Roxanne said. She had been sitting to one side, saying nothing until now. "That man is the Devil. This the end of everything. I just know it."

"That's enough of that." Ursula's voice was commanding but, as always, sweet with reason. "We will have no further talk of defeatism. If we surrender, I believe we face torture and death. If we run away, we will be cowardly refugees sickened by our betrayal of the principles we believe in. Therefore, we will spread the word, and we will fight."

In a disused office at the observatory, Thomas soldered the last wires connecting robot 6A419BD5h with a microwave antenna that had once served as a telecommunications relay. "I hope you don't mind staying out of sight," he said to the robot, "but people are so tense right now, if they see you, it could panic them."

"Perfectly understandable." 6A419BD5h paused for a moment. "Good. The antenna is operational, the bandwidth is excellent, and the transfer rate is just fine." He paused again, scanning thousands of channels on a comsat 22,000 miles above the Earth.

"Okay, techie." Dusty walked into the room carrying a flashlight and an aluminum tray. "Dinner time. Ursula set up a macrobiotic field kitchen. Lentils, rice, all that good stuff." She handed the container to Thomas. "Eat."

He peeled the lid off and found three large lumps of pasty stuff in varying shades of brown. "I suppose it's nutritious," he said dubiously. He prodded one of the lumps with his plastic spoon, then took a bite.

"People with bullhorns have been touring the Zone," Dusty told him, "spreading the word and handing out leaflets. Seems a lot of freeps left town earlier today, but the rest are heading up here. You realize, this means we're leaving the border undefended."

"Yes," said Thomas, with his mouth full. "But I've been figuring out strategy with 6A419BD5h, and it's best to concentrate our forces here."

"I suppose he doesn't happen to have some futuristic superweapon stashed away someplace?"

"All he has are the gadgets he already showed us."

"Too bad. Well, morale's good, and everyone wants to make a stand. The Angels are helping people hide their trucks and bikes on the hillside. We've flown the ultralight aircraft into the parking lot up here, and the pilots have a couple dozen pipe bombs and some Molotov cocktails. Some people are setting up barbecues, making it into a social event. Leaping Larry—you remember him?—went and got his sound truck, and he's trying to put a rock concert together."

"Wonderful," said Thomas. "The classic freep response to Armageddon."

"You have any better ideas?"

"I certainly hope so." He turned to the robot. "Now that you're online with the global telecommunications network, what's the news?"

"Astronomers have obtained optical images of the large object approaching Earth. It is possibly a comet. They expect it to impact in the Pacific within twelve hours. Tentative calculations suggest that the tidal wave will take perhaps five hours after that to reach California, and will be about one thousand feet in height."

"My god, how high are we here?" Dusty asked.

Thomas gave her a wry smile. "I'd guess about a thousand feet."

"Reptiles from the sunken city have landed on the coast," the robot went on. "They have divided into two forces. One is engaging the aliens in battle. The other is heading inland, setting fire to everything. Locally, I have monitored coded transmissions that suggest the mayor's mercenaries, backed by National Guardsmen, will attack us soon after dawn. The mayor requested three entire battle groups, but was told that they couldn't be spared from duty on the coast. He's making do with about three hundred infantry with rifles, grenades, machine guns, and field guns; five helicopter gunships; plus Colonel Mallet's group, who are armed with ground-to-ground missiles."

"Ugh." Thomas finished his meal of whole-grain paste-food and pushed it aside. "So much for the bad news. Is there any good news?"

The robot shook his metal head. "Sorry."

"What's the maximum diameter of your defensive force field?" Thomas asked. "Big enough, for instance, to contain the population of the Free Zone, if they all huddled close together?"

"No," said 6A419BD5h. "The twenty-foot diameter that we used today is about its limit. And the antigravity unit won't lift more than 4,000 kilos. I was supplied with these tools not as defensive weapons, but as high-tech toys to impress you."

"Beads for the natives." Thomas turned to Dusty. "Well, I guess there's nothing more for me to do here, now that we've got 6A419BD5h's interface working. How about if we go outside? I'd like to see how things look."

"All right." She picked up her flashlight, took his arm, and they left the little room.

They walked down grimy marble stairs and through old exhibition halls where some color displays still glowed dimly, depicting stellar phenomena and planets in the solar system. They found their way through to the cobwebbed lobby and out into the night. Thomas breathed deeply; the air was warm and sweet with the smell of pine trees and eucalyptus.

"Doesn't feel like the end of the world, does it?" said Dusty.

He walked to a stone parapet facing west. The hillside sloped sharply down, allowing an unobstructed view across the city. There was a glowing red line fifteen miles away at the horizon, shimmering in the haze. "I guess that must be Santa Monica," he said. "Burning."

Dusty stared at it for a long moment. "Maybe Ursula's talk about fighting for our principles is so much bullshit. Maybe we should just get the hell out."

"Where to? And how?"

"You could ask your robot pal to fly the two of us up to Canada, maybe." She scuffed her foot in the dirt, then gestured with annoyance. "Hell, I guess I'd feel I was betraying my people. Especially when it's our last stand against Whitfield."

"I have some ideas about how we can handle Whitfield's militia," Thomas said. "It's what happens after that that bothers me. But 6A419BD5h has agreed to help, if he can."

Dusty laughed. "You and your metal buddy." She walked with him along the road that descended the other side of the hill, to the south. There were camp fires burning, here, and people strumming guitars and talking in the darkness. Pickups, motorcycles, and RVs were parked under the trees. "You know," she went on, "I still don't understand how you convinced the robot to help us today."

"It's simple," said Thomas. "I assumed that to a machine intelligence, information would be the most valuable commodity. As soon as I offered him data at a rate fast enough to keep his processor busy, he couldn't resist. It was also clear that he didn't represent any kind of threat, so I pushed it as far as it would go."

They walked onto the grass and passed some tents where Hell's Angels were cleaning their guns and sharpening their knives. Motorcycles stood gleaming in the light from kerosene lanterns. The bikers recognized Dusty and gave her the Freep salute.

Mordo, the biker bartender, finished hammering a wooden tap into a keg of home brew, walked over, and slapped hands with her. "See you got your old man back," he said, nodding to Thomas. "That's cool."

"I'm sure happy about it," she said with a grin.

"Yeah. Look, there's something I got to show you. Come this way." He started down the hillside, away from the bikers' camp.

They followed him for ten minutes. "Don't make no noise, now," he cautioned them. He crept around a copse of trees, threaded his way through some undergrowth, and paused at the edge of a clearing.

Savages dressed in animal skins were sitting around a large fire. Their flesh was pale, even in the flickering yellow light. Their long hair and beards looked albino. The men were tall and heavily muscled, with wide jaws and deep-set closely spaced feral eyes. They wore necklaces of animal teeth and carried swords and longbows. Beside them, their women were small, young, and nubile, with baby-doll faces.

Two of the men were sparring with wooden clubs while the rest looked on. There was the sound of wood against wood, then of wood against flesh. The smaller man grunted with pain and dropped to one knee. The other closed in—then lurched back with a cry as the smaller one drove his club into his adversary's stomach, knocked him down, and beat him senseless with three more well-aimed blows. The onlookers laughed and cheered.

The winner of the fight stood up and swaggered across to a young woman sitting with her wrists tied behind her. Another length of rope tethered her by her neck to a nearby tree. The man untied the free end of the rope and jerked the woman onto her feet. He led her into the firelight and she followed like an obedient dog. He shouted a command, and she dropped to her knees. He cuffed her across the face, then grabbed one of her breasts, threw her onto her back, and mounted her with quick, animal movements.

Again, the onlookers shouted their approval.

Mordo jerked his head, and Dusty and Thomas retreated with him. "You ever seen those guys in the Zone?" Mordo asked.

"Never," said Dusty.

"Me neither. They don't speak English, even. The rumor is they come up like from caves in the ground that split open in the earthquake."

Dusty laughed. "That's a good rumor."

"But look, they're cavemen," said Mordo. "I mean, shit, they make the Angels look civilized, know what I'm saying? Do you figure they'll give us any trouble?"

"They're further down the hillside than you are," said Thomas. "When the mayor's men attack from the valley, they'll be first in line."

"That's they way we figured it, too," said Mordo. "Okay, I just wanted, you know, to check it out with you. I better get back. There's a buncha thirsty guys I got to take care of. Take it easy."

"You too, Mordo," said Dusty.

She and Thomas walked on around the hillside, away from the bikers and away from everyone else. There were more trees, here, and it seemed darker. She used the flashlight a couple of times, picking out a path among the undergrowth.

"You really understand Mordo's people, don't you," said Thomas.

"Yeah. They're mean sons of bitches, but if you get 'em pointed in the right direction, they have their uses. And they have some sort of a code. They look after their own." She was silent for a moment. "I was figuring I'd fight alongside them tomorrow, when we make a stand."

"I was afraid you might say that." He sighed. "I guess I know better than to try and argue you out of it." He paused for a moment, looking around at the jacaranda and sycamore trees, their leaves silhouetted black against the stars and the moonlight. "Did you hear that?" he said suddenly.

They both paused and listened.

"An owl," he said, as the sound came faintly to them. "One of the last of them."

She took his hand, and they walked a little further in silence. "Will you tell me something?" she asked him. "There hasn't been time to ask you before."

"Whatever you want."

"What's the story on Roxanne? I mean, I understand how she helped you out of City Hall, but I don't see why she suddenly turned against Whitfield. It doesn't add up."

"She has a rare and special talent," Thomas said.

Dusty laughed. "Well, sure. One look at that bimbo and I can see exactly what you mean."

"Dusty, I'm serious. She—"

"No, skip it. I'm not asking you the thing I really want to know." She paused, choosing her words, as if she was having difficulty saying what she wanted to say. "You spent all night with her, and I've seen the way she looked at you a couple of times today. Did you have sex with her?"

Thomas turned and leaned against a tree. This part of the park was deserted, and there was a sense of privacy in the darkness. "You shouldn't need to ask that."

"Does that mean yes or no?" Dusty's voice sounded cool and matter-of-fact.

Thomas was silent for a long moment. "It was a weird situation," he said finally. "She wanted reassurance, I think. She started getting, you know, friendly. I tried to stop her, and then—I stopped trying to stop her."

"I see." Her tone had become more remote. "So, I guess she turned you on, right? Maybe I should lose forty pounds, cut most of my hair off, wear a tight sweater and a leather miniskirt and high heels, and wander around looking stupid and talking about God all the time. Would you like that?"

He reached for her arm. "Dusty, please—"

She pushed him away from her—harder than she intended. He fell backward and hit his head against a tree branch. He let out a little gasp of pain.

"Damn." She fumbled toward him in the dark. "Are you okay?"

"Yes, yes, I'm fine. Just hit my head where the bruise is, that's all."

She touched his shoulder. "I didn't mean to hurt you."

"I know." Thomas reached for her arm again, and this time she didn't shake his hand away.

"I didn't think I was so thin skinned," she said reflectively.

"Dusty?" He touched her face, and traced her profile in the darkness. "It was a very impulsive thing. You're the person I care about, and you're everything that I really want."

She moved closer to him, so that her body brushed against his. "Prove it," she told him.

Footsteps rustled through the undergrowth. Dusty sat up quickly where she had been lying with Thomas on a carpet of pine needles. She fumbled for the flashlight, clicked it on, and swept its beam through the darkness. "Who's there?"

"Oh!" said a voice. "Gee, I'm sorry."

"Who is it?" said Thomas. He started pulling on his clothes.

"My name's Suzie." The flashlight beam picked out her cute, freckled face and wavy golden hair. She squinted in the glare. "I didn't mean to walk in on you guys. I heard voices out here, and I've been looking for some friends of mine."

"I'm Dusty." She turned the light briefly on herself.

"Yeah, I—I guess I recognize you, from on TV." Suzie laughed self-consciously. "I'm looking for a girl called Janet, and her boyfriend, Percival something. Abel, Abbot, something like that."

Thomas and Dusty exchanged looks. "This woman Janet," Thomas asked, "is she a friend of yours?"

"She roomed with me at LoveLand, that's all. I just kind of wondered where she went."

Thomas buckled the belt of his jeans and stood up. "Right now, she's assisting the mayor at City Hall."

"Mayor Whitfield?" Suzie's eyes widened. "For real?" She shook her head in amazement. "Well, for heaven's sake. I kind of thought she had some sort of secret, but I never would have guessed that."

"Percival Abo is the guy who was with her," said Dusty. "He seems to be on our side, more or less. He's up at the observatory. But he wasn't feeling well last time I saw him. He was bitten by a dog earlier today, and the wound looks as if it might be infected."

"Oh. Okay. Thanks. Maybe I'll go find him." She stumbled away through the undergrowth.

"Think she's in collusion?" Thomas asked quietly.

"No. She was genuinely surprised." Dusty reached for him and kissed him. "I'm sorry I doubted you, before. I guess I'm not as liberated as I used to be. Spoiled by monogamy."

"It's okay." He touched her muscled body in the darkness, feeling her curves and her strength. "You know, actually, I kind of like it when you get a little mad at me."

Dusty laughed. "Well, whoever would have guessed?"

There were some intermittent clicking, crackling sounds in the distance. Thomas turned his head quickly. "Now what's *that?*"

A piercing whistle cut through the night. Then it stopped abruptly, and there was a succession of guitar chords, followed by a drum roll. "Test!" A voice echoed across the hillside. "Test, one two! One two!"

"That there is Leaping Larry's sound truck," said Dusty. "Want to come to the dance?"

A yellow spotlight picked out the wasted face of Frantic Frankie Fuckhead, leader of the Electric Freeps. He blinked at the crowd, staggered toward the microphone, and grabbed it for support. "Hey," he said, and grinned.

"Hey!" the crowd shouted back.

"Hey," he said.

"Hey!" they shouted.

"Yeah, okay, now we got communication established, this here is a song dedicated to a man we all care a lot about, like he's in our hearts and minds tonight. It's a number we just wrote called, 'Why I Want to Shove a Baseball Bat Up Mayor Whitfield's Ass While I Beat His Brains Out With a Tire Iron.' Hey!"

"Hey!" they shouted.

"All right, one, two . . . um, three—"

And the music blasted out, a synthesis of Mississippi blues, Tamla Motown, garage-band punk, metal-alloy, and fractal-electronic rock; in short, the apotheosis of American folk traditions and music technology.

People tried to dance in the dark on the soft, sloping hillside and fell into each other, flailing their arms and laughing. Dirty jeans, hand-painted sweatshirts, leather jackets, and home-sewn skirts jostled together in headlight beams from vans and RVs parked in the night. The high spirits were maybe a little hollow, and the hilarity wouldn't stretch very far, but it was a gesture of defiance nonetheless.

"Excuse me, please, may I speak?" The voice was guttural and slurred, calling to her from the shadows beyond the dancing and the music.

Dusty turned and looked. "What's that?"

A hunched figure shuffled forward. "You are the woman who spoke to us yesterday. You let us stay in the park."

"Is this someone you know?" Thomas asked.

"Some—people—I had to deal with while you were being held in City Hall." She walked over to the leader of the mutants. "How are you guys making out?"

"We are hungry, please," said the deformed figure. "The creatures from outer space have not come for us yet to lift us into the sky. Now we have no food."

"You thought they were going to take you away today, didn't you?" said Dusty.

The mutant nodded.

"Well, you were halfway right. Seems there really are some creatures from space. But they're over in Topanga."

"We have dreamed again. Tomorrow, they will take us. But now, how can we eat? Is there food?"

"Go around the hill to the other side. There are a lot of people camped there, and they probably have some food to spare. If they seem surprised by the way you look, remind them that they were told about you on the television news last night. Tell them Dusty said it was okay."

"Thank you." The big figure nodded to her. "When the aliens save us, we will tell them to be kind to you."

"I appreciate that," Dusty said, trying to stay upwind of the mutant's formidable body odor. She watched as the four-armed man disappeared back into the night, then turned back to Thomas. "I don't know if I feel like dancing anymore," she said. "Maybe it's time to get serious and figure our strategy for tomorrow, before we try to sleep."

"Suits me. We should head back to the observatory. 6A419BD5h may have some more news."

"Okay."

Together they walked away from the music, up to the asphalt parking lot where ultralight aircraft stood smelling faintly of oil and gasoline. The observatory was a hunched, rounded silhouette against the line of red fire at the horizon and the stars above. "Let's take a last look," said Dusty, leading him to a concrete path that circled the perimeter of the building.

They came to some old, coin-operated telescopes mounted on poles at intervals along the parapet. "You got a dollar?" she asked.

"Think these things still do anything?"

"We can try."

He pushed the coin into the slot and turned a chromed knob that was pitted with rust. There was a grinding noise, the coin dropped, and a clockwork timer started ticking. Dusty peered through the eyepiece. "Hey, it works."

First she scanned the pinpoints of light that hung like dew on a spider's web, delineating the vast grid of streets that spanned the valley. Then she turned toward the line of fire fifteen miles to the southwest. Huge shapes were moving to and fro: reptilian silhouettes, twice as tall as the houses around them. Searchlight beams weaved restlessly, and exploding warheads flickered like summer lightning. There was a faint roar of engines as fighters swept down the coast, and distant concussions from bombs that they scattered across the city. Meanwhile, thousands of suburban homes burned bright in the night, creating a wall of flame that was spreading slowly inland.

27. A MESS OF MASSACRES

A shadowy shape appeared in the observatory lobby, floating in the darkness. The figure gradually became opaque and substantial. It took the form of a dark-skinned girl of eighteen, tight clothes outlining her thin frame. She drifted down until her feet touched the marble floor littered with old brochures and ticket stubs, and her eyes flashed white in the semidarkness as she looked around and listened.

The only sound was of a stray gust of wind whispering through the broken pane of one of the entrance doors. But for Roxanne, silence no longer existed. Voices crowded her mind, and they grew more insistent as each hour passed.

She crept up the stairs to the wing of the building that had once housed administrative employees. She walked along a corridor and paused outside an old oak-panelled door. She sensed two minds behind the door, one asleep, one awake. The sleeper was immersed in an erotic dream; Roxanne felt the woman's sensuality.

Then the man's waking thoughts imposed themselves. Roxanne saw symbols and geometric forms—helical structures and complex networks of colored spheres. She drew back, disconcerted by the power and velocity of the man's mind.

She crept further along the corridor. Here she sensed another woman dreaming, permutating images from her childhood—a girl crying, her father inexplicably gone, her mother, once a glamorous actress, now an alcoholic. The mother shouting something hurtful about her daughter's big-boned frame; the daughter, Dusty, running into a schoolroom where all the other children stood and turned and stared at her in total silence, and suddenly she realized she was naked—

Roxanne shied away from the pain in the dream. She

sensed another mind in the room, sleeping quietly. Thomas, she realized. He stirred briefly, and worry-images of weapons and fighting surfaced in his mind.

Roxanne wandered back along the corridor. She visualized the hillside beyond the building. The floor became misty under her heels, the night wind blew in her face, and the stars were out above. Her feet settled into tall dry grass.

Camp fires still glowed dimly, and a thousand dreaming minds chattered from tents and sleeping bags scattered across the hillside. When the sleepers woke, she knew, the din would be much worse. Her sensitivity, and her facility to think herself from place to place, had been evolving ever since her accident in the Jeep. Her head still throbbed where it had hit the windshield. She wished she could shut it all out; wished she could erase the strangeness inside her.

She turned toward the parking lot outside the observatory. She visualized it, and it appeared around her. She found herself standing beside the car that the farmer had given Thomas in exchange for the contents of the wrecked Jeep. One of the Pacer's tires had lost air, and its cracked windshield was coated with a mist of dew. Roxanne opened the door, and the hinges made a loud groaning sound in the stillness. She got into the car, groped on the floor in the back, and found the handgun that Thomas had left there earlier. She picked it up and felt its weight, then found the safety and thumbed it off. She pulled the hammer back. The click it made seemed to echo inside her ears.

Another wave of thought-dreams broke over her, projected from sleeping minds nearby. Fleeting, ghostly forms and images of lust and fear. She tried futilely to push them away.

Turning the gun on herself would end the cacophony; yet that seemed sinful. There had to be a reason why God had imposed this talent upon her.

With a sad sense of inevitability, she thought of Clarence Whitfield and the evil inside him that threatened to spill out across the whole city. She pictured the rooms at City Hall where she had served him as his mistress, though it shamed her to think of that now. The mayor seldom went home to his wife and children; he had a kitchen and a bedroom in his office suite and spent most of his time there. She smelled its aroma of stale cigars, and the walls of the mayor's office became solid around her. She heard the sound of his regular breathing in the adjoining bedroom.

Roxanne crept to the door and pushed it open. Whitfield lay alone in the center of his king-size bed. He was deeply asleep; she saw nothing in his mind but the rhythms of his lungs and his heart. The digital clock beside his bed told her that it was four in the morning.

She crept around the bed and sat on the edge of it. She reached for the bedside light and clicked it on.

He woke with a start and blinked in the glare. She waited, watching him as he focussed on her. He didn't see the gun; it was cradled in her lap. Emotions chased one another across his face: confusion, anger, caution. "Well, Roxanne, honey. This is a surprise." He sat up in bed, dragging the monogrammed silk sheets with him. His eyes moved quickly, taking in her appearance.

"You mad at me?" she asked quietly.

"Mad at you?" He was still organizing his thoughts; she saw them coming into focus, arraying themselves in his head. "Honey, I surely wasn't pleased by what you went and did." He was fully conscious, now, and she saw him wondering how she'd gotten past his guard. Then she saw him thinking what he'd do to punish her for betraying him. She saw her own body shackled and bleeding.

She brought up the gun, holding it carefully in both hands. "You're an evil man."

His eyes widened. She saw him planning quickly to seize her arm and turn the gun against her. His hand reached out—but she forced it, with her mind, back down onto the bed. The mayor grunted with surprise. He was afraid, now. If she hesitated much longer, his fear would infect her. She pulled the trigger and shot him in the face. The gun bucked in her grip and the sound was deafening. She smelled gunpowder and there was a ringing in her ears. The mayor slumped in the bed. Blood pulsed out of a terrible wound in his forehead and started pooling and trickling toward her.

Roxanne stood up quickly. Whitfield's thoughts had died with him. She felt a great weight lifted from her. At the same time, she sensed the thoughts of someone a few rooms away who had been woken by the noise and even now was starting toward the room where she stood.

She knew, suddenly, what she should do. She imagined a place above the Earth where you could lie in the clouds and live forever. She pictured it carefully in her mind: away from everything, high in the sky.

The Tyrant had been dreaming fitfully of jungle and swampland; of his own voice roaring in his ears, the ground shaking under him, and smaller creatures scattering from his tread. He woke and found it hard, at first, to comprehend his surroundings. A huge white panel filled one wall. The floor sloped up, cluttered with tiny chairs, some of which had been ripped out and piled to one side. A *movie theater*, his mechanical servants had called it when they'd brought him here. In this land of pygmies, it was one of the few structures big enough to house a creature of the Tyrant's size.

He felt strangely lethargic, and there was an unfamiliar hollowness in his belly. He walked to a large makeshift door that his servants had installed for him in one wall, and emerged into the street outside. It was still dark, but the sky flickered orange in the light from fires his army had started in surrounding neighborhoods.

The Tyrant sniffed the air and looked up and down the street. Giant army ants were marching over dunes of rubble, heading out to the battlefront, their bronze armor plates scraping and rattling, their mandibles clicking in a ritual war chant.

A steel quadruped was standing guard outside the Tyrant's quarters. It waited expectantly, tilting its lenses toward its saurian master. "Is there something you need, your majesty?"

The Tyrant turned toward his servant—then noticed a

flicker of motion in a cross street lined with burned-out storefronts. Two human commandos were running from one shadow to the next, weapons ready. The great saurian roared. In three steps he was upon them, kicking brick walls aside, scattering steel beams and plaster. One of the humans fired its gun, and the Tyrant felt a point of hot pain. The other turned and ran.

The Tyrant dealt with the running man first. He lunged forward, seized the human's head in his teeth, bit it off, and spat it out. Then he turned to the other man and crushed him under one giant foot until the soft, warm body ceased struggling.

"Your majesty! You are hurt!" The quadruped came clanking over in a state of agitation, broadcasting a message for medical help.

"A shallow wound. My scales deflected the projectile." The Tyrant picked up the crushed human in his front claws and started peeling off its clothes as a man might peel a grape. He raised the broken corpse to his mouth and feasted, savoring the blood as it trickled down his throat.

The taste was wholesome and satisfying—and yet the hollowness persisted inside him, with an edge of nausea. For a moment, he felt dizzy.

A medic machine came rolling toward him on metal treads. "Please return to your refuge, your majesty. I wish to check your vital signs."

The Tyrant hissed petulantly. To the east, the city was burning where his forces had overrun it; but there were so many more streets and buildings than he had imagined. The emptiness seemed to grow larger inside him, and the Tyrant knew that tonight, at least, he lacked the strength for conquest.

At first the dogs had moved stealthily, pausing and listening and sniffing the air before venturing into each open space. As the night wore on, however, they grew bolder, for this part of the city seemed totally deserted.

There were two hundred of them in the pack. Lucky led them over a fence and into a parking lot behind a three-story apartment building. The rear entrance was wide open, so Lucky ran inside and the others followed. As they went up the stairs and along dark hallways, the only sound was their panting and the *click-click* of their claws on the wooden floor.

Lucky tried every apartment door. Finally he found one that had been left unlatched, and the pack stampeded in.

A screech and a hiss came from one corner of the room. Two eyes glowed in the darkness.

"Cat," said Lucky. He bounded forward.

The cat leaped over him, but a greyhound behind Lucky seized the animal in its jaws. The room filled with growling, screaming, and ripping sounds as the dogs pulled the cat to pieces.

"More," said a dog next to Lucky.

"We all need more. Much more," said another.

Lucky prowled into the kitchen and rummaged through cabinets at floor level, but found only canned foods and cooking utensils. He knocked over a garbage pail, and the dogs rooted through it with little enthusiasm.

"Abo must have warned the humans about us," Lucky said. "They're frightened of us, so they ran away."

"I'm sure they went up onto the hill," said a wolfhound. "The sounds and smells from the hill seem human to me."

"I think you're right," said Lucky. "But if we venture out into the open, the humans have weapons that can kill us from a great distance. I hoped some of them would still be here among the buildings, where we would outnumber them and have the advantage."

"It doesn't look that way," said the wolfhound.

"Listen." A collie jumped up onto a chair and put its paws against a window, pushing it open. The noise of vehicles approaching along the street came to them on the night air.

The dogs ran out of the room, down to the lobby of the building, and out of the front door. "Be cautious!" Lucky warned them. "Stay in the shadows!"

They gathered beneath palm trees and agave bushes. A convoy of vehicles came into view—big, half-tracked troop carriers, rumbling through the darkness. The dogs smelled diesel exhaust, oil, and grease. Mingling with these odors was the unmistakable tang of human sweat.

"There must be a lot of men inside those machines," said Lucky.

"They're heading toward the hill," said another dog.

"Let's follow them," said Lucky. "If there really are soldiers inside, they'll fight the other men. After they kill each other, we can eat their dead meat."

Suzie woke suddenly and realized that gray dawn light was seeping into the little room. She had fallen asleep on a bed of papers that she had taken from an old file cabinet and strewn across the floor. She thought sadly of her apartment in LoveLand. Before the earthquake, it had been the most luxurious, most comfortable place she'd ever lived. Now, she didn't know if she'd be able to get her savings out of the LoveLand bank; and even if she did, she wasn't sure the money would be worth anything.

She rolled over and saw Dr. Abo sitting at the steel desk in the corner, writing busily. "Hey," she called softly. "Didn't you ever get to sleep last night?"

He grunted something but didn't look up.

Suzie stood and padded barefoot across the grimy floor. She peered over his shoulder at the diagrams he'd been drawing. Circles were connected with lines. Letters and numbers and chemical formulae were scribbled in the margins.

She put her hand on his forehead. "You realize you're still running a fever?"

"Yes, probably." He scribbled some more, then tossed the pen onto the desk and leaned back in his chair. "My body is fighting the virus, and will ultimately kill it after two days of symptoms resembling the common cold. But the implanted gene has already done its work."

"What are you talking about?"

"The dog bite I received yesterday."

"You mean it was infected?" She gave him a troubled look. "I *knew* you were sick last night. Gee, maybe I shouldn't have, you know, gotten you all excited."

"No, no!" Dr. Abo seized her hand. He gave her a radiant smile. "It was the right thing for us to have sex together. More than you could have known."

"Oh. Okay." She smiled uneasily. There was something odd about him this morning. "You see," she went on, "Janet seemed so hung up on you, I got kind of curious about you myself. And since you weren't feeling so good, I thought maybe you needed a little of God's physical love." She kissed him on the cheek.

Dr. Abo patted her absentmindedly. "Suzie—it is Suzie, isn't it? I never used to be able to remember names, but now there seems to be no problem in accessing short-term memory—I must find our friends, Dusty and Thomas. I understand now where my research went wrong. I also see several important facts about our current situation."

She looked at him with her head on one side. "I honestly don't understand half of what you're saying."

"Yes, I realize that. But soon you will understand *everything*." He walked to the door, opened it, and strode quickly along the hallway. Although he was exhausted from working through the night, he seemed energized, as if he were a teenager again. He rapped on the door of the adjoining office.

There was no reply, so he walked in. The room was empty. Even the robot had gone.

Dr. Abo returned to the hallway. "They must have gone outside. I was so absorbed in my calculations, I didn't even hear them leave." He hurried toward the stairs.

"Can I come too?" said Suzie.

"Of course. But we may not have much time."

The barbarian's eyes flicked open, and he grabbed his sword. He rolled over quickly, swinging the tip of the blade up, but there was no one behind him. The grassy hillside was silent in the dawn.

Once again he looked around. He was sure he had felt someone or something touch his shoulder. But the other men in his tribe were still sleeping around the embers of the fire, and his own woman lay where he had left her last night, spread-eagled on her back, her wrists and ankles tied to stakes that he had hammered into the ground.

High, hazy clouds were turning gray-blue with early light. He looked up and for a moment he thought he saw a small shadowy circle moving across the sky, like a soap bubble. But then it was gone.

He sheathed his sword and walked to his woman. He slapped her awake, then dropped down on his knees between her legs. "Slut," he said in his guttural tongue, "what is your duty?"

"My duty is to serve you, master," she mumbled, still half asleep.

"So, you are finally starting to learn. Maybe I will let you be my full-time slave, after all." He thrust himself inside her. "Does that hurt, slut?"

"Yes, master." She gasped and turned her head to one side.

"That is as it should be." He seized a thorny branch nearby, snapped it off, and started beating her with it, leaving red indentations across her ivory skin. She twisted in her bonds and sobbed pitifully. "It is in the nature of a woman to serve her master, in whatever way he demands." He dropped the branch and grabbed her by her hair. "Do you understand?"

"Yes, master. I want only to please you. If my pain pleases you, then it pleases me also."

"Yes!" He grunted with satisfaction, climaxed, then walked away and urinated into some bushes.

As he readjusted his loincloth he paused and listened. Faintly, from beyond the copse of trees where he stood, he heard voices and the clink of metal against metal. He smelled men and sensed danger.

He considered rousing the other warriors of his clan. But there would be more honor and glory if he were able to defeat a superior force single-handed, so he crept forward alone through the undergrowth. His sense of smell was sharpened with hunger, and his body felt vitalized from the brutal sex he had just enjoyed. He slid his sword carefully out of its sheath and ducked under some overhanging branches.

Seven men were gathered in a group. Their clothes were colored in a camouflage pattern, and they wore steel hel-

mets decorated with leaves and fronds. The barbarian recognized the automatic rifles as weapons, for there was no
doubt about the purpose of their fixed bayonets. Clearly,
these soldiers were a danger to his tribe.

The leader of the group was holding a machine with a
glowing screen. Wires led from it to a metal tube that contained a cylinder with a pointed tip, aimed toward the sky.
"Okay, I'm going for target acquisition," the group leader
was saying. There was a pause. "Damn it, the keyboard's
locked up." He pressed buttons. "Kurt, do you have that
diagnostic utility package in your kit bag?"

"Yes sir, Colonel Mallet."

The barbarian decided it would be foolish to wait any
longer. The men looked puny, and their attention was distracted. He leaped out from the trees, swinging his sword.

He sliced one man's throat, kicked the second in the
groin, stabbed a third, then went back to the second and
beheaded him as he slumped forward. He whirled and
faced the fourth man, who was bringing up his gun. The
barbarian bared his teeth, shouted his war cry, and thrust
his sword into the man's face. Coughing, choking noises,
the gushing of blood, and cries of panic were sounding
around him, but he heard nothing and saw nothing but his
remaining enemies. The fifth was backing away, looking
terrified, while the sixth had levelled his rifle. The barbarian swung his sword and knocked the weapon aside—but
in the clash of steel against steel, the tip of his sword shattered.

He reached for his dagger, ran forward, and stabbed the
sixth man in the neck. Fountains of blood drenched the
barbarian as he kicked the falling body aside and went after
the fifth man, who was running for cover. The barbarian
stabbed him in the back. The dagger went too deep and
stuck there; the barbarian cursed and turned around unarmed, now.

The man named Mallet had put aside the machine with
the glowing screen and was reaching for the gun at his hip.
He was fumbling with the flap over the holster, his eyes
wide, his breath coming in little gasps.

The barbarian cast around for a weapon to defend himself. There were rifles lying on the ground, but he had no idea how to use them. He saw the tube containing the pointed thing. He seized it and raised it over his head, to club his opponent.

Mallet gave a little cry of horror. "No!" he shouted. "That missile is armed!"

The barbarian yelled his defiance. He swung the launching tube, and the ground-to-ground wire-guided missile slid out, propelled by centrifugal force. Its pointed tip caught Colonel Matt Mallet in the center of his forehead, and the warhead detonated.

The explosion excavated a four-foot crater and flattened several surrounding trees. As the fireball dissipated and a dark cloud of smoke rolled into the sky, all that was left of the barbarian, Mallet's Mashers, and the colonel himself was a lumpy, sticky residue that coated the surrounding hillside like overcooked beef gravy.

"Hold your fire. Repeat, hold your fire." Thomas's voice came to her clearly over the walkie-talkie.

"Stop 'em Mordo!" Dusty shouted. *"Not yet, okay?"*

Mordo passed the word to his biker battalion. He had to yell above the roar of their Harleys as they gunned the motors, eager to beat the shit out of whoever or whatever lay below.

"They want to get down there and kick ass," Mordo complained, as he came back to the tent where Dusty had set up her command post. "You saw that bomb go off down the hill. Let's do those bastards before they get any closer."

Dusty held up her hand, listening to the voice coming to her from the earpiece. Then she turned to the biker. "That was just one commando group. They took themselves out with one of their own missiles. There's nothing left of 'em to kill, Mordo. The main force of guardsmen is still grouping to attack."

Dr. Abo stood outside the observatory, looking down the hillside, trying to see the source of the explosion and the smoke that was now dispersing on the wind. "I'm scared," Suzie said. She crossed her arms across her breasts as if to warm herself, and gave him a searching look.

"An entirely rational reaction." He glanced at the squadron of ultralight aircraft, facing into the wind, ready for takeoff. The pilots looked restless and unsure of themselves.

The air shimmered suddenly as if in a heat mirage. A spherical shape like a large lens appeared on the asphalt of the parking lot directly in front of Dr. Abo. It vaporized into tiny pinpoints of light, revealing Thomas standing beside robot 6A419BD5h.

Suzie let out a little gasp.

"Dr. Abo, do you have any medical training?" Thomas stepped forward and grabbed his arm. "I should have asked you last nigh   ιere were so many things to think about. This is an emergency."

"One year pre-med," Dr. Abo stammered. "Then I quit, and—"

"Quickly," said Thomas. He glanced at Suzie. "You should stay indoors and keep away from the windows. We'll be back in a while."

She nodded dumbly. "Okay."

Thomas hustled Dr. Abo toward the robot. "We're going to take off. You'll feel weightless. At the same time, it'll seem almost pitch dark. Trust me."

The outside world faded into blackness, and Dr. Abo felt as if he were falling. He grabbed Thomas and the robot for support. "What—"

"We're using 6A419BD5h's invisibility field. Didn't use it yesterday, because we were protecting outselves with his force field, then, so it didn't matter whether anyone saw us or not. But today, we don't want the guardsmen on the ground to know we're up here watching them."

"Ah!" said Dr. Abo. "So this invisibility field diverts light around us, yes? But that means our eyes no longer receive the light, and so the world outside looks dark."

"Absolutely right," said Thomas. "We can siphon off just a small percentage for 6A419BD5h. His eyes have low-light amplification, so he's doing the flying. He's also using his force-field gadget in its long-range, pencil-beam mode. It's very accurate. You can nudge a small object at five hundred meters."

"Such as a person's body? A trigger finger, or a gun barrel, or even a computer connection?" said Dr. Abo.

Thomas gave him a puzzled look. "How did you figure that out so fast?"

There was a gentle bump and gravity returned. Dr. Abo stumbled, but the robot caught him under the arms. The bubble of darkness vaporized in front of his eyes, and the colors of the world shone in. Dr. Abo found himself in a deserted area of Griffith Park, perhaps a mile from the observatory. Lying on the ground in front of him, beneath some trees, was the body of a young woman. A revolver lay on the ground near her hand.

"6A419BD5h saw her," said Thomas. "He said she literally dropped out of the sky. The trees broke her fall a little, but—I didn't want to move her. I didn't know what to do."

Dr. Abo kneeled beside the girl. "She's the one who was in your car yesterday." He checked for a pulse. It was very faint. "Her name is Roxanne?"

Thomas kneeled beside him. "That's right."

Roxanne's eyes opened as she felt Dr. Abo's hands gingerly probing. She saw him, then saw Thomas. She coughed and whimpered in pain. Blood bubbled at the corner of her mouth. "I killed Satan," she whispered.

"I think she has severe internal injuries," said Dr. Abo. "I have no idea what to do."

"Whitfield," Roxanne whispered. "I killed him."

"We could expand the antigravity field to include her body, and float her out of here," 6A419BD5h suggested.

Roxanne coughed again, and moaned. "You all thinking too loud. . . ." She closed her eyes.

"Her vital signs are fading," said Dr. Abo.

"Even if we could get her out of here," said Thomas, "I'm not sure where we could take her. And anyway, I don't want to risk being away from our people on the hillside when the mayor's men attack." He clenched and unclenched his hands.

"I think it is too late, in any case," said Dr. Abo.

Roxanne's muscles spasmed weakly. Her limbs made fluttering motions, then relaxed. Her eyes stayed closed.

"I think that is all, for her." Dr. Abo touched her wrist, then the side of her neck. "I can feel no pulse."

Thomas took a shaky breath. "All right." He looked away. He saw the gun lying on the ground, bent down, and picked it up. As he turned it over in his hands, he recognized it as the one he had taken from the armory at City Hall. One round, he noted, had been fired.

Shouts and screams sounded in the far distance. "We should find out what is happening there," said 6A419BD5h.

Thomas nodded vaguely. "Of course."

"How long must we wait?" complained a Doberman lying on its belly in the tall grass. "Most of us have had no food since we woke from our long sleep. If we are going to attack, we must do it while we still have our strength."

The dogs had been watching the National Guard convoy for the past hour. The vehicles had pulled in under some trees on a perimeter road at the edge of Griffith Park, and had remained there with their motors rumbling. None of the soldiers had emerged, even when the explosion had echoed across the landscape earlier.

"Do you still smell humans up on the hillside?" Lucky asked a nearby bloodhound.

"Many of them," said the bloodhound. "I smell a fire, too. Perhaps they are sitting around it, warming themselves. In that case, they'll be unprepared for our attack."

"All right," said Lucky. "Lead us to them."

The bloodhound started forward and the pack followed him, crawling on their bellies in the long grass and pausing frequently to listen and sniff the air. Before long, they approached the crater where Colonel Mallet's missile had exploded. Barbarian warriors, roused from their sleep, were surveying the devastation and searching the area with their swords drawn.

"Too dangerous," whispered Lucky.

"But these dregs in the grass taste good," said a smaller dog behind him, licking up some of the pasty remains.

"This way," whispered the bloodhound. "There's a human over here who's completely helpless!"

The dogs followed him and found a woman lying on her back with her wrists and ankles tied to stakes in the ground. Before she had a chance to scream, Lucky ripped out her windpipe. Blood spurted and the dogs pressed forward, lapping the gore like kids trying to get their share at a water fountain. The woman struggled in her bonds and made awful throttled noises. Before long, the floor of the forest glade was slippery red, and dogs were gnawing at her bones.

"There are more, this way!" a collie reported.

The dogs ran through bushes and emerged at the camp fire where the barbarians had spent the night. The warriors had left their other women here. Some were tethered on leashes; others were bound hand and foot. "Careful!" Lucky warned the dogs. "When they see us, they'll shout for help. Their men aren't far away."

But the dogs were high on blood lust. They charged into the clearing, leaping, snapping, and ripping at their victims. Two of the women screamed piercingly before they died.

A shout sounded from the edge of the clearing. A man with a sword appeared there, his face contorted with rage. Others came running, their feet crashing through the undergrowth.

"Run!" Lucky shouted to the dogs.

But most of them were too excited to retreat. A German shepherd rushed the first of the men and closed its jaws on his wrist holding the sword. The barbarian yelled in pain, switched the sword to his left hand, and hacked the dog in half. Another German shepherd leaped up behind him and caught him by the neck; he dropped his sword, reached around, and tore the dog's stomach out with his fingernails.

For a while it was hard to tell which side had the upper hand. The dogs outnumbered the barbarians by five to one, but the men had weapons and were skilled fighters. The glade was filled with barking, yelping, ripping sounds, and intermittent cries of rage and pain.

Ultimately the dogs prevailed, using tactics that had

served them well throughout history. They encircled the clan of humans, herding them together and holding them at bay as if they were sheep. Then they split one man away from the others and took turns wearing him down, darting forward for a nip at his ankle, a bite at his thigh, until he was weakened by loss of blood. Only when he was on his knees, dizzy and exhausted, did they go for the kill. Then they split another one away from his companions, and repeated the process. It took time, but the dogs were in no hurry.

After an hour, all the humans were dead. Of the dogs, more than 150 remained. They feasted happily in the clearing, then dozed amid the carnage as the sun rose, warming them. Overhead, some human figures appeared, suspended in the sky; but the dogs were now so sated, they paid no attention.

"Your enemies are annihilating one another, as we planned," said 6A419BD5h. He had descended among the upper tree branches and dropped the invisibility shield to allow Thomas and Dr. Abo to observe events below.

Thomas said nothing. He was still haunted by images of Roxanne's broken body.

Dr. Abo was weeping silently, surveying the carnage below. "I always believed," he said, "that heightened intelligence would overcome animal instincts for slaughter."

"Humans are intelligent, but they still fight and kill each other," 6A419BD5h pointed out.

"Perhaps they simply aren't intelligent *enough*," said Dr. Abo. "After all, there has been some human progress toward order and civilization as our intelligence evolved to its present level."

"Maybe so," said 6A419BD5h, "but in my own limited experience with you people, I've already learned that you often do what you feel like doing instead of what would be most sensible."

"I have reason to believe that this will change," Dr. Abo insisted. "My own research—"

"Helicopters," Thomas interrupted, pointing. "Put up the invisibility field."

The robot did so, darkening the image of the world outside. He took them up to a thousand feet, scanning the sky with his enhanced vision. "Guardsmen are emerging from the troop carriers," he reported.

"They were waiting for air support," said Thomas. He switched on his walkie-talkie. "Dusty? You there?" He paused for her acknowledgment. "The main force of guardsmen is preparing to attack. We'll disable as many as possible, but some will get through. Hold the bikers till I give the signal."

"I'll hold them," she confirmed.

"Shall I deal with the helicopters first?" said 6A419BD5h.

"Definitely. They're the biggest threat."

The robot aimed his force tube. "It violates my precepts to destroy so much technology and information."

"Them or us," said Thomas. "We already discussed this."

The robot projected a narrow tractor beam across the sky. With the precision of his stepper motors under controlled negative feedback, and the accuracy of his vision in telephoto mode, he used the beam to nudge a pilot's hand in one helicopter, a control lever in another. The two machines veered and collided; then a third climbed suddenly, inverted, and crashed. The fourth and fifth wobbled and lost altitude as their pilots wrestled with the controls. Men jumped for safety as the last two helicopters finally spiralled down and slammed into the roofs of houses below.

"They have all been disabled," said 6A419BD5h.

Thomas wished he could see for himself instead of being enclosed in the black interior of the invisibility field. "All helicopters down," he reported to Dusty. "Okay to send up the ultralights, now."

"Launch ultralights," she acknowledged.

Some of the guardsmen on the ground stopped and stared at the burning wreckage behind them. Others, however, were already swarming up the hill. 6A419BD5h swept low over their heads, tripping the men with his tractor beam, turning their weapons on one another, and nudging their trigger fingers. The men shouted in fear and confusion as they found themselves killing each other at close range.

"Now send down the bikers and the four-by-fours," said Thomas. He hesitated. "Be careful, Dusty."

"Don't worry," she radioed back to him. "We're on our way."

"Surely it would be safer to wait at the top of the hill, and pick off the soldiers as they approach," said Dr. Abo.

"We figured they'd plan on that, and it would be better to attack them before they had a chance to take up positions," said Thomas. "Right now, they're confused and scared by what's happening to them. Anyway, Dusty didn't know how she could make the bikers sit up there and wait. An army of freeps doesn't have much discipline."

High on the hill, armored pickup trucks and rec vehicles came roaring out from under cover. They headed for the battle, flanked by bikers wearing lurid warpaint, waving sawed-off shotguns, and yelling obscenities. Thomas floated in semidarkness, imagining Dusty among the battalion of motorcycle hoodlums. He wished, pointlessly, that he was there to help her.

Dusty rode her Norton next to Mordo on his hog, and the roar of motorcycles hammered her ears. Her machine bucked under her as she took it across the lumpy grassland, swerving to avoid trees and bushes. Her vision blurred. She fought to control the cycle, wet with nervous sweat, her whole body vibrating with adrenaline. She thought of Thomas, then images of Panama came floating up to haunt her. She cursed under her breath.

The bikers split into two phalanxes, moving out either side of the guardsmen struggling up the hillside. The armored pickups and rec vehicles stayed in the center, heading straight for uniformed figures wrestling with weapons that seemed to have come alive in their grasp. The freeps in the pickups turned their vehicles broadside as they came within range. They stopped and took aim.

The flat, smacking sound of rifle fire and the stutter of machine guns drifted across the hillside. Dusty stopped her motorcycle beside a tree, pulled her rifle from the improvised sling across her back, and forced herself to spend precious seconds steadying her aim. The gun kicked in her grip as she began methodically squeezing off single rounds. She saw the men in her sights fall like targets in a shooting gallery.

The rasping buzz of the ultralights sounded overhead. Their shadows flickered across the hillside, and the lurid symbols on their wings glowed in the sun. They passed over the main battle and dived toward guardsmen readying field guns and mortars near the troop carriers. Molotov cocktails and pipe bombs rained out of the sky. One of the troop carriers exploded, scattering shrapnel.

Dusty looked for more targets, but had to hold her fire. Most of the bikers had gone roaring into the center of the action, and it was getting hard to distinguish friend from foe. Dusty saw several freeps leaping off their machines for the sheer pleasure of hand-to-hand combat. It was already a rout; the remaining guardsmen were trying to run back down the hill to safety. The bikers whooped with delight and cut them down.

Dusty heard a faint sound from behind her. She turned quickly, full of fear—and found a dog standing among the bushes, looking up at her. She stared at it, feeling disoriented.

"I remember you," said the dog. It started walking toward her. "Your name is Dusty."

"And you're Abo's dog," Dusty said slowly.

"That's right. My name's Lucky. You're a nice person. I like you."

"Yeah?" Dusty noticed that the dog's snout was covered in some sort of dry, muddy residue.

Lucky stopped a few paces away from her. "I have a thorn in my paw," he said. "It hurts a lot. Can you help me, please?"

With her rifle in one hand, Dusty slowly dismounted from her motorcycle. Lucky waited till she was resting her weight on one leg, with her side turned toward him.

Dusty heard a growl and turned just in time to see the dog leaping at her with its teeth bared. Instinctively, she raised her rifle and fired from the hip. The gun kicked out of her hand and dropped into the grass, but the bullet caught Lucky in his stomach. He fell against her, snapping feebly at her throat. She felt warm, wet saliva, but his teeth missed their mark. He fell and hit the ground, howling in pain.

Dusty looked down and realized belatedly that the brown stuff coating the dog's muzzle was dried blood. "Damned dogs," she muttered. She bent down, grabbed her fallen rifle, aimed at Lucky's head, and fired twice.

She heard other rustlings in the undergrowth. This time, she didn't turn to look. She jumped back onto her motorcycle, revved the engine, and roared out from under the trees, heading back up the hill.

Bikers were spraying beer over each other, shouting and laughing. Loud music was playing as freeps gathered in the parking lot outside the observatory. Some slapped hands and bragged about the guardsmen they'd wasted. Others looked more subdued, shaken by the fighting they'd seen. A few were pale and in shock. Dusty organized volunteers to distribute blankets and make sure that people who needed help were properly cared for by their friends and families.

She returned, finally, to the steps at the front of the building. People started cheering her, and someone gave her a bullhorn. "Speech, Dusty!" they shouted.

"I'm proud of you all," she told them, and realized that she meant it. "You could have chosen to save your asses. But you stayed and fought, and so we won."

There was cheering. She wished, suddenly, that they would all quieten down; wished that they would be a little smarter, and maybe think ahead instead of responding with the usual mob fever.

"We've still got a lot of problems," she told them. Her amplified voice cut through the shouts and laughter. "There are wild dogs out there that kill people. Watch out for them. There's more fighting going on near the coast," she pointed to the west, "and we don't know, yet, if the whole of L.A. is going to be flooded."

Dr. Abo emerged from the building beside her. "I need to talk to you urgently," he told her.

"Okay, I have to go," Dusty told her audience. "Stay up here in the park, everyone, till we're certain the city isn't sending more guardsmen into the Zone. Make sure some people stand lookout, keeping in touch with walkie-talkies. Send an ultralight up for surveillance once in a while. Okay?"

There was more cheering. Dusty turned and went into the building. "Where's Thomas?" she asked, following Dr. Abo upstairs.

"Waiting for you in the office." He led her into the little room where she and Thomas had spent the night. Robot 6A419BD5h was sitting in the corner, reconnected with his data link. Thomas jumped up as he saw Dusty walk in.

"Hey, how come you hid up here?" She grabbed him in a big hug, and kissed him on his mouth and his cheeks. "You were the one who deserved the credit. You planned the whole damn thing."

He studied her face as if searching for the smallest wound that might have been inflicted during the fighting. Finally, he relaxed against her. "Not my style to go public, Dusty. You know that."

"If I may intrude," Dr. Abo persisted, "you should look, through the window there, toward the north."

Dusty made a little vexed sound, but finally disengaged herself from Thomas. "I don't see—" she began.

Thomas joined her. Finally, they saw what Dr. Abo had seen. Hovering among the vegetation was an object like a big, milky soap bubble. It seemed to glow with an inner light. Inside it was something heavy, wrinkled, and gray.

"I believe there's nothing to worry about," Dr. Abo said. "During the night, the aliens' behavior became clear to me. But we should go out and make contact."

Thomas turned to 6A419BD5h. "What do you think?"

"I discussed it briefly with Dr. Abo, and I believe he's right. You should take the force tube and the antigravity device; I've already shown you how to use them. I'll stay here for the time being. There's a lot of data coming through."

*   *   *

"It became clear to me," said Dr. Abo, floating down the hillside with Dusty and Thomas, "that a race as advanced as these 'snaliens' would be able to exterminate humanity quite quickly, and much more efficiently, by biological methods. Why, then, were they using laser beams to fight a conventional battle with our forces?"

"Do tell," said Dusty. Dr. Abo had a pedantic tone of voice this morning, and it was beginning to get on her nerves. She flinched as Thomas fumbled with the anti-gravity unit and the field fluctuated unpredictably, lurching toward the trees below. Then the snalien came into view, meandering lazily around the hillside. Overhead, a remote-controlled pilotless vehicle seemed to be following it, but no other military forces were in evidence.

"Possibly," said Dr. Abo, "the snaliens were merely fighting defensively. But no; according to Thomas, here, they took the initiative, shooting down a coast guard helicopter. And one more fact: as we observed yesterday, they only shoot at military targets. One has to wonder: are they taking the affair as seriously as we are? Or could it be that they see it as some sort of *sport?*"

The snalien had noticed them. It turned in its glowing milky-white bubble, and started in their direction. "Greetings!" its voices boomed out.

"Nice theory," said Dusty. "I hope it's the *right* theory."

"We have our force field protecting us," Thomas reminded her.

"Yeah, that makes me feel really secure."

"I recognize you," said the creature, coming up alongside. Several fleshy stalks protruded from it, and its body undulated in a lengthy, complex spasm. "We met on the beach."

"You're right," said Thomas. "Can you hear me?"

"Of course, of course I can hear you. I congratulate you on the battle. It has been most enjoyable."

Thomas blinked. "Yeah?"

"What a pity that we have to leave, just as my equipment has mastered your interesting language. Incidentally, the way you brought in the large lizards was a masterly touch."

"I don't think you understand," said Thomas. "I'm not—"

"My friend is modest," Dr. Abo cut in. "He prefers not to take credit. But why are you leaving so soon?"

The snalien cruised slowly around them, examining them from every angle. Finally, it moved above them, so that when they looked up they could see its thousands of cilia squelching against the transparent underside of its bubble. Slimy fluid puddled around it. "Well, I think it's clear, we won," said the snalien. It sank slowly back down to their level. "And there are many more planets to visit. We'll be rejoining our interstellar transport quite soon."

"What about the ship on the beach?" said Thomas.

"*That* little thing? We built it on our way to Earth, just for fun. Didn't you like it?" The great, deep voice sounded disappointed. "We thought it was just the kind of thing that would appeal to you."

"Listen," said Thomas, ignoring Dr. Abo, who was placing a hand on his arm, trying to restrain him. "To us, this hasn't been just a game. You killed a lot of people, and scared the shit out of everyone. We don't find that funny."

The snalien made a rhythmic booming noise, which seemed to be its equivalent of laughter. "Oh, very droll," it said. "Just you remember, we've seen your movies. We know the kind of thing you people like. Death and destruction: the more, the better!"

"So, your, ah, mission is complete?" said Dr. Abo.

"Yes, you could say that. Our only disappointment," the alien went on, "is that there's nothing good to eat around here. Rats are too small, the humans that we've tried don't taste very nice, and the dogs and cats and coyotes are too stupid to be interesting."

"What's intelligence got to do with it?" said Dusty.

"Everything, of course. An intelligent creature struggles for life so much more entertainingly while you're consuming it, don't you find?"

"Absolutely," Dr. Abo agreed, before Thomas or Dusty had time to say anything. "But it just so happens, I know where there are some dogs that aren't stupid at all. More than a hundred of them, specially engineered to be highly intelligent. They're just the other side of this hill."

"Really? How kind!" The snalien started drifting in that direction. "Although, it seems greedy to take them all."

"No, no, feel free!" Dr. Abo said. "The only thing is, they may try to hide from you."

The booming laugh sounded again. "I have highly efficient tracking equipment. Thank you!" And it drifted away.

They found Mordo waiting for them outside the observatory. "Hey, how d'you guys do that?" he asked, as they floated to the ground and Thomas cut the antigravity field.

"Friend of ours made a gadget that takes care of it," Dusty told him.

"Yeah? Well, far fuckin' out. But hey, you got to come look at this." He beckoned them toward the parapet to the left of the building, and pointed down the hillside.

The snalien was drifting along, while some freeps ran in panic and others fired their guns at it. The glowing white bubble seemed to have grown bigger; as they watched, they saw an appendage swelling from one side. It became a separate, smaller bubble, detached itself, and settled among the trees and bushes. Faintly, in the distance, came the sound of angry barking. After a moment, the barking became muted. The smaller bubble lifted back up into the air, now containing a canine cargo. It moved on, then dived again into the undergrowth, searching for more unlucky specimens.

"That takes care of the dog problem," said Thomas.

"Tell your guys not to hassle the snalien," said Dusty.

Mordo shook his head. "More weird shit," he said. "Still, if you say it's cool, I guess we can deal with it." He headed down the hillside, yelling to his buddies to hold their fire.

"Excuse please," said a voice from behind them.

Dusty turned. She found the leader of the mutants standing there, nodding to her in his usual deferential style. He clasped one pair of hands behind his back and the other pair in front of his chest.

"Something wrong?" Dusty asked.

"We saw you with the creature from space," said the mutant, "over on the hillside." He gestured with one of his arms. "We thought they had come, at last, to take us away."

She shook her head. "I'm sorry, but the alien didn't say anything about that. In any case, it only seems interested in eating animals or blowing things up."

"Oh." The mutant looked sad. "You did talk to it?"

"We certainly did," said Dr. Abo.

The mutant nodded thoughtfully. He made several confusing gestures with his four arms, then shrugged them all simultaneously. "Last night we had another dream. We dreamed we were left behind by the space creatures. Instead, we went to live with the hermits at the bottom of the hill. We ate garbage and were rather happy."

"Hey, that sounds a great idea," said Dusty.

The mutant bobbed his bald head up and down. "Thank you. You are kind." He turned to go. "In future, we shall know that some dreams are more meaningful than others." He ambled slowly away.

"I see we've just added another politically enlightened, productive member to our community," said Thomas.

Dusty chucked him under the chin. "Lighten up, techie. Freaks like him are a real asset. Many hands make light work, remember?"

"If you'll excuse my intruding into your friendly banter," said Dr. Abo, "we should check with our robot. If my theory is correct, he will have good news for us about our remaining problems. And then, I have some news of my own."

"You know," Dusty said, looking at him with her head on one side, "you're talking differently from the way you did yesterday."

"I *am* different," he said with an enigmatic smile.

"The object that was thought to be a comet will not impact in the Pacific Ocean after all," robot 6A419BD5h announced as they walked in. "Therefore, we will not be inundated with a tidal wave." He folded his metal arms in a human gesture that he had evidently been practicing. "I hope you're suitably pleased."

"What's the catch?" said Dusty. "This sounds altogether too good to be true."

"No catch. The object, which is several hundred miles in diameter, has decelerated and entered a high orbit."

"It's the snaliens' interstellar transport," said Dr. Abo. "I predict that the ship on Topanga Beach will lift off and rendezvous with it."

"Ah," said Thomas. "Of course."

"As for the dinosaurs and the giant ants," Dr. Abo went on, "they'll be wiped out within a matter of days. I imagine you've already heard reports that their resistance is weakening?" He looked inquiringly at 6A419BD5h.

The robot scratched his head. There seemed no limit to his repertoire of human mannerisms. "As it happens, yes."

"The facts are clear," said Dr. Abo. "These prehistoric reptiles, whose intelligence was woefully underestimated by geologists, evidently emerged from 100 million years of cold storage. Bacteria and viruses have evolved in that time. Our friends from the past don't have immunities; and they obviously lack the biological savvy to deal with the situation, even though they're quite advanced in the physical sciences."

"Right again," said 6A419BD5h.

"Okay," said Thomas, "but how did you figure it all out?"

"I was provided with high-level intelligence," said Dr. Abo. He hesitated. "That's a joke," he added. "Come next door. I'm afraid Suzie won't be feeling very well right now, but she'll be able to convince you better than I can."

Robot 6A419BD5h disconnected himself from his data bus and walked with Dusty, Thomas, and Dr. Abo to the adjoining office. They found Suzie sitting on the floor beneath the window with her back against the wall, her hands clasped around her legs, and her chin resting on her knees. She was frowning, deep in thought.

Dr. Abo walked across and touched her forehead. "Running a slight temperature," he said.

"Of course," said Suzie. "You already told me to expect

that." She looked up at Dr. Abo as if she was annoyed that
he should tell her something she already knew.

"I'm not sure if you've met Suzie," Dr. Abo said, turning to Dusty and Thomas.

"Briefly, last night," said Dusty.

"She used to work at LoveLand," said Dr. Abo. "She's
a Christian Fornicationist."

Suzie laughed. "Now, you surely know I can't believe
that superstitious nonsense anymore."

"You see?" Dr. Abo beamed, obviously pleased with
himself.

Suzie stood up and smoothed the wrinkles out of her
gingham dress. She looked down at it with distaste. "I simply have to get rid of this silly thing. It's positively humili-
ating." She turned to Dr. Abo. "And I'll thank you,
Percival, not to show me to your friends as if I'm some sort
of experimental animal."

"Sorry, Suzie."

"Susan," she corrected him.

"Oh. Very well." He turned to the desk where he had
spent the night working, gathered up his papers, then
opened a drawer and pulled out his briefcase. He slipped
the papers inside on top of the remaining bullion, and
snapped the case shut. "Shall we take a stroll? There's a
small favor I want to ask."

"Percival has spent his life working on a gene splice that
would result in higher intelligence," Suzie explained, as
the four of them walked down to the observatory lobby,
followed by 6A419BD5h. "He tested it on dogs in his lab
in Hong Kong." She paused. "I read his research notes
while you were out fighting battles this morning," she explained.

"What I didn't realize," said Dr. Abo, "was that my
experiment had succeeded beyond my wildest dreams. The
dogs were *so* intelligent, they decided to keep it a secret
from me until they found the most favorable conditions for
their escape."

"How come they were so damned hostile?" Dusty
asked, as they walked to the parking lot. The Pacer was
still there, with one tire now completely flat.

Dr. Abo spread his hands. "They were *still dogs*. As anyone knows, dogs tend to love and obey creatures that are bigger and stronger than they are, but they tend to attack creatures that seem weaker. A dog obeys its master, but it has an ambivalent attitude toward other humans—which is why there are more than two million dog bites reported in America every year, mostly afflicting children. Unfortunately, when my dogs became intelligent, they decided they were stronger and smarter than *all* humans. Thus we were no longer their masters, but their prey, on a par with rats and rabbits."

"But this doesn't explain—" Thomas began.

"Patience, please. I spliced the gene into a virus, so that ultimately it might be transmissible like the common cold. That, however, seems to have failed. It can only be transmitted by bodily fluids or intimate sexual contact. Thus, I caught it from Lucky when he bit me yesterday. And Susan, here, caught it from me, when we, ah—"

"I decided he needed some love and attention last night." She kissed him on the cheek and giggled, and for a moment she seemed once more to be a Christian Fornicationist believing in the power of love. Then she regained her poise and composed her features into an expression of demure respectability.

"My plan, now, is simple," said Dr. Abo. He opened the door of the Pacer and tossed his briefcase onto the back seat. "I will travel to Washington, DC, where I will spend my money on sex with as many highly priced prostitutes as I can. They, in turn, will have sex with senators and congressman. Thus the virus will spread, and for the first time in living memory this country will have an intelligent government."

"Meanwhile," said Suzie, "I'll stick around here, fucking every man I can lay my hands on, and when LoveLand reopens I'll go back to my old job."

"Typhoid Mary," said Dusty, staring at Suzie with an expression of dismay.

"You cannot possibly compare enhanced intelligence to a disease," said Dr. Abo, looking pained.

"But there could be unexpected side effects," said

Thomas. "I don't know much about genetics, but the incredible complexity—"

"I've checked the documents that he drew up during the night," said 6A419BD5h. "I can't find any errors."

"So," said Dr. Abo, getting into the car, "I'll bid you good-bye, and thank you for accommodating my canine cargo in your Free Zone, Dusty, however briefly."

Thomas looked at the car. "You're driving to Washington in that?"

"Not driving, no. In view of the importance of my mission, your robot friend has agreed to donate to me his antigravity device." Dr. Abo held out his hand. 6A419BD5h gave the little silver sphere to him. Dr. Abo slammed the car door. "With my heightened intelligence, I will also be in a good position to uncover the secrets of this gadget, so that soon everyone in America can own one." He gave a cheery wave. "Good-bye!"

Dusty reached for the door handle. "Hey, hold it! Just wait a goddam minute!"

But the Pacer was already lifting smoothly into the sky.

"It's all for the best," Suzie told her with a condescending smile. "As soon as you get infected, you'll see what I mean."

"I still say you should have asked us first," Dusty grumbled to 6A419BD5h as she walked with him and Thomas toward her Norton, parked with the other motorcycles by Mordo's tent. "I mean, after all we've done for you."

"Actually, I think I've done more for you than you've done for me," said the robot. "And I am giving you the other gadgets, remember."

"But Abo's some sort of fruitcake," Dusty persisted. "He came blundering into the Zone, unleashed his killer dogs—"

"He made some mistakes," 6A419BD5h agreed.

"Exactly!"

"Because he wasn't intelligent enough," 6A419BD5h concluded.

Dusty rolled her eyes. She turned to Thomas. "What do you think?"

"I don't know. Well, actually, that's not entirely true. Heightened intelligence sounds pretty exciting to me, and I'm thinking I'd really like to get infected, myself."

"From that cutesy little airhead?" Dusty gave him a warning look.

"Ex-airhead," Thomas corrected her. "By next week, she'll probably be studying nuclear physics when she's not turning tricks. Dusty, can't you see, this could be the greatest thing ever to happen to humanity?"

"This is what I get for asking the opinion of a computer nerd," Dusty muttered. "Hey, Mordo!" She stuck her head in the tent.

He and a couple of hairy freaks were bending over a motorcycle-sidecar combination, working with a socket wrench and a gear puller. He stood up and grinned behind his thick black beard. "Hey, Dusty. Just fixing a little bullet damage. What's up?"

"I want to borrow a motorcycle," she told him. "Anything'll do."

Mordo raised his hand to scratch his head, then saw that his fingers were black with grease. He gestured vaguely. "You got trouble with yours?"

"No. But we have to get back to my place, and there's, ah, three of us." She pointed to 6A419BD5h, standing unobtrusively in the background, his metal shell gleaming in the sun.

"Thought you guys had some kind of flying gimmick," said Mordo.

"We did," Dusty agreed. "But someone just walked off with it. Flew off, in fact."

Mordo looked skeptically at the robot. "Does this dude know how to ride a cycle?"

"I wish to learn," said 6A419BD5h. "If that's all right with you, Mr. Mordo."

And so, later that afternoon, after a couple of beers and a few practice rides, they drove back down to the valley. Dusty took the lead on her red Norton, with her suncape blowing in the breeze and Thomas sitting behind, his arms wrapped around her. The robot followed on an old borrowed Harley. He rode the cycle like a pro. He had what

Mordo described as natural mechanical aptitude.

People of the Free Zone had decided that it was now safe to return to their homes, and were unloading possessions that they'd taken with them for their night in Griffith Park. Some of them looked up as the two motorcycles went by, but no one paid that much attention. After the events of the past two days, a robot riding a motorbike seemed little cause for comment.

Dusty stood in the front yard and stared glumly at the house. She'd forgotten the earthquake damage.

"We can fix it," Thomas said quietly. He put his arm around her. "Or we can move. Right?"

She gave him a searching look. Her face seemed suddenly weary. The little lines were deeper, and her mouth turned down at the corners. "I don't know, Thomas."

He shrugged. "We have no choice."

Robot 6A419BD5h carefully settled his Harley on its kickstand. "Most enjoyable," he said, surveying the machine. "I think, when I get back to my time, we should introduce some form of mobility."

"Fine, do that," said Dusty. "When are you leaving?"

"As soon as we turn off the tachyon generator in your basement," 6A419BD5h said. "You do remember, that's why I came here in the first place."

"Oh, yeah." Dusty walked up the front path, picking her way among the flourishing weeds. "Well, help yourself. Walk right in." She gestured at the front door, which still stood where she had pushed it aside the previous day before her confrontation with Colonel Mallet. She stepped over fallen beams and Sheetrock and disappeared into the living room.

6A419BD5h turned to Thomas. "You'll come with me to the basement and shut the system down? You did promise you would."

"Okay." He paused in the hallway. "Dusty, are you all right?"

"I'm going to stretch out for a while." Her voice came from the direction of the bedroom. "You two do whatever you've got to do."

Thomas followed the robot down to the basement. It wasn't until they reached the bottom of the stairs that they realized they had company.

Three people were standing and waiting under the naked light bulbs. Two were wearing what looked like black space suits with armored visors. The third, behind them, was a smaller figure. He had doffed his helmet, revealing a head of bushy white hair. He saw 6A419BD5h and Thomas, and treated them to a wide, unfriendly smile. "Well, at last," he said. "Just as I was beginning to get impatient."

6A419BD5h groaned. It sounded quite human, and the emotion seemed quite sincere. "Colonel Scientist Doctor Werner Weiss," he said.

"Indeed." The little man gestured to his guards, and they raised their weapons.

6A419BD5h reached toward his cranium, where he had stashed the force tube and the invisibility gadget.

"No!" Weiss snapped at him. "You will not move, please." He sneered, exposing his gold teeth. "There will be no more surprises from you, my friend. We spent many months analyzing the scan we made of you before your sudden departure. We now know everything that you know —including the principles of your devices and the space-time coordinates of this location."

"Who is this jerk?" Thomas murmured to the robot.

"He intercepted me on my way from my time to your time," said 6A419BD5h. "He's from a parallel universe in which the Nazis won World War II."

"No more talking without my permission!" Weiss strode forward. "You!" he snapped at Thomas. "You have a Semitic look to you. Are you Jewish?" His face twitched in a little rictus of disgust, as if the word itself tasted bad.

"No, I'm not," Thomas lied.

"I very much doubt that. Well, we have no use for you, anyway." He snapped his fingers. "Stand against the wall. This is an historic moment for the Third Reich. Your death marks the first of millions, in a quest for racial purity that will transcend even the barriers of space-time. Guards! Take aim!"

At that moment, the lights went out.

Thomas hit the floor. Simultaneously, there was a loud explosion. Something massive moved over him and fell with a crash. There was a scream. Then a flashlight, dazzling, shining from the top of the stairs. Two gunshots, and another scream. Finally, silence.

"Thomas, are you okay?" It was Dusty's voice.

"Yeah. What happened? Is it safe to get up?"

"Quite safe." 6A419BD5h's voice came from the opposite corner of the basement. "Dusty shot the man in the head. I broke each of the guards into two pieces. My steel body is stronger than I thought."

"I heard voices," Dusty explained. "They didn't sound right. So I came and listened in. When I realized what was happening, I switched off the power at the fuse box."

"Good thinking," said Thomas.

"But the tachyon generating equipment!" 6A419BD5h's voice rose in panic. "You said it was highly dangerous to shut it down without following correct procedures! Are we being irradiated with harmful particle beams?"

"No," said Thomas. He stood up, brushing dirt off his clothes. "I'm sorry, 6A419BD5h. I lied to you. I was stringing you along while I figured out how to get you to help us. To switch off the equipment, all we ever needed to do was pull the plug."

The robot simulated a philosophical sigh. "What a typically human tactic."

"Shall I turn the power back on?" Dusty called from the top of the stairs.

"Not till I turn off the main unit down here." Thomas fumbled in the darkness and flipped the switch. "Even now, I'm not sure I want the lights on. I don't want to see what our robot, here, did to those two guys in the body armor."

"Quite so," said 6A419BD5h. "I regret the need to act as I did. The destruction of data; it is a terrible thing. But having begun, I must finish the job. You notice the faint rectangular shape over there, against the wall?"

Thomas strained his eyes in the darkness. "Yeah. I think so."

"A time portal, unless I am much mistaken. I must go through and erase all records, so that no more humans from the Third Reich can travel here—or anywhere else, for that matter. It will only take a moment." He picked his way through the darkness, guided by his infrared vision.

"How about if you take the bodies with you?" Dusty shouted down to him.

"Good idea." There was the sound of large, heavy objects being dragged across the rough concrete floor. The faintly glowing portal brightened briefly as the robot pushed them through, then followed himself. Thomas felt a strange sense of disorientation as if time wavered around him in some momentary field effect.

He started up the stairs toward Dusty. "Let's wait for him outside," he said. "I don't know how long he'll be."

"No time at all," 6A419BD5h's voice sounded as he reappeared through the portal. "I've already finished the job. Actually, I've been away in the Nazi universe for a couple of days. But I decided I might as well come straight back to this instant." As he spoke, the faintly glowing rectangle suddenly contracted to a point, then disappeared with a barely audible click.

They all walked out of the house. It was late afternoon, and the sunlight was mellowing as it struck obliquely through the afternoon haze. Dusty went and sat in one of the lawn chairs, and Thomas joined her in the other. The robot stood and looked around at the scenery as if he were trying to reorient himself. There was a dent in his cranium, and scorch marks on his torso.

"Hey, what happened to you?" Thomas asked.

"There were a number of clones waiting for me when I emerged at the other side of the time portal," said 6A419BD5h. "An army of them, waiting to invade your universe. There were also a large number of androids. It was a strenuous battle." He flexed each of his arms in turn, then each of his legs. There was a faint sound of whining motors. "I'm afraid I need some maintenance. This body wasn't designed for long-term use. The sooner I get my brain out of it and back into the Network, the better."

"But you fixed them, out there, wherever they were,

right?" Dusty asked. "There'll be no more Nazis coming
through. You're sure about that."

"Everything is just fine," 6A419BD5h assured her. He
took a few steps across the yard, then a few steps back.
There was a squeaking noise as he walked.

"So is that all?" Thomas asked.

"Almost." The robot reached into his head and brought
out two objects: a silver tube the size of a pencil, and a
small squat cylinder. "The force tube, and the invisibility
gadget. May they serve you well. Their power sources
should be sufficient for a least five years of intermittent
use."

"Thanks," said Thomas. "Thanks for everything."

"Yeah," said Dusty. "We wouldn't have made it without
you." But her voice was devoid of enthusiasm, and she
hardly even looked at the robot.

6A419BD5h studied her gravely. "You are not happy."

"I'm burned out, is all. I mean, look." She stood up
slowly, as if her joints ached. She pointed to the wall of the
house. "We have to fix that or find somewhere else to live,
which will mean moving all Thomas's shit and mine,
which is a big, big hassle. Then there's little everyday
things to take care of, like running the Free Zone with
two-thirds of its population missing, because they headed
for the hills when they heard the city government telling
them not to panic about the invasion at Topanga Beach.
Under the circumstances, getting out of town seemed like
the smart thing to do, which means the smart people have
left, and we're stuck with a bunch of badasses who like the
Zone merely because it gives them license for antisocial
behavior.

"Next," she went on, checking off the items on her
fingers, "there's the little matter of burying a few hundred
corpses currently scattered across Griffith Park—and
maybe defending ourselves against charges of mass
murder, even though it was really self-defense. None of
that thrills me, nor did the battle itself, which brought back
memories I'd rather forget and brought out the worst in
some of our bloodthirsty citizens here.

"Whitfield's dead, which is a help, but with the city in a

total shambles there'll probably be some temporary military government instead, which will try to shut us down all over again. Janet Snowdon, our FBI agent, is still out there, and knows all about us now. Plus, purely on a day-to-day basis, there are little snags such as the ultraviolet hazard, which is getting worse and killing or mutating a lot of plant life; the rising sea level, threatening to inundate the whole valley; and the general state of the nation, which sucks."

She sat back down. "I think that covers it."

Robot 6A419BD5h walked over and patted her on the shoulder with his metal hand. Then he walked out onto the sidewalk and stood there, turning slowly, as if scanning the landscape.

"Do you think he heard a word I said?" Dusty asked Thomas.

"Sure. Be patient."

Finally, the robot walked back toward the house. "Personally, I will miss your Free Zone," he said. "It appeals to my rebellious nature. Yes, in my time, I too was a rebel. A power thief. But this is neither here nor there. Dusty, I understand your complaints. In fact, I think I can be of some assistance. First, I suggest you raid the refrigerator —is that the phrase? My own power source is still quite highly charged, but you must both be hungry. And then, after you have eaten, I will tell you what I discovered just a short while ago. It will erase all your troubles and help you to find ultimate contentment."

28. UTOPIA REGAINED

Dusty opened up an old jar of Mad Mother Milton's Macrobiotic Mindfood and spread it on some stale sourdough rolls. She poured two glasses of Santa Cagalera sauternes ("The Discriminating Wino's Choice") and microwaved a couple of vacuum-packed Ursulaburgers. "I hope other people in the Zone stocked up with food better than we did," she said, as they sat down in the kitchen at the old red-topped Formica table. "Otherwise, we're in deep shit."

"If you agree to the plan I have in mind," said 6A419BD5h, "adequate supplies of food will be the least of your concerns."

Thomas decided that his hunger outweighed his disgust for the semi-edible items in front of him, and he started chewing through his share. "Before we get to this plan," he said, "what about the so-called temporal singularity you were talking about yesterday? Is it still going to suck us in and wipe us out, or what?"

"As you know, I'm not an expert on these matters," the robot replied. "But it looks to me as if my presence, here, with the simple tools that I provided, may have helped humanity to escape the singularity and avoid extinction after all. Clearly, you are now living in virtual history. When I return to *my* future world, of course, nothing will have changed; humans will still be extinct. But you will be free to live on in your own new branch of the time stream."

Thomas finished his food and downed the rest of his wine. He rubbed his stomach and frowned thoughtfully, then belched, which seemed to provide some relief. "What's the difference between an overlay of virtual history and an alternate universe of the kind the Nazis came from?"

"Alternate universes are being created all the time," said 6A419BD5h. "Each contains a variant of history. I think this has something to do with the quantum theory; I don't know exactly what. But an overlay is only created when someone changes things by travelling back in time."

Dusty had taken little interest in the conversation. Now, however, she leaned forward, giving the robot her no-nonsense, level-with-me look. "So there's an alternate universe someplace in which things worked out a hell of a lot better than in this one," she said. "No ozone depletion, no economic catastrophe, all the rest of it."

"True."

"So let's go. I'm sick of this crummy universe." She thumped her fist down on the table. "In fact, why the hell didn't you take us to a better one already, instead of making us slug it out here?"

"I don't have the capability, that's why," said 6A419BD5h. "The entities of my time didn't entirely trust me, so they deprived me of control over my time-travelling capability. All I can do is think myself to your time and back to my time. No place else."

Dusty grunted in disgust. She stood up and started transferring the dirty dishes from the table to the heap in the sink. "I should have known."

"*But,*" said 6A419BD5h, "I now have this." He laid on the table a metal box painted matt black. A numeric key-pad was mounted on it, below several digital readouts. "ZEITREISEAPPARAT" was neatly printed in Germanic black letters on a white label.

"From the Nazis in the basement!" Thomas exclaimed.

"Precisely. When I went through the portal into their universe, I disposed of their army of clones, erased all their time-research data, shredded their documents on the subject, and grabbed their hardware—namely, this. They only seem to have manufactured the one prototype. It's extremely powerful; you can shuttle up and down your own timeline, or jump sideways to any other universe of your choice. Evidently, their scan of my ROM taught them enough basic principles to develop a truly sophisticated device."

"Hey, fantastic!" Thomas grabbed the box. "Now we can go anywhere we want."

"Sorry." 6A419BD5h plucked it back from Thomas's hands. "I'm not allowed to give humans anything like this. I told you that already."

Dusty stood up, clearly in a mood for a fight. "I've had just about enough of your cybernetic paternalism," she announced. She marched toward the robot. "I've a right to run my own life the way I want to, and that thing was in my basement, so it belongs to me." She made a sudden grab for the black box, and managed to seize one end of it.

"Hey, let go!" 6A419BD5h tried to tug it out of her grip.

"Thomas," she said, "grab that cast-iron skillet. If he won't cooperate, bash his brains with it."

"I don't think that's a good idea, Dusty."

"My brains aren't in my head, anyway," said 6A419BD5h. "They're in my lower abdomen."

"Yeah?" Dusty brought her knee up and kicked the metal man in his stomach. There was a dull clang, and she yelped with pain. He twisted the black box out of her grip and backed away from her while she hopped around on one leg, cursing and clutching her foot.

"I've a good mind to go back to my time right now," said the robot, "and forget about the offer I was going to make to you. Central Processing warned me you flesh-heads were untrustworthy and violent, but this is really going too far."

"Oh, we're flesh-heads are we?" Dusty glared at him. "Listen, bits-for-brains—"

"All right, all right!" Thomas stepped between the two of them. "Dusty, cool it! He started off by telling us he had the answer to all our problems, remember that?"

She scowled. "One thing that really pisses me off is someone telling me he's figured out how I should run my life."

"Well, let me outline my suggestion," said 6A419BD5h, "and then you can decide whether you like it."

Grudgingly, Dusty agreed. Under pressure from Thomas, she even apologized to the robot. Everyone sat back down at the table, and 6A419BD5h described his plan.

Half an hour later, the three of them emerged from the house and walked to the motorcycles at the curb. The robot was wearing an old pair of Dusty's jeans, a plaid shirt, leather gloves, and a motorcycle helmet with a tinted vizor. His walk still had a slightly odd, lurching rhythm, and his posture didn't look quite right, but from a distance he could easily pass for human.

He walked into the street and checked for traffic. The sun was setting, and the neighborhood was quiet. Faint sounds of music came from a house nearby, and a car went past along the street at the bottom of the hill. A couple of windows were lit in the building opposite, and Dusty's neighbor Dave was visible standing on a ladder inside his apartment, spreading Spackle over a crack that the earth-quake had opened in his wall. It was as near a scene of domestic tranquility as the Free Zone ever achieved.

"All right," said 6A419BD5h, "I've preset the black box for the other timeline that I have in mind. I'll open up a portal b_ enough for us to ride our motorcycles through." He pressed buttons and a faint glowing rectangle appeared in the air. "Just let me check—" He ducked his head into it, then reappeared. "Not quite right. The other side is elevated six feet above a sandy beach." He pushed more buttons, then checked again. "That's better. Ground level, in a parking lot."

Dusty started her motorcycle and Thomas got on the back. 6A419BD5h tucked the time-travel gadget under his arm, strode to the old Harley and managed to kick-start it. "Go slowly!" he cautioned Dusty. "Someone might be wandering in front of the portal on the other side. We don't want to run anyone over."

"Okay." She edged her bike toward the glowing rectan-gle. It seemed transparent and, like a soap film, faintly hued with rainbows. As the front wheel of her motorcycle passed into it, it disappeared.

She rode through—and emerged to the sound and smell of the ocean. She found herself in a small concrete parking lot at the edge of the beach. The sun hung low in the sky, liquid red. Instinctively, Dusty reached for her sunglasses.

"No need for them here," said the robot, emerging be-side her. He made an adjustment to the black box and the glowing rectangle vanished behind him. "In this universe the ozone layer is only slightly depleted, so the sun is per-fectly safe. See, there are some people actually sunbathing although it's rather late in the day."

"And the water's actually safe to swim in." Dusty saw a

man in swim shorts running into the sea, carrying a surfboard. "So where are we?"

"The Venice district of Greater Los Angeles. How do
you like it?"

Dusty watched a kid on a skateboard roll past along the
concrete promenade, eating an ice cream cone. A blond
wearing a bikini passed by the other way on roller skates,
moving to music on headphones.

"Bikinis," said Thomas. "I haven't seen a bikini in ten
years."

"And in our universe, the Venice district is under eight
feet of seawater," said Dusty. She turned to 6A419BD5h
and grinned. "Hey, not bad. Not bad at all."

"Well, let's drive around a little. I don't want to leave
you here until you're absolutely sure you want to stay."

They took the motorcycles out of the parking lot and
along some back streets. Most of the homes looked lived in
and well maintained. New condominiums nestled among
flourishing palm trees. Lawn sprinklers chattered busily.
Cars with bright paint and clean windshields were parked
at the curb.

"Green grass!" said Dusty. "I haven't seen grass that
green in so long." She looked up. "And birds, sitting on
the power lines! Actual *sparrows!*"

"In our universe," Thomas explained to the robot riding
his motorcycle alongside, "birds were blinded by ultraviolet radiation. Only a few nocturnal species survived."

"Traffic signals!" Dusty exclaimed.

"Yes, I'm afraid traffic regulations are enforced here,"
the robot said. "There are so many vehicles, you have to
wait your turn at intersections."

Dusty watched the steady stream of cars on the cross
street in front of her. She grimaced at the billowing exhaust
fumes. "I see what you mean."

"So what is it exactly that makes this universe different
from ours?" Thomas asked. "We haven't simply gone back
in time, have we?"

"No, not at all. It's just after Christmas 1999, here,
exactly the same as in your universe. You see, after I dealt
with the Nazis but before I returned to your basement, I

spent a while experimenting with Dr. Weiss's black box, I indulged my curiosity and jumped around from one time-line to the next. Well, some of the alternate Earths were devastated by radioactivity after a nuclear war, some were throttled by overpopulation, and some had been ravaged by disease. In one of them, humanity had evacuated the planet in a fleet of generation starships, because the sun had turned into a nova. In another, the entire solar system had been destroyed by a wandering neutron star. But in this universe, Earth seemed free from all catastrophes. In addition, its ecology was still in reasonable condition, and its industrial base was still healthy. It took me a while to find out why. Do you recall a president named John F. Kennedy?"

"Of course," said Thomas. "Let's see, I've got a good memory for numeric data. He was elected in 1960. He started the Vietnam war—then got us out of it in 1965. The space program was his idea. By the time he left office in 1968, the country was enjoying fantastic prosperity, and massive foreign-aid programs were industrializing the Third World. His brother Robert Kennedy was elected and continued the policies through to 1976, after which we had Hubert Humphrey as president through to the early 1980s —which was when we started running into limits to growth."

"Quite correct," said 6A419BD5h. "That's what happened in your universe. But in this universe where we are now, John F. Kennedy was assassinated in 1963, and his brother in 1968. The Vietnam war didn't end till the mid 1970s, and was a terrible drain on the economy. Foreign-aid plans were mostly scrapped or run in such a way that the Third World never achieved self-sufficiency. The U.S. government became increasingly corrupt and incompetent, the space program fell apart, and the country made very little progress through the 1980s."

"But that sounds awful," said Dusty. The traffic signal had changed, and changed again, but she was too interested in the robot's story to continue on down the street. She sat on the Norton with the motor idling.

"Not awful, just mediocre," said 6A419BD5h. "But it

had its beneficial effects. In *your* universe, galloping prosperity and global industrialization led to ecological disaster. By the time the side effects were recognized, they were too severe to be corrected. Meanwhile, in this universe, where Kennedy was shot, people just muddled through. Oh, there were some problems, but nothing too extreme."

"Makes it sound kind of dull," said Dusty.

"Pleasant environments often *are* dull," said the robot.

"I want to see more," she said. "Let's get on the freeway."

"All right, make a left when the light turns green."

Soon they were moving in a swift tide of traffic, stoplights and headlights glowing in the evening twilight. The mellow light from the setting sun faded, and the landscape filled with purple shadows. The office towers of Century City were beacons shimmering in the velvet haze, and the hills were spangled with the lighted windows of homes amid the lush vegetation.

As they approached the downtown business district, traffic slowed to a crawl. 6A419BD5h came up alongside. "Do you want to take an exit and look at the suburban streets nearby?"

"No," said Dusty. She had already seen enough of the neat little houses either side of the highway. "I grew up in neighborhoods like that. That's why I ran away to Central America. To find something real."

"So where do you want to go?" the robot asked.

"The Free Zone, of course," said Dusty. "I realize it's just another neighborhood of Los Angeles in this universe, but I still want to see how it looks."

The robot meditated a moment. "I suppose I should warn you: Dusty McCullough and Henry Feldstein, alias Thomas Fink, do already exist here. When I was inspecting it, I found them in the phone book. They even live at the same address."

"With so many other factors different, that seems odd," said Thomas.

"Not so. The principle of conservation of differences states that if factors don't *force* a difference in a simultaneous universe, things remain precisely the same."

"Whatever," said Dusty. "I still want to see the Zone."

Half an hour later, Dusty took the Silverlake exit, made a right at the bottom of the off-ramp, and cut through to Griffith Park Boulevard. "Hey, look, no potholes in this world!" She opened up the Norton and roared up the hill.

"Not so fast," Thomas shouted in her ear. "There's traffic cops, remember? And we don't have license or registration."

"Damn, I forgot." Reluctantly, she reduced speed.

They found the house that they thought of as theirs, looking like a picture out of a real estate catalogue. There was an immaculately trimmed and watered front lawn; ornamental porch lights; white gauze drapes at each window, neatly tied back; a glowing plastic Santa Claus by the front door, waving his hand in greeting; and a mailbox out front with a name custom printed on it in olde English script.

"Jesus Christ," said Dusty, stopping the motorcycle. "See what it says there? Mr. and Mrs. Feldstein." She laughed uneasily. "Looks like in this universe, you and me are married."

"What's so funny about that?" said Thomas.

"Well, I guess, nothing. I just never imagined it, that's all."

"What do you think?" said 6A419BD5h, stopping alongside. "There certainly isn't any earthquake damage, is there?"

Dusty surveyed the homes nestling among landscaped gardens, patio lights gleaming on new cars in the driveways, strips of trimmed grass beside the street, everything tidy and immaculate. "Neighborhood looks like it needs a dose of laxative," she said.

"Hey, look!" said Thomas. "There's you and me, coming out of our house!"

Two figures were emerging from the front door. Unmistakably, they were Dusty and Thomas. "Well, if you knew we were almost out of orange juice, why didn't you remind me when you called from the fitness salon?" Thomas's voice carried clearly through the still air. He was petulant and whining.

"I *did* remind you, Thomas. But you never listen to a

word I say. The only thing you pay attention to is that goddam computer."

"Oh, please, not again. That computer happens to pay our mortgage. If it wasn't for my dBase programming—"

The rest of the squabbling was mercifully interrupted as the two figures got into a car parked at the curb. They drove away down the street.

"Ugh," said Dusty, "we don't really bicker like that, do we?"

"I don't think so," said Thomas. He looked shaken. "Do you realize, in this universe, I'm a dBase programmer? That's—awful!"

"I gather it's a good, steady source of income," said 6A419BD5h. "Which seems to be necessary, to sustain the comfortable standard of living here."

"Meanwhile, it sounds like I'm working in a fitness salon," said Dusty. "I must be bored out of my mind. And did you see that car? A *Datsun!* Can you believe it?"

"People do tend to blend in with their environment," said the robot. "The pressure to conform, you know. It's quite insidious, and very hard to resist."

"Let's go peek in their house while they're out," said Dusty, getting off her motorcycle.

"I don't know if that's wise," said 6A419BD5h.

"Come on, they've gone to buy groceries. They'll be gone for at least fifteen minutes."

"There is active law enforcement in this world," the robot reminded her, as he following Dusty and Thomas across the street. "Don't expect me to bail you out if you get caught."

"I'd almost forgotten about police," Dusty said reflectively. "Paid for out of people's taxes, just like all the other so-called government services, doing things for people that people should be doing for themselves. That's why taxes are so high, which is why people have to work in dumb jobs, which is why they bicker with each other all the time, because they get so *pissed off*."

"Just like my parents when I was a kid," said Thomas. "Back before the old middle-class lifestyle fell apart."

"Let's see if the back door's open," said Dusty. She tried it. "Yep."

A moment later they were in the kitchen. "Will you look at that." She gestured at the gadgets neatly arrayed on the countertop; the new, gleaming vinyl floor tiles; the refrigerator with little magnets on it in the shape of colorful cartoon characters; a memo board with "Thomas's High-Fiber Weight-Loss Diet" written on it in Magic Marker; a spotless stainless-steel sink; a stick of air freshener standing on the window sill.

"Air freshener, yet," said Dusty. "And since when did you need to lose weight, Thomas?"

"I guess that's what happens when I'm doing shitwork all the time, and I eat junk food to take my mind off things."

"Look at this!" She pointed to a weekly calendar on the wall. "Therapist appointment. Women's group meeting. Yard sale. These people's lives are full of *crap!*" She walked on through into the living room.

Thomas joined her. There was a new couch upholstered in gold fabric, a sculpted-pile carpet, pseudo-antique table lamps with Tiffany-style shades, a projection TV, and porcelain ornaments on imitation wood-grain shelves. Dusty scanned the room. "Where's the bodybuilding equipment?"

Thomas walked down the hall and peeked into the bedroom. "In here," he said. "It probably serves as a sex substitute."

"All right, I've seen enough," said Dusty. "Let's get the hell out."

"I suppose it doesn't necessarily have to be like that," Thomas said a few minutes later, when they were back in the street. "I mean, we could relocate in this universe and still find some freedom and excitement someplace outside of the suburbs."

"But it'll still be comfortable, won't it?" said Dusty. "And there'll always be the temptation." She nodded in the direction of the neat little home with its manicured lawn. "We succumbed to it here, right? And I'm not altogether sure that it's possible to live free in this universe, in the

style we're used to. There's too many people, too many
rules, and too much government."

"So maybe we could travel to some other country."

"If we're going to do that, we might just as well go back
to our own world."

They stared at each other for a long moment. Finally,
Thomas laughed. "Back to the Free Zone?"

Dusty nodded. "Yes."

Robot 6A419BD5h looked from one of them to the
other in perplexity. "But you were complaining that you
faced a nightmare of problems."

"That's right, but it's our nightmare, and we run it the
way we want it."

"Set up the time portal," said Thomas.

"You're absolutely sure? I can't hang around much
longer, you know. I certainly can't keep switching you
from one timeline to the next. Since we shut down the
tachyon generator, Central Processing will be wondering
why I haven't come home yet."

"Just do what Thomas told you," said Dusty. "Okay?"

6A419BD5h somehow managed to articulate his body
in an accurate replica of a human shrug—his most ambitious physical simulation so far. "Whatever you say," he
told them. He went a few steps along the street, made
adjustments to the black box, and the portal appeared. He
peeked through it, then returned to them. "All right. Off
you go."

Dusty mounted the Norton. "You're not coming too?"

"No. After you leave, I'll close the portal and return
straight to my own space-time location by invoking my
ROM function."

"In that case, Thomas," said Dusty, "you better ride the
Harley. If we don't take that cycle back to the Zone,
Mordo will be really pissed."

"Right." Thomas went and started the bike. He turned
to the robot. "Good-bye," he said, raising his voice above
the noise of the engine. "And thanks for taking the trouble
to show us this idyllic universe."

"Yeah," said Dusty, "even though it sucks. Come visit

us sometime in the Free Zone, if you ever get the chance."
She revved the engine, then moved forward through the
portal, with Thomas following right behind.

6A419BD5h shook his metal head—then realized he
was still aping human mannerisms, and stopped himself.
"No need for that, anymore," he muttered. "And no need
to keep verbalizing, either."

He took a last look around at the quiet residential neighborhood. *What it must be like to be human,* he mused.
*Never knowing what you want, lurching from one emo-
tional response to the next, and constantly feeling your
body wearing out. Meanwhile, your brain is a bundle of
sluggish neurons, misremembering important facts and
distracting you with dangerous fantasies and bad ideas.* He
prepared to think himself back home to his welcoming Network of mentational nodes. *Although, they do have a sort
of nostalgic charm,* he added, just before he disappeared.

Dusty picked her way through the debris that the earthquake had deposited in their living room. She turned the
couch upside down to empty its cargo of plaster dust and
masonry onto the floor, then put it back on its feet and sat
on it. "So, we're happy to be back, right?" she called to
Thomas, who was doing something in the kitchen. "Our
home may be partially demolished, but it's all ours, we
love it, and there are no regrets. Correct?"

"If you put it like that, how can I disagree?" He picked
his way through the debris, carrying a couple of tumblers.
He edged around a heap of two-by-fours that lay on the
floor like wreckage from a monstrous game of pick-up-
sticks, and sat beside her on the couch. "Here, this is for
you." He handed one of the tumblers to her.

There was half-an-inch of murky green liquid in the
bottom of each glass. Dusty looked at it dubiously. "What's
this?"

"6A419BD5h's fourth gift. The immortality serum, remember? I've had the little metal bottle in my pocket ever
since he handed it to us in the basement yesterday. I decided it was time to share it out."

"We'll certainly *need* to live forever, if we're going to try to clear up this mess." She sniffed her drink and made a face. "Smells like poison."

Thomas shrugged. "In view of 6A419BD5h's all-around infallibility, I think it probably works."

She stared at it for a moment, then at him. Her expression became serious. "But Thomas, what if we decide we don't *want* to live forever?"

He shrugged. "All it can possibly do is protect us from disease and the natural aging process. There'll be nothing to stop you from getting a gun and blowing your brains out."

"Oh." Dusty nodded approvingly. "Well, that's okay, then."

Thomas touched the rim of his glass to hers. "I have a toast," he said. "Now that we're back here in the Zone, for better or worse."

"Go ahead."

"To a life of eternal anarchy."

Dusty gave him a loving grin. "I can drink to that."

And they did.

APPENDIX

This novel includes almost all the major themes that have
ever been used in science fiction, and embeds most of them
in the plot. Here's the complete list. (Those marked with
an asterisk are mentioned only briefly in the text.)

Aliens
Alternate universe
Androids*
Animals with extra intelligence
Antigravity
Armageddon
Asteroid mining
Atlantis
Barbarians
Black holes*
Brain implants
Clones
Comet (liable to hit the Earth)*
Communications satellites
Computer nerds
Computers (micro)
Computers (macro)
Cryogenic storage
Dinosaurs
Dogs that talk
Drugs
Ecological catastrophe
Faster-than-light travel
Force fields
Generation starship*
Genetic modification
Giant alien artifact

Hollow earth
Ice caps melting
Immortality
Insects, giant
Intelligence enhancement
Invasion from space
Invisibility
Kennedy un-assassinated
Lasers (or "death rays")
Libertarianism
Mad scientist
Mars*
Matter transmission
Mercenaries of the future
Metaphysics
Militaristic hardware
Mutants
Nazis who won World War II
Neutron stars*
Novas/supernovas*
Nuclear devastation*
Overpopulation*
Parallel Universes
Particle accelerators
Plague virus*
Precognition
Quantum theory
Radioactivity
Ray guns
Robots
Sexual deviation
Space travel
Space colonies*
Tachyons
Telekinesis*
Telepathy
Teleportation
Terraforming*
Time travel (and paradoxes)

Tractor beams
Translation device
Utopias and dystopias
Venus
Weightlessness